The Perfect Deception

APR -- 2015 CH

Also by Lutishia Lovely

The Hallelujah Love Series
Sex in the Sanctuary
Love Like Hallelujah
A Preacher's Passion
Heaven Right Here
Reverend Feelgood
Heaven Forbid
Divine Intervention
The Eleventh Commandment

The Business Series
All Up in My Business
Mind Your Own Business
Taking Care of Business

The Shady Sisters Trilogy
The Perfect Affair
The Perfect Deception
The Perfect Revenge

Published by Kensington Publishing Corp.

The Perfect Deception

LUTISHIA LOVELY

Dafina BOOKS

KENSINGTON PUBLISHING CORP.
www.kensingtonbooks.com

DAFINA BOOKS are published by

Kensington Publishing Corp.
119 West 40th Street
New York, NY 10018

All Kensington titles, imprints, and distributed lines are available at special quantity discounts for bulk purchases for sales promotion, premiums, fund-raising, and educational or institutional use.

Special book excerpts or customized printings can also be created to fit specific needs. For details, write or phone the office of the Kensington Special Sales Manager: Kensington Publishing Corp., 119 West 40th Street, New York, NY 10018. Attn. Special Sales Department. Phone: 1-800-221-2647.

Dafina and the Dafina logo Reg. U.S. Pat. & TM Off.

ISBN-13: 978-0-7582-8668-0
ISBN-10: 0-7582-8668-6
First Kensington Trade Paperback Printing: December 2014

eISBN-13: 978-0-7582-8670-3
eISBN-10: 0-7582-8670-8
First Kensington Electronic Edition: December 2014

10 9 8 7 6 5 4 3 2 1

Printed in the United States of America

This one is for the brand-new, first ever online book club hosted by myself and Zuri Day, already nearly one thousand strong! Thank you for joining us in having . . .

A LOVELY DAY EXPERIENCE!

(To join us, go to Facebook and type above group name into search box. Thx!)

Acknowledgments

It's three a.m., and I sit here deliriously excited . . . or deliriously exhausted (semantics—you know—po-TAY-to, po-TAH-to?) but so very grateful to have finished book two in the Shady Sisters Trilogy! I love these shady women and the chance to be a bad girl vicariously through their muddled, messy lives! What a blessing to have an editor and friend who's as crazy as I am and gets a kick out of these devious plots. Thanks, Selena! ☺ As always, Team Lutishia is the village that helps raise this literary child: Natasha, my Kensington family, you guys are the best. A special thank-you to Rebecca Cremonese, who handled a sinful amount of last-minute edits without putting out a contract on my life! Heading to New York soon, girl. Drinks on me!

To my family and my secret lover (long story . . . stay tuned . . . might end up in a book). ☺ Thanks for your patience while I was chained to my computer, a socializing outcast who rolled through twenty-four-hour workdays and tried to hold conversations after having no sleep. Either "I take back everything I said" or "I didn't mean it," whichever is most appropriate. Drinks on me!

Readers, supporters, fantastic fans: If I began thanking all of you who've supported/promoted/encouraged/kept me sane during the writing of this novel, I'd run out of room and leave out too many names. The book clubs, bloggers, reviewers, literary magazines, and everyone who promotes my books with as much enthusiasm as I do . . . thank you. Again and again. You are the wind beneath my wings. Let's keep flying!

PROLOGUE

"If forced to choose, would you pick your family . . . or your man?"

The question caused Jessica Bolton to look up from her cell phone to the reality show turned on mainly for background noise.

The show's star and most vocal character was the first to respond. "Are you kidding? My family comes before anybody, including my baby's daddy!"

"Not me," countered the one viewers loved to hate. "I didn't choose my family. I chose my man and he means everything to me."

"More than your mama?" the quiet Southern belle asked.

"She said *everything*," Star sarcastically replied.

"And I meant it," Hated retorted, totally unapologetic. "Everybody didn't have a mother as wonderful as the one who raised you." The little smirk that accompanied this statement was enough to suggest it hadn't quite been a compliment.

Star jumped up. The requisite reality fight scene had been cued. "What the hell does that mean?"

Unfortunately, Jessica was all too familiar with the feelings about which Hated spoke, a passionate comment that took her back to when she discovered that the woman who raised her was not her mother and life was not always so wonderful.

"Where's Mommy?" Six-year-old Jessica wandered into the room where several children played. She used a stubby finger to poke the leg of the boy sitting at the end of the couch. "Where's Mommy?"

He watched cartoons for several more seconds, then leaned toward her, his face in a scowl. "She is *not* your mommy."

"Is too."

"Is not."

"Is too."

"Is not."

"Is too!"

"Uh-uh. You're a foster child. Your parents are dead!"

Dead. Jessica flashed back to the year before and the incident that gave that word meaning, the bird she and her sister had found on the sidewalk, the one that couldn't fly. The one that was almost as stiff as plastic, and had eyes that did not move. As foggy as was the memory of her mama and dada, surely they weren't like that.

"No they're not!" she screamed, punctuating the declaration by connecting the foot of her naked Tammy Lifelike doll with the eight-year-old liar's cheek. "They went to heaven!"

Enraged, the boy grabbed the inside of her leg and pinched hard. "Stupid foster kids," he muttered amid her yelping.

"Oww!"

"Stop it!" Mommy's obviously unhappy command reverberated through the wall before her face—red and disfigured by poverty, bitterness, and lack of sleep—appeared in the doorway. "Jessie, go to your room, *now.*"

"But Mommy, he pinched me."

"She hit me with that stupid doll!" the boy countered. As the foster mother's only biological child, Dennis's word was truer than the Bible.

"Give me that," she hissed, snatching the doll from Jessie's hand.

"But that's my Sissy!" Jessie cried.

"Maybe next time you'll learn to not use Sissy as a weapon. Now get upstairs."

"I'm hungry!"

"What have I told you about that? It's either food or fighting. You chose the latter. Now go!"

"But Dennis—"

Mommy's raised hand put a period on the thought and encouraged little Jessica to head toward the stairs.

Later that night her new sister, Francine, handed her two biscuits and a slice of ham before crawling into bed. "William never cleans his plate," she whispered, once they were safely beneath the heavy quilt where their voices didn't carry. "I snuck it when Mommy said to scrape it into the trash."

Though only two years older than Jessica, Francine had been in the system since birth, in this house since the age of two, and knew all the ropes. Francine reminded Jessie of Sissy, the older sister who'd gone away and the inspiration behind the name of Jessica's doll. That sometimes made her sad, but not ungrateful.

"Thank you, Franny." Jessie turned back the quilt, sat up, and carefully spread out the napkin. She tore the ham slice into two even pieces and placed the meat between the sliced biscuits. Her stomach growled, but she ate slowly, deliberately, savoring each bite. She thought to save the second biscuit should she get in trouble tomorrow, but almost before she'd wrapped the idea in a napkin and placed it under the pillow her mind changed, and she relished the taste of strawberry jam on her tongue.

"Franny, you awake?" Jessica lightly shook her bedmate once the second biscuit and the last bit of jam had melted in her mouth, and the quilt covered them both once more.

"Yep." Franny turned to face her.

"What's a frosted mom?"

"*Foster*, not frosted. That's a woman who acts like our mommy but is not our real mommy . . . like Mrs. Lewis."

"Why can't she be our real mommy?"

"Because we didn't bake in her tummy."

"Why did my real mommy go to heaven?"

"Go to sleep, Jessie," Francine said with a sigh as she turned over. "And be glad she's not in hell where my mommy ended up."

By the time Jessica was ten years old her natural beauty was striking: long curly hair, almond eyes, pouty lips and flawless tan skin. Fourteen-year-old Dennis's torment went from pinching to probing, from fighting to fondling, threatening to kill the family pet if she said a word. He needn't have bothered. One year before, Francine had confided in Jessica that she and Dennis were "boyfriend and girlfriend." So anyone finding out about what he'd forced Jessica to do was the last thing she wanted. But someone had found out, stumbled across them in the laundry room when all were supposed to be outside helping Mommy gather pinecones for holiday decorations. And not just anyone but the worse possible person—Francine. This revelation had cost her the dearest friend she'd known since Sissy, and one month later, it forced Mommy to send Jessica away from the relatively comfy foster home and back into the system. What happened was all her fault after all.

Francine was the last female Jessica trusted, her one and only best friend forever. Forever was an illusion in foster care. At sixteen Jessica was reminded of this lesson and learned that no matter the sex, friendship was fleeting. The first boy she willingly slept with, the one who loved her and only her ("No, really, I mean it, you're it for me, girl") also *only* loved fellow classmates Oneida, Felicia, Tess, Jill, and Shannon . . . that she knew of. This eye-opening "he's not your man" conversation—*is too, is not, is too, is not*—couldn't be assuaged with a ham-filled biscuit topped with strawberry jam, and taught Jessica that both mommies and men could be a pain in the chest.

★ ★ ★

When Jessica came out of memory lane, the drama-filled reality show was ending. She muted the volume and refocused on the vague request in the out-of-the-blue e-mail that had rocked her world. If she refused outright, would there be any chance of a relationship? She doubted it. But if she answered yes, her purposely designed, solitary world could once again be filled with family and love . . . the illusion that came with painful consequences, and vague, hazy memories of a time when she was happy, when someone else cared.

Ironic that the raucous dialogue from a lowbrow reality show had aided her decision. Jessica fired up her iPad and began to type.

Hey Sissy: Sounds interesting. I want to hear more. Whatever it is, of course I will help you. Still can't believe you wrote me! So much has happened. So happy you did and you're right—there's nothing like family. I love you. Your real! sister . . . Jessie.

CHAPTER 1

Several months later . . .

A beautiful couple walked up the immaculately landscaped entrance to a large home in a tony Alexandria, Virginia, suburb. The woman, Jessica, was nervous. It was Thanksgiving, which, for various reasons, was one of her least favorite holidays, second only to Christmas. More importantly, it was the first time she was meeting her boyfriend's family, the amazing man with whom she'd enjoyed a whirlwind courtship for the past two months. Life had turned out better than she could have dreamed when shortly after moving to Atlanta she'd spotted the handsome stranger among a happy-hour crowd and made a bold move. If she played her cards right and impressed his next of kin, who knew what type of sparkly bauble Santa might place under the Christmas tree and change her feelings about holidays?

He knocked on the door and after a moment, it swung open.

"Nathan!" An attractive woman dressed in black stretch pants and a colorful sweater opened the door.

"Hey, Sis!"

"Come on in!" She stepped back so the couple could enter the massive foyer with a high vaulted ceiling and chic chandelier.

The siblings hugged. Nathan Carver turned and beamed at the woman standing by his side with a hesitant smile and downcast eyes. "Sister, this is Jessica Bolton. Baby, this is Sherri Atwater, my sister and best friend."

A genuine smile lit Sherri's face. "I've heard so much about you." They shared a light hug. "You're as pretty as my brother bragged that you were."

"It's a pleasure to meet you." Jessica's eyes darted behind them to the hallway from which jovial voices traveled.

"That's my crazy family," Sherri explained, "and a few of our friends. They're pretty lively, but no one bites."

Nathan put his arm around Jessica and gave her shoulder an affectionate squeeze. They started down the hall. Halfway to their destination a handsome man rounded the corner and walked their way.

"I thought I heard the doorbell." He reached them and gave Nathan dap and a shoulder bump.

"Hello, Bro." Again, introductions all around.

"Where are you from?" Randall Atwater asked Jessica once they'd been introduced. "You look familiar."

Private by nature, Jessica's brow arched in surprise. "Me?" She quickly added, "I live in Atlanta but am from California." This was basically true. She had lived in California for many years, before her divorce.

"Southern California?" Randall inquired as they continued down the hall into the great room where the adults had gathered.

"Northern. Oakland."

They stepped into a comfortably decorated space where Nathan's mother, Elaine, was recounting a funny incident from when Randall and Sherri first began dating. Listening were

Randall's mother, her male companion, Randall's brother and sister-in-law, Sherri's best friend, Renee, and a few others.

"It was thoughtful for him to buy me a bouquet," she finished. "He went on about how he'd searched the city for just the right type of flowers. I didn't have the heart to tell him that the price tag was still on it from the store where he worked part-time, along with the receipt that was time-stamped to show he'd bought them right after finishing his shift!"

Various responses echoed around the room, laughter sprinkled among them. "Come on, Mom Elaine." Randall stopped just inside the door. "Haven't I lived that one down by now?"

"Yes, but it's worth retelling." She'd answered him but her eyes were on Nathan and his date, as were all other eyes in the room. "Hello, Son."

"Happy Thanksgiving, everybody." Nathan gave a general wave before crossing over to give his mom a hug. "Hello, Mom." He reached back for Jessica's hand, bringing her forward. "Mom, this is my friend, Jessica. Jessica, this is the best mother in the world, Elaine Carver."

"Hello, Mrs. Carver." Jessica's outstretched hand reached Elaine's. "It's wonderful to meet you."

"Nice meeting you too, darling. Congratulations on making it to a family function." With a side glance at Nathan, she continued, "It's been awhile since my son has invited a guest."

Jessica split her smile between Nathan and Elaine. "I'm happy to be here."

Nathan then addressed the room. "Everybody, this is Jessica."

With a nervous giggle, she scanned the room. "Hi, everyone."

"We'll make the rounds for a personal hello," he said, still holding her hand. "But don't worry about remembering everyone's name."

"I was hoping there wouldn't be a quiz once we're done."

He lowered his voice. "I'll definitely test something later . . . but not your memory."

"What are y'all drinking?" Randall asked. They followed him over to the bar.

And with that, conversation resumed, more drinks were poured, soft music played, and Nathan and Jessica made their way through the rest of the personal greetings.

"This is a beautiful home," she commented after they'd circled the room.

"Come on. Let me give you a quick tour."

Nathan was a perfect guide as they navigated the large yet cozy abode. Upon seeing the upscale setting and a grouping of plaques, certificates, and photos that filled almost an entire wall in the downstairs office, Jessica was even more impressed with her honey's in-laws than when he'd told her about them. Randall, his brother-in-law, was a prominent scientist who'd won awards for his groundbreaking research. A picture of him with President Barack Obama placed the man in very high company. The day was already overwhelming and now she felt intimidated, too.

Nathan immediately noticed her change in attitude. "What's wrong?"

"Nothing."

"Tell me about nothing."

She smiled. His sensitivity and astute observational skills were just two of the many things that she both loved—and feared—about him. "Your family is so . . . accomplished."

"You already knew that."

"Yes, but to be here, to meet them. I just hope that I'm not . . ."

"Shh. Don't even go there. Yes, there are those in my family who are highly successful. But we don't judge people based on awards and degrees. We're more interested in a person's character, their integrity, their family values." He reached over and pulled her into his arms, gave her one kiss, and then another. "So you don't have anything to worry about."

Jessica nodded, and entwined her arm in his as they walked toward French doors that led to a solarium. She knew that Nathan meant what he said when he told her not to worry. He'd meant to be soothing. Little did he know it was exactly his upstanding views on character, integrity, and family values that worried her most of all.

CHAPTER 2

"What do you think?"

Dinner was over. Various family members had broken off into smaller groups. Nathan and Sherri were in the kitchen, sitting at the island, eating second slices of sweet potato pie that neither needed but couldn't refuse.

"She's cute, I'll give you that." Sherri took a sip of cold milk. "But she's so quiet, Nate, and"—she paused, searching for the right word—"reserved. Not the type of woman you usually date."

"She is different from anyone I've dated in the past. That's part of what attracted me to her."

"How did you guys meet?"

"I told you, remember? At the sports bar in Buckhead where I like to hang out."

"Was she a friend of a friend, someone's sister . . . ?"

"No. She was at the bar, alone. We'd noticed each other throughout the evening and at one particular point, when my friends and I were in a heated debate, she walked up and said, 'I don't know what you guys are arguing about, but you win,' looking at me."

Sherri gave her brother the side eye. "Really? You win? That was the line that did it?"

"It wasn't so much what she said as the way she said it: sincere and straightforward, with the merest twinkle in her eye."

Sherri finished her pie, pushed back the plate. "And then she whipped out the card containing her phone number."

Nathan shook his head. "And then she walked back to her bar stool and pulled out her phone."

"And waited for the bait to take hold."

"Not at all. In fact, if one of the guys hadn't observed her leaving, I would have missed my chance. She was almost out the door when I caught up to her. I liked her style. Considering the types of bold and aggressive women out there and the lame, tired, and insulting ways I've been approached, her compliment delivered with no ulterior motive was refreshing." Nathan finished his pie as well. "See, you've been out of the game too long to know what it's like out here right now. Married for fifteen years and with Randall for what, three or four years before that? Hell, I think the Cabbage Patch doll was all the rage the last time you had to flirt with someone not your husband. That or the Model T." He dodged Sherri's punch. "I'll admit that men in Atlanta have women coming at us every way and every day; beautiful, successful, educated. It's easy to get jaded, to tell you the truth. Which is probably why I find Jessica so intriguing. She's never tried to impress me by being anything other than herself."

"Where'd she go to school?"

"She didn't."

"No degree?" Nathan shook his head. "Wow. That's different, too."

"If you'll remember, your dual-degreed brother was temporarily unemployed not so long ago."

"Only because your company downsized and could no longer afford you. And only because you could afford to be selective in choosing your next job, which if I remember correctly is netting you a cool six figures." She looked around, lowered her voice. "Does she know this? That you own your own home, and how much you're making?"

"Sherri . . ."

"I know your nose is wide open and all, but you haven't known her long. I'm just throwing up the caution sign. That's what big sisters do."

"I know a gold digger when I see one and trust me, I've seen plenty."

"You're a good judge of character, baby bro, and normally I wouldn't be concerned. But given what happened to me and Randall last year . . ."

"You have every right to be skeptical, and I have every intention of listening to your advice. I'll be careful. But it's been a long time since I've felt about someone the way I feel about Jessica. That's why I wanted her to meet the people most important to me."

Sherri stood and hugged her brother. "I want nothing more than to see you happy, Nathan. I'll be keeping my fingers crossed that this one works out and that Jessica will be everything you desire . . . and more."

On the other side of the tastefully appointed home and one level up, a conversation similar to what Nathan and Sherri were having was happening with Jessica and Sherri's best friend.

"Nathan is like a brother to me," Renee said as the two ladies watched the dancing flames in the sitting room's fireplace. "He's one of the good ones. So if you mess with him, then you're going to have to deal with more than his family." Her tone was light, she chuckled even, but there was something in her eyes that suggested she was as serious as a brain tumor.

Jessica's response was guarded. "I see."

Renee's eyes narrowed a bit as she eyed the attractive woman with flawless sun-kissed skin, luscious lips, mesmerizing eyes, and hourglass figure. It was easy to see why Nathan would have been tempted by the package. However, considering the type of women he usually dated—vivacious, outgoing, and supremely confident—Renee couldn't understand why he'd fallen so hard for the contents inside this pretty wrapping. Wanting to find out, she tried to lighten the mood.

"How did the two of you meet?"

"At a sports bar."

"You're into sports? I am too, mainly because of the fine men who play them." This time her light laughter elicited a brief smile.

"Honestly, I barely know a layup from a field goal. But I like the establishment's ambiance. Plus, they make the best martinis in town."

"I love a good drink. I'll have to make sure and go there the next time I'm in Atlanta. You do live in Atlanta, correct?"

"Yes."

"For how long?"

Jessica took a sip of the spiced tea that the two ladies were drinking, except that Renee's had been enhanced with a liberal shot of brandy. "Renee, it's understandable that you're curious about me. But I'm an extremely private person and your interrogation is making me uncomfortable."

Renee reared back, incredulous. "Interrogation? Girl, that's a strong word for simple chitchat."

"Don't take it personally." Jessica stood. "It's not you. It's me. Nice meeting you, but it's been a long day. I'm going to find Nathan."

With that, Jessica turned and left the room. Renee watched her exit, her mind whirling with questions from front to back. For this Chi-Town to Sin City transplant, life was pretty much an open book. There was very little about her that friends didn't know. On one hand, Jessica had every right to not answer

Renee's questions. But on the other, the woman's response left her feeling uncomfortable and just a tad pissed. Yes, she was very attractive. Yes, she seemed nice enough. But there was something about her that made Renee's brow crease. She slowly sipped her brandy-spiced tea and tried to figure out why.

She was still pondering the conversation when a short time later Sherri walked in. "Hey, Sis. What's got your face all scrunched up?"

"An interesting conversation I just had with Nate's friend." She put emphasis on the last word. "Are they gone?"

Sherri rushed over and took a seat beside Renee. "Girl, yes. And I couldn't wait to get your take. What happened?"

Renee told her. "I am direct and straightforward, as you know. But it wasn't like I asked for the girl's birth date and social security number, just making conversation. It was odd that she was so guarded."

"I thought it was me. Throughout the day—while setting up the dessert table, when I found her and Nathan alone in the solarium, after the guys had come back from playing ball—I went out of my way to engage her. She was nice enough, and seems genuinely taken with my baby bro. But . . ."

"Who wouldn't be?" Renee fluttered her lashes.

"Stop it! You've never been interested in Nate!"

"Before, he seemed too young and immature, but brother man is growing up nicely. He's what, seven or eight years younger than me?" Sherri nodded. "Hmm . . ."

"You know good and darn well you're not going to step to my younger brother."

"Never say never."

"I think you're serious." Renee raised a brow. "Well, good luck in getting past Jessica. All day that girl stuck to him like wet on water." They were both silent a moment. A log broke, causing the fire to pop and flare as the wood rearranged itself in the large hearth. "Do you think I'm overly paranoid because of all the drama that happened to my family last year?"

"Probably," Renee said with a sigh, an involuntary shudder accompanying the memories of that unspeakable event. "None of us will ever look at strangers quite the same way again. But that doesn't mean we're not picking up on something, either."

"That's true. But you know what? Nathan is intelligent. And he's grown. So I'm going to trust his instincts and give Jessica the benefit of the doubt until or unless she does something that causes me to think otherwise."

"I don't know. A man's thinking isn't always straight when he's using the other head. And trust me, one look at that girl's cute bubble booty and you already know. His other head is getting a workout."

"Nay, really? I needed that information? It's my brother we're talking about!"

Renee answered, nonplussed. "Like you said, we're all grown and we both know what grown men do with asses like that."

The women continued talking well into the night, their conversation going from Nathan to Renee's latest boo possibility, to Sherri's new part-time teaching job, to Randall's upcoming trips. In the back of both of their minds, however, was the topic that had begun this latest chat. The guarded, private Jessica . . . and what was up with that.

CHAPTER 3

She'd failed the test. The signs weren't glaring like they'd be on a school paper, when one expected a gold star and instead received red marks and a minus sign. They were subtle, like the way Sherri gave her brother a big bear hug and Jessica's arm a little squeeze. Or how Sherri's friend Renee offered a skeptical smile when Jessica said it had been good to meet her. Nathan's mother, Miss Elaine, was definitely the kindest of the bunch and probably the nicest as well. The men, especially Nathan's brother-in-law, Randall, had been cordial but kept their distance. The other wives and girlfriends were friendly enough. Not that she cared about them. The ones she wanted to win over were Miss Elaine and Sherri. In this instance, one out of two wasn't good enough. Especially given what was at stake, and what she'd promised.

If only I hadn't . . .

Jessica jumped from the couch and walked to the window of her second-floor condo near Five Points. Of all the things she'd been thinking about since the weekend she'd spent with Nathan—first with his family in Virginia and then with his DC friends—what could, should, and would have been wasn't part of the process then and wouldn't be now.

It was Sunday evening. Nathan had dropped her off less than an hour ago. It felt much longer. Being practically inseparable from him for four straight days had provided some of the happiest moments of her life, especially when they partied in DC. After all of the holiday hoopla, her home was too quiet, and she too alone.

She turned on the radio. One of Nathan's all-time favorites was playing, or so he'd told her the first time they'd heard it together. Jessica walked back to the couch, plopped down and grabbed a pillow as her mind drifted back to the night she'd spotted him across the room.

There ought to be a law.

That's what Jessica thought as she looked across the crowded restaurant and beheld a table filled with caramel and chocolate testosterone. She lazily sipped a pomegranate martini, swinging a stiletto-clad foot as she watched them laughing, scoping, sipping, too. They were all handsome, but one stood out, and for more reasons than the fact that he was the one she wanted: tall, at least six feet—which, although she was only five-foot-three, she preferred—nattily dressed, expressive eyes and easy smile. The group of four men was in a lively discussion. The one she watched spoke little, but when he did, the others listened attentively.

A couple times their eyes had met. After hearing snatches of conversation as she passed their table on her way to and from the bathroom, she stopped and boldly made her move. At her declaration that he'd won the argument, Nathan nodded with a casual smile. One of the guys blatantly flirted. But she walked away from the table as quickly as she'd come, returned to her seat, and became engrossed in something online. She'd finished her drink and believed a rendezvous with the handsome stranger a lost cause until she'd reached the door, felt a hand on her shoulder, and turned to find that same sexy, self-assured smile from across the room now on display in front of her.

They'd gone to dinner the next night, and dancing the night after that. The following weekend they'd enjoyed a neosoul concert and the weekend after that they'd enjoyed each other. Nathan was a skillful, thoughtful lover, which she'd expected. What she hadn't expected was to develop real feelings for him. Nor had she expected such feelings to be reciprocated.

No, that hadn't been a part of the plan at all.

Her ringing cell phone brought Jessica out of her musings. Seeing the name on the caller ID only further muddled her mood. "Hey."

"Hey. What's wrong with you?"

"Nothing." A sigh and then, "just thinking and wondering what all this is about. And why you can't explain."

"My limited communication has to be frustrating. I know it's a lot to ask but please, just trust me. Okay? How was Thanksgiving?"

"He has a nice family." This elicited a snort and a curse word from the other end. "I knew you'd react that way, but it's true. His mother was very nice to me, his sister, too."

"Sounds like you've made quite the impression. His taking you around the family is a sure sign that he's falling for you, that he trusts you. His absolute trust is very important."

"That's just it, Sissy. His trusting, caring nature makes your intense dislike for him uncomfortable to hear. That and the fact that I'm falling in love with him."

"That's real peachy, but *love* has nothing to do with why you're with him. Then again"—a humorless laugh spilled from the phone's speaker—"I guess it does."

"Being with him over the holidays showed me that what I've never had but always wanted is possible, a close-knit, happy family. I used to talk about it. Remember?"

"Yes, in those letters we traded before I got caught. You always were the dreamer, the believer in fairy tales. But as your ex clearly showed you, life is not a storybook that ends with happily ever after, and blood is thicker than water. The man you now think is Mr. Wonderful is part of the reason I'm here. Remember that."

Tension crackled like wood in a fireplace, heated by seconds of angry silence.

Jessica sighed. "I still don't know what you want."

"What I've always wanted: for us to be together and for you to be okay. That's what all of this is about."

Jessica smiled. In these infrequent, tender moments with her sister she felt protected and loved.

"I've got to go, but I'm sending you a letter. Read it for fun, like how we communicated when we were in different foster homes. Understand?"

"Yes. I got it."

"Good. This is a huge favor, Jessie, and you're the only one I can ask for help. Trust me when I tell you it's the only way I can get out of here so that we can be a true family again."

"I want that more than anything but . . ."

"But what?"

"Not knowing what you need is making me nervous."

"It will soon be made very clear. When it does please, *please* don't change your mind."

"You're the only family I have left in the world. Whatever you need, I'm here."

CHAPTER 4

"Nate Carver." His voice was all business as he eyed the unknown caller ID on his dashboard.

"Nathan, it's Renee."

"What's up, Renee? This is a surprise."

"Yeah, I was hoping you'd pick up. Sherri gave me your number. I hope you don't mind."

"Not at all. What's going on?"

"Thought I'd call and check on you. All the snow and ice . . . for Atlanta that's crazy!"

"It was pretty bad earlier in the week. The streets are fine now."

"That's good. I wish I could bottle this eighty degree weather and send it to you."

"We could use it right about now. What else is happening in Sin City?"

"Not much; just sitting home bored on a Friday night."

"A pretty lady like you? That doesn't sound right."

"Brothers don't know what they're missing."

"They need to recognize."

She laughed. "I tried to get your attention at Sherri's house. But you were preoccupied."

Nathan switched the call from his car to his earbud, parked in front of a wine shop, and went inside. He entered the aisle stocked with a variety of cabernet sauvignons and eyed the labels.

"I've been known to leave men speechless but . . ."

"Sorry about that. I just walked into a store for a bottle of wine."

"Romantic night planned with your girl, Jessica?"

"Something like that."

"I still can't get over you being with someone like her."

"That's what Sherri said. Is she the other reason why you're calling?"

"Yes and no. We barely talked in Virginia. I wanted the chance to really catch up. It wasn't until we were together at Thanksgiving that I realized how long it had been since I'd seen you, and that Sherri's baby brother is all grown-up. You're my main reason for calling. But since you mentioned it, your sister and I got the same impression about your friend."

"She told me how y'all felt about her. Hold on a minute." He swapped calls. "Hey, baby."

"Where are you, Nate?"

Jessica's light and flirty voice put an instant smile on Nathan's face. "On my way home, ready to shut out the world and spend time with you."

"I'm ready for you, too. And I have a surprise."

"Oh really? What?"

"Ha! Good try. It's a surprise, silly, but I think you'll like it."

"I can't wait. Hold on, Jessica. Let me end this other call." He switched again. "Renee, I need to take this."

"No worries. We'll talk later."

"All right. Good-bye." After choosing a bottle he walked to the counter, once again tapping the screen. "Baby, you there? Hello?"

She wasn't. Nathan paid for the wine, returned to his car

and sent Jessica a quick text. Even with rush hour traffic, he was home in ten minutes.

It had been a busy week since the Thanksgiving celebration in Virginia. For Nathan and the consulting firm where he was employed, it was time to wrap up cases for the year and handle all the business that could be concluded before December 23rd, when the entire firm shut down for the holidays. His boss, Broderick Turner, had been increasing his responsibilities for the past three months. Nathan relished the challenge, but it was time to unwind. He'd put in a grueling twelve-hour day and was looking forward to a quiet evening of takeout, movies, a bottle of wine, and good loving from the woman he'd not seen all week. He placed a food order with instructions that it be delivered in an hour, stripped off his clothes, and headed to the shower.

Is that my doorbell? Nathan turned down the gushing shower-head and cocked his head toward the door. Another sound of the chimes had him turning off the water and reaching for a towel. No more than five minutes had passed since he stepped in the shower; too early for either Jessica or the food to have arrived. Curious, he looked through the peephole, then opened the door.

"You're early."

Jessica untied the belt wrapped around her waist. The coat fell open. Besides high-heel boots she wore nothing but a smile. "I couldn't wait."

The temperature was dropping but Nathan heated right up. He stepped back and dropped his towel. "Well, come on in."

Their "greeting" took almost an hour, leaving just enough time for a quick duo shower before the food arrived.

After he donned PJ bottoms and she the top, they went into the dining room. "Hope you're hungry."

"Starving."

"Can you grab the wine? It's on the kitchen counter."

"Sure."

He pulled lasagna, garlic bread, and salad from the bags. She returned with the bottle and two glasses. They made their plates and dug in.

Jessica swirled a piece of bread in the thick sauce. "This is delicious, Nate."

"I agree." He licked his fingers. "Tastes almost as good as you."

The look she gave him was filled with love. "I missed you."

"It was a busy week. I'm glad it's over."

"Did you finish everything you wanted?"

"No. It's going to be crazy until Christmas."

"I just hope it doesn't snow anymore."

"I wouldn't count on it. I believe another cold front is supposed to move in next week." He reached for more salad. "Maybe we should move to Vegas, where Renee lives. She told me it was eighty degrees over there."

Placing down her fork and picking up her napkin were Jessica's only outward displays of her inner angst. "When did you talk to her?"

"Today," Nathan said around a forkful of lasagna. "I love the spicy sausage they add to this dish. Do you think you can make this, baby?"

"Maybe, if I cooked." She took a sip of wine. "I didn't know you and Renee were so close."

"I told you she is my sister's BFF. I've known her since high school."

"Hmm."

"What does that mean?"

Jessica shrugged. "I just didn't know you guys talked, that's all."

"We normally don't. She heard about the weather and called to see if I was okay."

"How thoughtful of her."

Nathan paused, reaching for his own wineglass. "Do I detect a little jealousy?"

"Would you think less of me if I said yes? I trust you, but her calling you has me feeling some kind of way. I don't have the best track record with women, or with men who have them as good friends. When we met, it was clear that she didn't like me all that much."

"Baby, you have to understand something. She and my sister are used to seeing me with loud, aggressive women. Women who are more like Renee." He reached over and ran a finger down her cheek. "You're quiet—reserved, is how Sherri described you. It'll just take them a while to adjust to your personality, that's all. Once they get to know you, I'm sure they will love you just as much as I do. Well, probably not that much, but they'll understand why you've stolen my heart."

Jessica reached for her wine and relaxed against the chair with a satisfied smile. "Is that what I've done?"

"Right out of my chest, and I'm not even going to file a police report. Because you're the sexiest thief I've ever met."

Placing down her glass, she walked around to Nathan's side of the table and sat on his lap. "I really want the acceptance of your family and friends," she said, placing kisses on his cheek, chin, and mouth while grinding against his burgeoning erection. "But knowing you love me is what's most important. You mean the world to me."

Nathan reached beneath the pajama top and tweaked her nipple to hardness. "Don't worry about them, baby. You've got this."

CHAPTER 5

Bright sunlight crept between the blinds. The day lived up to its name. Nathan ran an errant hand across the bed, seeking warm flesh. A cold sheet greeted his palm. His eyes popped open. Then he remembered. Jessica left earlier to go home, take a shower, and put on that which was delightedly missing when she showed up Friday night. He lazily pulled the cover over his naked torso, watching a mental replay of the love they'd made using different positions and almost every room. There'd been plenty of women in Nathan's life, a couple of them continued to call even now, long after the romance had ended. But when it came to giving pleasure, all of them together didn't match one Jessica Bolton.

Just as he decided to roll out of bed and take a shower, his phone rang. He checked the ID and pushed the speaker button. "Good morning, Mom. How'd you know I was planning to call you?"

"Because you're always planning, just don't get around to doing it too much."

"Aw, Mom . . ."

"Just teasing you, Son. Good morning. I hope it's not too early."

"Never for you. How's life in North Carolina?"

"I'm blessed, honey. Just returned from the eight o'clock service with Constance. The pastor was on fire today!"

"I'm glad you enjoyed it. And you said with Ms. Riley?"

"Yes, she's back here checking on her house. You know she decided to rent it out instead of sell it, said she might move back some day."

"She was a great neighbor and is a good friend. But I'm sure she's enjoying her family in St. Louis."

"Oh yes. There's nothing like grands and great-grands to make us smile. Of course, where some are concerned I'm still waiting."

"You have Aaron and Albany. You'll always be a grand-mother even if I never have kids."

"Hmph. Speaking of Sherri's kids, have you talked to her?"

"No, not this weekend."

"Well, she'll be calling you. They want the family down to the island for Christmas."

Nathan got out of bed and reached for his bottoms, considering what his mother had said. He'd only visited the Bahamas once since his brother-in-law had bought his sister a house there. "That sounds great, Mom. Let me talk to Jessica and see if she can get the time off."

"How is your girlfriend?"

"She's fine."

"Tell her I said hello. She seems like a nice girl."

"We're going to brunch in a bit. I'll be sure and tell her."

He and his mother talked for several more minutes and when the call ended, he decided to call his sister.

"Hey, Sis. I hear that for Christmas we're Bahamas bound."

"So you can make it. That's great, Nate!"

"Yes, our office shuts down until after the New Year. I just have to make sure Jessica can get off."

"Oh, she'll be coming with you?"

Nathan barely paused before he answered. "Of course."

★ ★ ★

Jessica paired skinny jeans with a cream-colored mohair sweater. Her shoulder-length hair hung loose and she wore no makeup. Looking at the clock, she realized it had taken her less than an hour to shower and dress.

Still at least thirty minutes until Nate comes over. Let me check my mail.

She walked back to her condo, flipping through several pieces of mail. Coming to one postmarked from North Carolina stopped her in her tracks. *Sissy's letter!* She hurried to her door, throwing down the other pieces of mail as she entered, and ripped open her sister's letter.

> *Jessie! Good to talk with you the other day, as always.*
> *It's been months, but I'm still pinching myself that we*
> *are able to talk again. I thought you'd never get away*
> *from that controlling asshole. How long ago was it*
> *he changed your phone number so I couldn't reach*
> *you . . . six, seven years? Crazy how life has kept us*
> *separated for so long. But if we work together on this*
> *idea I have, that's all about to change.*

Hmm . . . nothing so far. Sissy's second paragraph detailed an incident that never happened. Confusing, until Jessica again tried the code. The average person would see a silly childhood story, but using the system Sissy had created, Jessica began to decipher the message within the message—the huge favor her sister needed that only she could do. Her jaw dropped, along with her stomach. To call this favor huge was a *huge* under-statement. She stared at the paper in disbelief. *What the hell?*

She read the entire paragraph again, then focused on the sentences where the real reason for Sissy's letter was deftly hidden.

> *Speaking of snakes—remember when I had to help our*
> *skittish neighbor catch and kill that snake? Remember*
> *the one who got blamed? Bobby caught and put it on*

the porch, blamed me, then lied. "She put it here!" I
wanted to slap him. So full of it. Didn't matter. I adored
him anyway. So hot! Can still see him sweat and get
dirty playing with his cousin out behind the old coot's
yard!!! To him I was just a kid. But he was my secret
crush. Good old Bobby Smith. Wonder whatever
happened to him. He's probably got several kids and a
few exes by now. Ha! But that was one gorgeous man.

Jessica clenched the paper as she walked to the couch and
sat. Surely there'd been a mistake. Perhaps Sissy forgot the nu-
merical sequence to create the secret message. *Maybe I forgot*
how to read it. Wishful thinking; Jessica knew this wasn't true.
When she was nine and living with a foster family in the
countryside, then fourteen-year-old Sissy moved nearby. Jessica
had been surprised and thrilled to see her at the local store. In
a strange twist of fate, Sissy had been placed in a group home
less than three miles away. Even stranger was the initial reluc-
tance and final refusal of the foster mom to let them visit each
other. That's when Sissy suggested writing letters. She quickly
created a code and taught it to Jessie. Only half a dozen letters
passed between them before Jessica was caught with the foster
mom's biological son, Dennis, and abruptly moved to another
home. Though lost long ago, those letters were special. Neither
would ever forget that time, or the code. Sissy had made what
she needed done very clear.

Jessica stood and paced the room. *How on earth can I do this?*
But considering that the end result would be her sister's freedom . . . how could she not?

The day she'd found Sissy's contact information online and
sent her an e-mail had been nerve-racking. The day she'd gotten a response had been the happiest one in a very long time.
They went from e-mails to phone calls and enjoyed short, rare
chitchats for almost a year. That all changed when Jessica's controlling and possessive ex-husband broke into her inbox and

read their exchanges. She still bore a small mark above her eye from that night's "discipline."

In a rare act of defiance, she had gone to the public library, created a fake Facebook profile and sent her sister a friend request. When Sissy found out about the physical abuse, she encouraged Jessica to end the marriage and said she would help. Two weeks later Jessica was living in Atlanta, and a few days after that they'd reconnected by phone. That's when Sissy first alluded to needing a huge favor. And that's when Jessica said she'd do it. To refuse never crossed her mind.

Returning to the couch, she read the letter a final time. The coded message made everything clear, just as Sissy said it would. The cryptic statements made during their phone conversations now made sense, the reason for secrecy obvious. The request caused Jessica to view everything that had happened since the Facebook friend request in a different light: the push from Sissy to leave Edwin and the money to do so, her suggesting Atlanta for relocation, the planned meeting with Nathan. Was all of that done because of what was in the letter, to put Jessica in her debt?

"Of course not," Jessica whispered. *Sissy would never use me like that.* She walked to her computer and opened a Word document. After a general greeting and small talk mentioned simply to throw off the nosy, letter-reading guards—Jessica got to the point.

> *Funny, the story about Bobby. The holidays have you feeling nostalgic. I can't wait to take a break. Work has been very hard, impossible really. I don't like the situation. But sometimes we have to do what we don't want to do. I guess now is one of those times. So I'll try and enjoy a little R&R, then after New Years, unfortunately, it will be back to work.*

She ended the letter abruptly, a part of her heart already breaking.

CHAPTER 6

"Did you suggest a background check on Jessica to Sherri?" Nathan was so chagrined that he'd reached past small talk for the heart of the matter.

"Hello to you too, Nate. And here I thought you were just calling because you loved me."

Renee's voice was way too cheerful for Nathan's mood. "Answer my question."

"Yes, but only indirectly. I was telling her about a recent situation where I should have done some checking, then jokingly suggested that you do one on Jessica."

"When she called me she wasn't laughing."

"I'm sorry if putting that in her head upset you. But is it such a bad idea? Maybe I watch too much Investigation Discovery, but how much do we know about the people we meet? Unlike the old days when we either grew up with, went to school or church with, or were introduced by someone who knew our whole family, we don't know who we're meeting now. I wouldn't think twice if someone wanted to check me out. I have nothing to hide. And with what happened to Sherri and Randall—"

"This isn't about what happened to my sister. Or to you. This is *my* life. And I don't appreciate y'all interfering."

Attitude met its match. "Dang, Nate. It was just a suggestion. If you don't feel like it, don't do it!" Then in a softer tone, "I can understand your being upset. That's your girl. But Sherri is like a sister to me. That makes you family. I'm always going to be concerned about both of you, and Miss Elaine, too."

Nathan took a breath and loosened his hold on the steering wheel. "Sorry for going off on you. I know you care. But I'm frustrated. It's been a couple years since I brought one of my girlfriends around the family. In one day, a matter of hours, you and Sherri have formed all of these opinions and suspicions when what I need is for y'all to be as happy for me as I am for myself."

"You're right, Nitpicky. I'll back off."

Nathan chuckled, low and deep. "Wow, I haven't heard that nickname since I was what, sixteen or seventeen years old?"

"Sixteen, and on the way to your first prom, remember?"

"Right. You and Sherri had come down to visit."

"And you were determined to not have one hair, thread, or kerchief out of place."

"Please, girl. You know I was styling in that double-breasted."

"Nobody could tell you otherwise! Looking like Wanya Morris."

"Those brothers in Boyz To Men wish they had it like I did."

"Getting invited by a senior when you were just a sophomore? Yes, you had swag, even back in the day, Mr. Nitpicky."

"Girl, you're a trip. And even though I want you to mind your own business and stay out of mine . . . I know your actions are because you care."

"All of us single people are looking for love, Nate. I hope you've found it."

"Thanks, Renee. Hey, how well do you know the Vegas club scene?"

"I know a little bit. What age group are we talking?"

"The grown and sexy crowd, thirty and older."

"I'd have to think about that. Most of the clubs here, especially those on the strip, cater to the younger, twenty-something crowd."

"I've helped one of my clients develop a successful club here for those I just described; mainly R & B music with some old school thrown in, an excellent specialty bar, and gourmet hors d'oeuvres. He's thinking about expanding."

"Here might be a good place to do it. We don't have anything like that."

"Okay, I'll keep in touch."

Later that night, Nate and Jessica were snuggling on the couch in Jessica's condo, located just minutes away from Nate's loft in the Atlantic Station neighborhood. In a rare move, Jessica had tried her hand at cooking and had made a fairly decent pot of chili. Now they sipped spiced apple cider while watching *Monday Night Football*.

Nate set his cup on the coffee-table coaster and wrapped his arms more firmly around her. "I know you moved here from Oakland. Is that where you were born?" A long pause. No answer. "Jess, did you hear me?"

"Hmm?"

"Where were you born?"

"New Orleans, but they lost my records in Hurricane Katrina."

"I would have never guessed you were from the South."

"We left when I was a baby—uh, I'm told not too long after I was born."

"Was this with your birth mom, before you were adopted?"

Jessica raised her head from Nathan's shoulder. "Why all the questions?"

"Just getting to know you better, that's all. Today I was thinking about how I enjoyed introducing you to my family and

realized that aside from your spending time in foster care before being adopted, I don't know much about your background."

I never should have told him I was adopted. She made a mental
note to correct that lie. She placed her head back on Nate's
shoulder and her arm went around his waist. "Those are sad
and lonely memories. I don't like to talk about it."

"I can understand that. We all like to put unhappy events
behind us. But sharing some of that experience will help me
feel more connected, like I know you inside and out, like nobody else does, like the way I want you to know me."

"I'm a private person. You already know more than most."

"If I were plucked away from my birth mother I'd forever
wonder about her, and whether or not I had siblings. Who my
father was . . . all of that. I don't even know your middle
name."

"Don't have one."

Her shoulders rose and fell on the waves of a silent sigh.
They watched as Russell Wilson threw a perfect spiral to Mar-
shawn Lynch for a touchdown; silently took in the Seahawks
cheering on the sidelines before the extra point was kicked
and the network went to commercial.

"From what I was told," she finally began, "my parents died
tragically when I was five years old. How exactly was never
made clear. My memories of them are vague, perhaps even
imagined. I was never formally adopted out of the foster care
system, but these people were the only family I really knew. I
have a sister out there, somewhere . . . but I haven't seen her
in . . . a while. After I got married my life revolved around
my husband, totally and completely. I was only eighteen then
and had been with him since just before turning seventeen. He
was twenty-eight when we met, thirty when we married—attractive, successful—my knight in shining armor. Or so I
thought. It turns out he was my warden, our palatial home my
prison."

"Was he abusive?"

The answer was soft, almost whispered. "Yes."

Nate's jaw clenched. "What's his name?"

"Why?"

"Because I would love to give him a taste of his own medicine, so he knows how it feels."

"He'll get his eventually. I'm just glad I got away. Now"— she turned and placed a soft kiss on his lips—"can we leave the past and come back to the present? Here . . ." She kissed him again, on the chest this time as she repositioned herself. "And now?" She unbuckled his pants and made quick work of the zipper, pulling out his flaccid member and licking it to life.

"Baby, I'm trying to watch the game." Perhaps, but nonetheless he helped pull down his boxers for better access.

Jessica chuckled, bent her head toward his groin and made a play of her own.

CHAPTER 7

A week later Nate sat in his office, his hands poised over the laptop's keyboard as he viewed the screen. For a search, there were several website choices: BeenVerified, PeopleSmart, Instant Checkmate, PeopleFinders, iDTrue, IdentityPI, and more. After another minute of contemplation he pulled his hands from the keyboard, leaned against his black leather office chair and gazed out the window. The forecast had called for the chance of a snowstorm, but right now the sun was bright and the ground was dry. The only storm was in his mind, brought on by the conversation with his sister when she called to discuss the holidays.

"I want to talk about our Christmas plans."

"Okay." Nate knew this had been his sister's main reason for calling but had patiently indulged her with small talk about her kids, his job, and the continued crazy snow season down South.

"Do you still intend to bring Jessica?"

"That's the plan."

"Okay, Brother. I don't want what I'm about to say to cause an argument, but if she's going to be in a home with the rest of my family, we have to talk about something you don't like."

"A background check."

"Yes. And it's not because of how I do or don't feel about her. I'd want to know as much as possible about anybody that was coming with us on a family vacation and staying a week."

"I understand, Sis. What happened to you and Randall last year had to have been traumatizing. I don't necessarily agree, and I definitely don't like feeling that I'm going behind someone's back and snooping on them—"

"Then tell her! Anyone dating these days should make it common practice. Heck, she needs to do one on your behind!"

"I wouldn't have any qualms about that."

"And neither should she. If you guys are going to be together long term, there should be no secrets."

"Sherri, if I do this, I need you to do something for me."

"What's that?"

"Be nice to Jessica. Stop judging her. Instead, get to know her. She just might become your sister-in-law."

"Wow, Nathan . . . it's that serious?"

"You and Mom have been on my case about settling down. Now that I'm thinking about it, you're acting shocked."

"I am, but I'm also happy that you've found someone to care about so deeply. Do the background check, Brother. And I'll welcome your girl Jessica with open arms."

His attention returned to the laptop screen. He scrolled down, clicked on a website, and after paying the fee for obtaining the report, typed a name into the search box. First glance showed there were dozens of Jessica Boltons in America.

After seeing how the categories were organized, he looked for her age, twenty-eight, and then over to the column for cities. Minutes later, the report was ready. With a hint of trepidation that surprised him, he began to read.

* * *

"Hey, pretty lady. Where's that gorgeous smile?"

Jessica looked up into the hazel-green eyes of Vincent Givens, one of the office's up-and-coming attorneys. His not-so-subtle flirting had begun within minutes of her being hired as their receptionist a month after arriving in the ATL. If not for her interest in Nathan, she would have acted upon the obvious attraction between them. As it was, she enjoyed their workplace friendship.

"Good afternoon."

"That's all I get? No smile to go with that greeting?"

Jessica turned and showed pearly whites.

"Ms. Bolton, on you even a fake smile looks good."

"There are no messages or mail for you here, Mr. Givens. So if you don't mind, I'll get back to work now."

"Why are you being so hard on someone who's trying to be nice to you?"

She hid a smile by turning to the memo she'd been typing, and resumed. "Because, like you, I have work to do."

"All right. But if you ever need anything at all, I'm here for you." He looked around quickly before leaning closer. "And I do mean . . . anything."

She didn't bother to watch him walk away. No matter, she knew how good that hard butt looked moving down a hall. In another life, she would have been on Vincent like white on rice, would have dated him in a heartbeat. She even wished she could confide in him, tell him about the promise she'd made that was driving her crazy. Unfortunately what she was about to do for her sister was something no one could ever know. If anyone found out, she'd join her dear Sissy; not exactly the type of reunion she'd envisioned. Unable to concentrate, Jessica called her backup and a few minutes later took a break. The downtown streets were as bustling as her thoughts.

Why was Nathan asking so many questions?

Is he angry that I was evasive?

Is that why he didn't call much last week, and chose to spend Sunday hanging out with his friends?

By the time Jessica reached a well-known deli and decided to grab a sandwich, she'd worked herself into a ball of walking worry, desperate to know if Nathan had found out something best kept hidden.

So much so that the vibrating cell phone in her suit pocket made her jump. Looking at the ID only increased her heart rate. "Hey, Nathan."

"Hey, baby. Are you all right?"

"I'm just . . . having one of those days, you know?"

"I thought the law firm's cases slowed during the holidays."

"Work is fine. It's just . . ."

"What's the matter, Jessica?"

"I don't know. You've been so quiet lately and we haven't hung out as much."

"That's why you're upset? Baby girl, I told you how my schedule would be until Christmas."

"Yes, but on Sunday you spent time with your friends instead of me."

"You knew about that days before and didn't say anything when I told you. What's got you acting insecure?"

"The holidays make me sad sometimes. That's all."

"Lucky for you I have just the type of information that will cheer you up. Why don't we meet for dinner around seven thirty?"

"That sounds good."

"Okay, baby." A pause before adding something he'd never before said in this relationship. "I love you."

When she exited the deli and stepped outside, her smile had returned and was shining as bright as the sun.

Nate ended the call with Jessica and immediately tapped another number. "Sherri, it's me."

"Hey, Brother."

"So . . . I did what you asked."

"What's that?"

"I did a background check on Jessica."

"And . . ."

"And I'm happy to say that everything she's ever told me checked out: her marriage, divorce, where she once worked in San Francisco . . . everything!"

"Jessica was married?"

"Yes, when she was very young. It was an abusive relationship that ended a year ago."

"How old is she?"

Nathan told her. She asked a few more questions. He answered those, too.

"So can you call off your deputy named Renee and turn in your own detective badge?"

"I haven't been investigating!"

"You've never put Jessica's name into a search engine."

"Maybe once," she mumbled.

They laughed.

"It's all good, Sis. The work schedule is crazy right now. I'm looking forward to chilling on the island."

"Me too, Nate. It's going to be a wonderful time."

That night Nathan and Jessica made quick work of their Thai-food dinner before returning to Nathan's loft. The night was short. Love was sweet. The next morning they left each other feeling happy and excited about the upcoming holidays. One big happy family. For now.

CHAPTER 8

She almost didn't take the call. The week had been wonderful. It was TGIF. Nathan had been busy with work, but they'd talked every day. Tonight they'd decided to stay in again—takeout and a movie. Tomorrow's plan was a club where a friend of Nathan's was performing. On Sunday, they'd watch football together at their favorite sports bar. And in less than a week—the Bahamas. In spite of the nefarious reason they were together, she enjoyed being with him. Given the situation he and his family had put her sister in, however, Jessica felt selfish for the thought.

"Hello, Sissy. How are you?"

"I've been better."

"I know."

"I got your letters."

"Then why haven't you answered my questions? From what I know so far, this situation doesn't make sense!"

"Does that mean you won't help me?"

"I said I would and I will, one way or another. But I need answers. And how I do it and when is up to me. Period."

"Listen to little Jessie, all grown-up. I apologize for not responding. You deserve to have your questions answered, and they will be, and the timeline should be up to you. You're there. I'm not. You know what's going on. I can only speculate and wait for your updates." Her acquiescence left Jessica no less conflicted. The silence was loud. "Hey, remember when I used to comb your hair and put it in ponytails? You were my doll."

Jessica sat on the couch and folded her legs beneath her, glad the topic had changed. "As I've often told you, I don't remember much."

"That's understandable. You were barely five years old when . . . everything happened."

"And you saved my life, right?"

"Twice. You don't remember them, or what happened at all?"

"Our parents?"

"If you can call them that."

"No, I don't."

"Trust me, that's a good thing."

"Maybe I've subconsciously blocked out the bad memories. Though I do seem to remember an old, gray-haired woman and . . ." Her brows scrunched with the will to remember. ". . . Being carried through clouds of smoke in someone's arms."

"The woman you remember is Mrs. Hurley. She seemed ancient but in actuality she just grayed early and was only in her late thirties, early forties when we were kids. I saw her a couple years ago."

"She's still alive?"

Her sister laughed. "Yes."

"Wow, I don't remember Mama and Dada but I remember her." Tears unexpectedly formed in Jessica's eyes. All her life this is what she'd longed for—family. With no memories of her mother, it was Sissy she'd missed and cried for the most. Years after Francine, she'd sought out girls her age to find a friend who could relate to the pain and loneliness she felt in her life. It always backfired, with the girl either lying on her, stealing from her, player-hating, or trying to take her man. Since the age of sixteen all of her friends had been male. But moments like this, girl talk with her sister, were what she'd longed for all these years. This was the only reason why she'd even for a second consider doing what her sister had asked.

"I have so many questions, so much I want to ask you, Sissy. Maybe I can come for a visit. I haven't seen you in person for well over ten years."

"I'd like that too, Jessie. But not yet. I'll explain everything some other time."

"Okay."

"Look, my time is up. I have to go. But I'm mailing another letter. We can talk more next week."

"Oh! That reminds me. You won't be able to reach me next week. I'll be in the Bahamas."

"Lucky you."

"I'm sorry, Sister, wish I could—"

"Hey!" A curt cutoff, but then her voice softened. "It's okay. Enjoy yourself. Because once you're back home . . . we get down to business."

"Right, down to business. Merry Christmas, Sissy."

"Sure, Jessie. Happy effing holidays."

Nathan sat chilling in his boss's office. Broderick wasn't much older, only forty-five, but his old-soul personality often made him seem much older. That and the fact that he'd married at eighteen and had a son just five years younger than Nathan. In the two years he had been with the firm, the two had gone from professional associates to good friends and confidants. Nathan's stellar performance probably had something to do with Broderick becoming the older brother that Nathan never had.

Broderick picked up a pen and twirled it. "Man, I'll be glad when this year is over."

"No doubt. I'm trying to close the deal on the Mc-Cormick account before it ends, but the bank is playing hardball, not wanting to lower their interest rate, or extend the terms."

"What about another bank?"

"I'm researching that as we speak."

"Of course. I knew you'd be on it. How is Kenneth Hall and the expansion of his business to Vegas coming along?"

"He's going for it. I talked with a contact who's lived there for about ten years. She says there's nothing out there like what he's is offering."

"She?"

"Yes, Renee Stanford. She's my sister's best friend, who I've known since high school. In the next few months, my client and I will probably be flying there to scout locations."

"Oh, okay. For a moment, I thought there might be a new lady in your life."

"Actually"—Nathan looked toward the door, then realized they were the only ones still there—"there is."

"Oh?"

Nathan nodded. "I met her a few months ago. So far, so good."

"Man, there's nothing like a solid sister having your back. Anita has always been there for me, Nate, through ups and downs, thick and thin. We haven't always agreed, and every day wasn't wine and roses. But at the end of the day we both knew we'd be there for each other. No matter what, know what I'm saying? Having that kind of security about a person is priceless."

"Y'all have been married for what, twenty-five years?"

"Almost. Twenty-two this past June."

"I can't even imagine it."

"If you're lucky, you'll do more than imagine it; you'll get to experience it for yourself. So when am I going to get to meet this new lady?"

"Jessica will join me at the Christmas party. After that we'll be heading to the blue skies and white beaches of the Bahamas. Is your family doing anything special for the holidays?"

"My son and his wife just bought a home in Texas. They've invited the family there."

"Sounds good."

"Not as good as the Bahamas. But when you're with family, and the love of your life, it really doesn't matter where you are."

Nathan checked his watch and stood. "I couldn't have said it better, Broderick. My mom and whole family will be there."

"Sounds like a merry Christmas indeed." He stood. They shook hands.

"Absolutely, man. I think this will be one of the best holidays I've had in a while."

CHAPTER 9

The company party was on December 23rd. The next day, Nathan and Jessica settled into their business-class seats for the flight to Nassau, the Bahamas.

Jessica gratefully accepted the mimosa offered by the flight attendant while waiting for others to board. "I'm glad my passport came in time. Vincent showed me how to get one quickly. It cost more to expedite, but to be on this plane right now makes it all worth it."

"Who's Vincent, one of the attorneys you work with?"

"Yes. He works in corporate law."

"With all those successful sharks swimming around, waiting for a chance to bite, I'd better keep my game up."

Jessica laid her head on his shoulder. "You have nothing to worry about."

"That's good to know. Buckle up, baby. This week is going to be one helluva ride."

It was early evening when they arrived at Château Sherri, located in a secluded, private section of the island. From the moment they came through the wrought-iron gates until the driver unloaded their luggage and started toward the house, Jessica didn't say a word.

Nathan reached for his laptop and noticed her staring. "Babe, are you all right?"

"This looks like a fairy tale." Her voice was a near whisper. "Your sister owns this house?"

"Yes, and I must admit that Randall outdid himself with this one." At her probing gaze, he continued. "This was his gift to her on their fifteenth anniversary."

"Wow. I've never seen anything like it."

"Wait till you see inside." He placed a hand at the small of her back and gently urged her up the walk.

While he paid the driver, Nathan's niece and nephew ran outside. "Uncle Nate!"

"Hey!" He picked his niece, Albany, up in his arms and twirled her around. "Girl, you're getting too tall for me to pick up!" He set her down and hugged his nephew. "What's up, Aaron? You're taller, too. What are they feeding you in Virginia?"

"Healthy food, something you probably don't know about!" All heads turned to see Sherri coming through the front door to greet them. "Welcome back to the château, Brother." They hugged. She turned to Jessica, her arms open to hug. "Welcome to my humble island abode, Jessica." After stepping back, she continued. "I hope you'll enjoy your stay."

"Thank you, Sherri. I'm sure I will. It's beautiful here."

"We absolutely love it. Come on in and let me show you to your room. You're just in time for dinner, which will be served within the hour."

After reaching their room, where Jessica continued to marvel at not only the décor but the red and silver holiday theme prevalent throughout, they showered, changed, and joined Nathan's mom, Elaine, in the dining room.

"There's my favorite lady!" Nate walked over and gave his mom a huge hug, slightly lifting her from the chair.

"Boy, put me down!" Eyes twinkling, she swatted his arm. "I didn't know y'all had made it down."

"We just got here."

"I must have been changing after taking my nap. The breeze coming through my windows is so wonderful." She looked behind Nathan. "I see you brought company. Hello, sweetie."

Jessica stepped forward. "Hello, Mrs. Carver. It's good to see you again."

"Likewise. I'm sorry, honey, but I've got a case of old age and don't remember your name."

"It's Jessica," Nate interjected. "And you're not old."

"What am I, middle-aged?"

"I never understood that phrase. One can't know they're middle-aged until the day they die. By then, who cares?"

"Not me. I'm old and glad to claim it."

"You're as young as you feel. That's why I'm going to get you started on a cardio routine. We'll take a run in the morning."

"You go ahead and run. I'll be watching from the rocking chair on the porch, cheering you on."

They laughed as Nathan and Jessica sat down.

Sherri and her family entered the room. "What's funny?"

"Your brother, that's what; thinking I'm going to live until I'm over a hundred."

"You're not?"

Sherri's husband, Randall, greeted Nathan and Jessica before taking his seat. Soon after, the young, dreadlocked chef brought out bowls of conch chowder: their first course.

After a bit of small talk about Sherri's lovely home and the beauty of the island, Sherri turned to Jessica. "You used to live in Oakland, correct?"

"Yes." She picked up her spoon.

"Were you born there?"

She shook her head in answer, pointing to her full mouth.

Nathan shot Sherri a look, but she either didn't see it or chose to ignore it.

"Oh, really? Where'd you grow up?"

Jessica glanced at Nathan, who used humor to intervene.

"Come on now, Sis. Don't grill my girl before she's even eaten her first meal!"

"Just trying to get to know your friend, Nate." Sherri smiled politely. "The only way I can find out what I don't know is to ask."

Randall reached for a warm roll. "How's business, Nate?"

And with that, the conversation blessedly turned away from Sherri's probing to everything from the economic climate to sports; and from the delicious entrée—baked fish served with peas, rice, and vegetables—that the adults ate, to the everyday hamburgers that the kids preferred.

Later, however, when Jessica went looking for Nathan, she found Sherri instead.

"Oh, I'm sorry. I thought Nathan was back here."

"No, he and Randall went for a walk. But come on in and join me. At the end of the day, this porch is one of my favorite places to unwind." She lifted her glass. "Would you like some wine?"

"No, thank you."

Sherri chuckled. "Girl, I'm not going to bite you. Have a seat. I know it can be uncomfortable meeting your guy's family, wanting to make a good impression, not knowing what to expect. With us, there's nothing to worry about. The château aside, we're pretty average folk who do regular things. Family is very important to us and my brother is my life, has been since he was born five years after me and followed me around like a puppy dog."

Jessica smiled.

"Do you have siblings?"

"I have a sister, but we didn't grow up together."

"Oh. Why not, if you don't mind my asking?"

Jessica looked out on the serene ocean view, listened as the waves crashed against the shore. "It's not that I mind. Of course you want to know about the person your brother is dating. My childhood was . . . difficult. I don't like to remember it, let alone talk about it.

"When very young, I was taken from my family, and for a very short time lived with an older lady. Later, I was placed in the foster care system where I remained until I was seventeen, when I met the man who became my husband. He was controlling and abusive, but after almost eight years he met someone to take my place. She probably thinks I hate her. But she was the distraction that made my leaving easier. I could have thrown her a welcome party." She leaned against the back of the chair. "I think I'll take that wine now."

Sherri reached for the bottle of pinot noir and poured.

"Thank you." Jessica took a long sip. Retelling these events had obviously drained her.

Sherri refilled her own glass as well. "That had to have been difficult, though I'd have no idea. I think those of us who grow up with our biological families take it for granted. Like I've said, Nathan is my heart. I can't imagine life without him. So the fact that you have a sister out there that you don't know has to be painful, or frustrating at the very least."

Jessica answered with a shrug. "It is what it is."

"Well, I can tell you there's very little about Nate that I don't know, so if you stick with me, you'll learn all of his secrets."

Jessica relaxed for the first time since that first spoon of soup. "I respect people's privacy, but"—she leaned forward in a conspiratorial whisper—"maybe you can share a few."

"Ha! Where to start? There was the time I caught him in the bathroom with the girl who lived down the street. They both had their pants down."

"How old was he?"

"He had to be all of seven or eight. Told me they were playing doctor."

"Wow."

"Jessica, my brother is a player from way back!"

The direction of the conversation created a delicate camaraderie between the women. Sherri did most of the talking. They finished the bottle of wine. By the time Nathan and Randall returned from their walk the atmosphere was tranquil while sounds of a reggae mix tape filled the air.

"You hear this, Ran? Our women have gone reggae." Nathan walked over and placed a kiss on Jessica's forehead.

"As long as they're not smoking ganja," Randall joked. "The only plants I mess with are in my lab." He sat next to Sherri, who was lounging on a chaise.

Jessie looked at Nathan. "You want to sit here, babe?"

"No. I've been up since five this morning." He stretched, his look conveying words not said. "I think I'm ready to call it a night."

"Me too." Jessica stood. "Thanks for the wine, Sherri."

"Thanks for the company. Breakfast is to order tomorrow so feel free to sleep in."

They said their good-nights, and after Nathan checked in on his mother, he joined Jessica in their beautifully appointed, spacious room. The various shades of blue blended perfectly with the tan and coral accent colors, conveying a beachlike atmosphere without being too obvious. As in all other rooms theirs held a Christmas tree, with blue, coral, and silver-colored bulbs to match the décor. The fresh pine smell mixed with a cinnamon-scented candle and created the perfect ambiance.

Jessica sidled up behind Nathan, who'd removed his shorts and sandals and was looking out the window. "Thanks for inviting me here."

When he turned around, he was surprised to see her eyes shining with tears. "Why are you crying?"

"I've never had this before. Everyone is so nice. And to think I might lose it . . ."

He stepped back, grasped her by the shoulders, and looked

deeply into her eyes. "Baby, I'm not like the men you've had in the past, who've used and abused you without a second thought. You're the best thing that's happened to me in a long time. I'm not going anywhere."

Jessica could only nod and hug him tightly. His assurance that he'd be there, and her knowledge that he wouldn't, is what made her sad.

CHAPTER 10

Jessica was dreaming; she had to be. Resting on a cloud in the middle of the ocean, the breeze ruffled her hair and brushed her skin. Music played, and she swayed to the rhythm. Happy sounds—laughter, bells, barking dogs—punctuated the air. She lay back and closed her eyes, imagining the one thing that would make this scene complete. And then he was there.

His touch was featherlight, like the wind. Large, strong hands softly caressed her body, becoming familiar with every delectable inch of her. He took his time. Kisses, light yet probing, began near a ticklish side of her neck. She squirmed and turned over, which only gave him access to her other side. The pressure of his lips intensified when they met hers. A stiff tongue demanded she part her lips. A strong finger demanded she part those lips, too. He drew her tongue into his mouth. She flicked it against his teeth, twirled it with his, moaned with raw pleasure when his finger found the door to her paradise and accepted her spread-legged invitation to go inside.

More kisses then, on her collarbone, breasts, nipples, tongue tracing the natural line that led to her navel. He shifted. Eyes fluttered. Jessica gained full consciousness just as Nathan eased his head between her legs, and his tongue between her folds.

The cloud was a feather-top mattress, the ocean was the sound of waves crashing below them, the happy sounds those she'd heard earlier on the beach.

This was reality, but felt like a dream.

He pushed her legs apart. "Wider," he commanded in a voice hoarse with need. She felt wicked, holy, powerful, defenseless, and there was no contradiction. The wind caressed her exposed feminine flower, which bloomed in response. He liked that. His mouth liked it more. His lips, soft; tongue, strong; finger, deep. Her senses roiled, crashed against themselves like the water beating the shore below, creating a storm in the core of her being that started out as an innocent funnel but quickly grew to an orgasmic hurricane, Category 5. She gripped the sheets. He lapped and kissed and nipped and sucked. Soft mewling became low guttural sighs. Grabbing the pillow, she shoved the pliable down fabric into her mouth. It met her scream, and pushed it back inside. Her legs trembled and body bucked with the force of her release. There was no time to catch her breath. He picked her up, wet and naked, and went outside to the private patio just off from their suite. She leaned against the balcony, her backside as vivid as the midnight moon. He gripped her hips, placed his hard yin into her soft yang, and settled into a steady groove. Soon another storm erupted. This time they both rode the wave.

"Did that just really happen?"

Nathan wore a look of satisfied confidence. "What do you think?"

Thirty minutes after their last round of lovemaking and long, hot shower, Nathan and Jessica sat against plush pillows with a bowl of fruit between them. A cutting board with various crackers and cheeses sat on a tray. Errant crumbs dotted the pristine white sheets. Neither culprit noticed. They were too busy assuaging the appetites all that dreaming had created.

Jessica popped a grape into her mouth, trying to recall how the spectacular sex got started. "I was dreaming, babe! And in the dream, I *thought* I was dreaming." She looked at him with curious eyes. He shrugged.

"I know it sounds crazy, but I swear it's true. I was dreaming and in the dream you came to me and started kissing my neck. Then you moved down and were kissing my body—"

"Baby, that wasn't a dream."

"It was, until you licked me. And then it wasn't."

"Oh, that woke you up for real, huh?"

"I guess. That was weird . . . but wonderful. Did you try these strawberries? They are so good. She held one up to his mouth.

He bit into it, then licked the juice from Jessica's fingers. "Mmm. That tastes very good."

By the time they settled down to sleep it was almost four a.m. Jessica snuggled next to Nathan, enjoying the contrast of their warm down bedding and the cool dawn breeze.

"Baby?"

"Hmm?"

"Can we stay here forever?"

"I wish."

"I want the way I feel right now to last a long time, like a vacation that never ends."

"I can't help with the vacation part, but that feeling I think I can get again."

"Hmm." Jessica's eyes fluttered closed. Her face held a smile. For these next few days she'd relish this dream. Soon enough, the nightmare would began.

CHAPTER 11

It was Christmas. Everyone had slept in, even the children, who'd enjoyed late-night fun with the chef's kids and their cousins. When Nathan and Jessica emerged from their love lair at around ten in the morning, the family was at the table.

"Good morning, everybody! How late are we?" Nate squeezed his mother's shoulders as he passed her before sitting down.

"We just got here," Sherri answered around a yawn. "But Mama got up with the roosters."

"It's too beautiful down here to sleep for long!"

After the greetings, Sherri tapped her fork against a crystal goblet. "Okay, guys. We've made plans to spend the day on the beach, so let's make quick work of breakfast—or brunch at this point—open gifts and then head to the seashore. How does that sound?"

Everyone voiced their approval and then set about ordering breakfast from the chef. Afterwards, they gathered in the living room and exchanged gifts. Jessica was stunned to receive presents from not only Nathan but also a spa certificate from his sister and brother-in-law and a hand-knitted throw from his mother.

She looked at what had been given her and her face fell. "I feel bad for not buying everyone gifts. I'm not used to being treated like this."

Miss Elaine quickly shushed her. "Don't worry about that. We just wanted you to feel included."

"And what woman can't use a massage, facial, and wrap," Sherri added. "The certificate is good for a year, so after one of those can't-stand-it weeks, go to the salon and enjoy."

When she received Nathan's gift, her heart sank the teeniest bit. Unless he'd concealed it, she knew by the size and shape of the box that it wasn't an engagement ring, which, considering the whole situation, was stupid to hope for anyway. As she opened the lid, revealing a heart-shaped diamond necklace with matching earrings, it was hard to keep real sadness at bay. After the New Year, everything would change.

"These are beautiful!" she gushed, leaning over to brush Nathan's lips with her own. "This is my best Christmas ever, babe. Thank you."

Nathan smiled when he saw that Jessica had gotten him the Movado stainless steel watch he'd admired while glancing through a magazine at her house. The matching business card case was a nice touch, but the card she'd placed inside it was the best gift of all.

"You chose the perfect gifts, Jessica." They shared a quick kiss. "I'll unwrap your other present later."

Jessica smiled. Her core tightened with the promise of that secret message.

After everyone had opened their gifts, Sherri stood. "Okay, gang. Let's move this party down to the beach. There will be surfing, Jet Skiing, and snorkeling available, so wear swimsuits!"

A short time later, the family converged on the sand. The kids headed straight for the Jet Skis and into the ocean, joined by their father. Sherri and Miss Elaine walked to one of two umbrella tables placed near the water. After setting a basket filled with refreshments on the table, Sherri took off her sandals.

"Mom, aren't you going in the water?"

She was met with a skeptical look. "That water right there?"

"Yes, Mom, otherwise known as the Atlantic Ocean."

"That's too much water for me, child. Best be glad you got me this close."

"You promised the next time you came down you'd at least stick your toe in!"

"Oh, all right." Miss Elaine slowly took off her sandals before standing. "A toe is what I promised and likely all that you're going to get!"

"Go on, Mom." Nathan wrapped both arms around Jessica. "Live a little!"

"Don't worry, Son. Your mama has already lived a whole lot."

He and Jessica watched the two women walk toward the shore and laughed as Sherri coaxed her mother to get closer to the water. After a tentative toe touch, she bravely allowed the water to cover her ankles.

"What do you say, baby? Do you want to go in?"

Jessica leaned against his chest. "Um, not right now. It's been so cold and wintery in Atlanta, I'd like to take the time to soak up this sun."

"That's cool." He walked over to one of the baskets and pulled out a large beach towel. "Let's go tan."

"Yeah, right." She playfully slapped his arm as they walked to a smooth area of the beach, spread out the blanket, and started playing footsie and kissy-face.

Nathan ran his hand along Jessica's curves. "You know I can't wait to unwrap the other gift you gave me."

She scooted closer. "Oh, really. The one mentioned on the card inside your case?"

"Yes, that gives me full access to your body and an unlimited supply of lovemaking." He ran a hand over her butt and moaned. "Woman, the way you're rocking that one-piece, I'm tempted to unwrap this gift right now!"

She slyly ran her hand between them and rubbed his hardening desire. "I want it, too. Waiting will only increase the pleasure, make you crazy with desire to make slow, sweet love."

"For sure, we'll do that. All night long."

She brushed him again. "I love it long. In fact I—" Jessica yelped as droplets of cold water were sprayed on her and Nathan.

The devious culprit was a water-gun-toting Aaron. "Sorry, Jessica. I was aiming for Uncle Nate!"

With this declaration, the love fest was over and the gunfight was on.

Jessica watched her lover frolic with the children. For her, adults and children playing together was a foreign concept. Her foster mother had been kind but stern. She couldn't remember the woman singing a song, laughing out loud, or having simple fun. *He'd make a good father. He's such a good man.* A twinge of guilt stabbed her heart, causing her to wonder about her loyalties and where they were placed.

"They love their uncle."

So engrossed had she been in watching Nathan, she hadn't seen Sherri walk up. She tried not to look as tense as she felt, flashed a smile to cover discomfort.

"Mind if I join you?"

"No." She moved over to make room on the towel.

Sherri sat down and an awkward silence settled around them. They watched the kids and Nathan, now joined by Randall, play along the beach. Miss Elaine sat under the umbrella, reading.

Sherri removed the sunglasses from her head and covered her eyes. "I could stay here forever."

"It's breathtaking," Jessica finally replied.

A pair of seagulls glided along in perfect synchronicity on the wind of the waves. In the distance, a sailboat bobbed. The gentle ebbing and flowing of the tide was background music to the scene.

"Is this your first trip to the Caribbean?"

"No. I went with my ex to Turks and Caicos. But that was a long time ago."

"How long were you married?"

"Too long."

Sherri stopped unscrewing the top, her focus on Jessica. "That's an interesting answer."

"I've had an interesting life."

"Do you feel my asking that question an invasion of privacy?"

Jessica offered a half smile. "I guess I'm not good at small talk, especially with women. No offense," she hurriedly added. "Growing up, I was a loner. Girls would normally rather dog me out or beat me up."

"I can understand that. You're a gorgeous girl. Kids can be cruel." Sherri offered the sunscreen to Jessica, who rubbed it on her legs and arms. "But you survived, thank goodness, and by the looks of it you're doing okay."

"I am now." Her smile was big and genuine as she watched Nathan and Randall coming to join them.

Their time at the beach was followed by dinner, drinks, and conversation. After Mom Elaine, Randall, and Jessica said good night, Nathan and Sherri walked into the kitchen.

She opened the fridge. "Water?"

"Sure. I'm probably dehydrated after drinking in the hot sun." He accepted the glass. "I want to thank you for making Jessica feel welcome. I saw y'all talking this afternoon."

"That's a bit of a stretch, though I tried to engage her in conversation."

"It takes her a while to warm up to people."

Sherri turned and faced him directly. "How long did it take with you?"

"That's different."

"How so?"

"You know your brother's got skills!" Sherri rolled her eyes and left the room.

Nathan followed her. "Come on, now, Sister. You set that up perfectly. I had to hit it out of the park."

"Seriously, though. I can't put my finger on it, but there's something about Jessica that feels . . . I don't know . . . uncomfortable."

"You're probably just picking up on her uneasiness. In time, she'll loosen up and you'll see the reason why I fell in love."

"Ooh, the L-word. So it's like that?"

"Yes. It's exactly like that."

Sherri turned toward the living room. Nathan kept on walking.

"Where are you going?"

"Upstairs to unwrap my last Christmas gift."

The following morning, Nathan and Jessica left for a four-day private rendezvous at the Sandals Royal Bahamian resort. Along with lots of rest and relaxation in their oceanside suite, they enjoyed windsurfing, billiards, live music, dancing, and a couples massage. During the day they'd assuage their appetites with a variety of cuisines from ten different restaurant choices. At night, they'd satisfy their appetite for each other. By the time they checked out and headed back to Château Sherri, Jessica felt relaxed and well-loved and Nathan felt like the luckiest man on the island.

Both were ready to celebrate the New Year, but the fireworks would happen earlier than expected.

CHAPTER 12

"Where's Jessica?"

It was New Year's Eve. Everyone was in the dining room, fixing plates from a small breakfast buffet.

Nathan served himself a huge helping of fried conch. "Good morning, Sis. My baby is going to sleep in this morning. I'll take a plate up when I leave."

"Hmph."

"What's that reaction about? She can't catch some extra z's without you tripping?"

Sherri bypassed the meat trays for a scoop of freshly cut fruit. "I'm sorry. I guess I can't expect her to be friendly toward me just because she's with my brother and staying in my home."

"She's been unfriendly?"

"She's been cordial, and definitely opens up more when she's with you. I guess I'm just used to seeing you with a different kind of woman."

"Here we go again. Like your girl Renee."

"Or your ex, Kaneka."

"Oh yes. You loved Kaneka, and look how that turned out."

"Who knew that her bubbly personality covered up a lying, cheating, conniving skank?"

Nathan cracked up laughing.

"Never mind. It's probably me."

"Give it time, Sister. Just give it time."

In early afternoon, Nathan met Sherri and Randall at the beach. The family had been joined by two couples who owned properties nearby. The children were off doing their own thing and Miss Elaine was talking on the phone to her good friend Ms. Riley, before joining the group later that day.

Sherri walked over. "Still no sleeping beauty?"

"Jessica's not down here?" Nathan looked around.

"Haven't seen her."

"She left the room. I assumed this is where she was headed. No doubt she'll be here soon." Nathan looked over to the umbrella-covered tables set up near the water and up to the cloudless sky. "Man, this is the life!"

Sherri linked her arm through his. "Yes, it's pretty amazing. Come on over. I want to introduce you to my neighbors. Good people. One couple is from Canada and the other lives in Michigan." They reached the table just as drinks were being poured. "Everybody, this is my brother, Nathan."

"How's everybody doing?" They all exchanged greetings. "Now, where is my drink?"

Jessica studied herself in the mirror, believing that she'd finally achieved the right look. After catching a side view of herself in the one-piece with matching wrap, she'd decided it didn't have the right amount of *wow* and had gone back upstairs to change into the other one she'd brought. It was the end of one year and the start of another. She was with a wonderful family and the best man she'd ever met. She wanted to please him, be the sexiest woman on the beach, and do him proud.

Donning her cover-up and slipping into low-heeled mules, she made her way down the rocky path that led to the home's private piece of paradise. Quickly spotting the group beneath the colorful umbrellas, she slipped out of the heels and relished the feel of warm sand beneath her pedicured feet. The view was as pretty as a postcard. A warm breeze tossed her shoulder-length curls. Looking up, she saw Nathan's gaze fixed on her. She offered a shy wave. He gave a nod. Her heart skipped a beat.

She looked like a goddess, or a nymph, coming toward him in dazzling white. Against her sun-kissed bronze-toned flesh the contrast was amazing. The cover-up she wore was long and sheer, so he could glimpse just enough of her juicy cleavage to make him want to forego the afternoon activities and return to the room. A sideways glance confirmed what he'd imagined: all eyes were on his girl.

She walked straight to him. "Hey."

"Hello, beautiful. I thought you'd beat me down here."

"At the last minute, I decided to change my outfit."

"Baby, I don't know what you had on before, but this right here is exceptional." He gave her a hug.

She whispered in his ear. "I hoped you'd like it."

"Everyone, this is my lady, Jessica." Everyone offered a hello. "I've been waiting on you, baby. I want to get in the water. Would you like a drink first? We've got a nonalcoholic fruit punch and another mix with a kick."

"No, I'm good. The water looks amazing, though. Let's go in."

"All right, y'all. We'll be back."

"Should I leave my cover-up here?"

"Sure."

She shimmied out of the see-through material and placed it on a lawn chair. Reaching for Nathan's outstretched hand, they turned toward the beach.

A gasp stopped him.

Nathan turned around. "What happened?" He watched his sister snatch up Jessica's throw and hurry toward them at the same time he witnessed the wives divert their husbands' pointed stares.

He followed their gaze to . . . Jessica's big bare ass.

"I can't believe you came out here like that," Sherri quietly hissed between clenched teeth. She moved them farther away from the group. This needed to be a private conversation. "That suit is not appropriate!"

"We're on a private island!" Jessica looked from Sherri to Nathan. "Babe?"

He took another peek at the round orb now competing with the sun for showiness. "She looks fine to me, Sis. The kids aren't here and we are on a private stretch of beach."

"With company." Sherri enunciated each consonant and vowel. "Women and their *husbands*."

Jessica shrugged, moving closer to Nathan. "And I'm here with my man. What's the problem?"

"If you don't know, I don't have time to tell you. Not right now. Just go change."

"We didn't know there'd be company, Sherri."

"Nathan's okay with it and that's all that matters." Jessica reached for Nathan's hand. "Come on, babe. Let's go swimming." She turned to leave.

Sherri grabbed her arm. Jessica snatched it back. Undeterred, Sherri took a step and got right in her face. "*I'm* not okay with it and this is *my* property. So you can either change or leave—your choice."

"Nathan?"

"It's not worth the drama, baby. Go change."

Jessica crossed her arms. "You're going to side with your sister?"

"This is her place and we are here at her invitation."

"Which doesn't excuse you from not having my back."

"Or backside," Sherri sarcastically quipped.

"This is just the type of bullshit that keeps me from having female friends. If I'd come down naked, you'd have a reason to be upset. But for showing just a little skin, you are seriously over-reacting."

Had Sherri been a piñata, this is when she would have burst. "Do. Not. Tell me how to react. Coming down here with your ass out is not cute. So like I said, you have two choices. You can go change, or you can go pack."

Sherri won the ten-second stare-down.

Nathan sighed. "Jessica, go put on something different."

"Okay," was Jessica's eventual reply. She took the cover-up that Sherri held, placed it over her arm, and started toward the path to the house. Nathan walked with her. Grumbling followed them both, no doubt the wives telling their husbands to place eyeballs back in sockets.

Nathan increased his pace to keep up with a fast-walking Jessica. "Sorry about that, babe. My sister is all about appearances." Silence, punctuated by huffing breaths and crunching sand. "I liked the one-piece you wore a few days ago."

They reached the top of the steps. Jessica whirled around. "I can't believe you!"

"What?" Nathan threw his hands up in surrender.

"Really? Your sister jumps down my throat, you jump on her bandwagon, and now you want to act like you don't know what's wrong?" She slipped on her heels and continued toward the house.

"That wasn't about taking sides. It was about keeping the peace."

Another stop. Another quip. "Do I look peaceful right now?"

Nathan stepped up and opened the door. Jessica stepped through and headed straight for the stairs and to their guest room, immediately stripping off the offensive thong swimsuit. After throwing on a pair of skinny jeans and a bright pink halter, she rolled out her suitcase, slammed it on the bench at the end of the bed, and then walked back into the closet to yank clothes from hangers.

Nathan looked on with mouth agape. "What in the hell are you doing?"

"What does it look like?"

"Jessica, baby, you need to calm down. This has gotten out of hand."

"No, what's out of hand was your sister being disrespectful. I'm not a child to be snatched and grabbed and told what to do."

"I'll talk to her about that. She shouldn't have put her hands on you, but—"

"For almost eight years I was controlled: what to wear, what to eat, where to go and how I should behave once I got there. Disobey and I'd get a black eye or fat lip for my trouble. Those days are over!"

She jerked open the dresser drawer to retrieve her lingerie.

"Don't you dare compare me to that monster you married. I'm not him, okay? But neither am I the man who's going to condone something that's wrong just to make you feel good!"

"When you saw me you said I looked amazing!"

"I believe the word was exceptional."

"However you felt changed as soon as your sister came over with her judgmental attitude. She was probably just mad because her husband saw something he wanted."

She marched into the en suite bathroom with Nathan close behind.

"And that makes you feel good? To get the attention of my brother-in-law?"

"There's nothing wrong with being appreciated."

"You can't be serious right now! After the way my family has welcomed you into our—"

A knock interrupted their increasingly loud tirade.

Nathan walked to the door. "Hello, Mom."

"What's going on in here, Nathan? I was headed to the stairway and could hear your voices all the way down the hall."

"Sorry about that. I didn't know we were so loud."

Miss Elaine removed her oversized floppy straw hat. "Is everything okay?"

"Yes, we're fine."

"Are you sure?"

"Yes."

"Is Jessica with you?"

"Yes. We're, uh, getting dressed."

"Okay. I'll see you two down at the beach."

By the time he turned around, Jessica was finished packing and had closed her bag. "Where do you think you're going?"

"To the airport."

"On New Year's Eve? You think you're going to get a flight out?"

"If not, there are hotels nearby."

"Baby, don't run off like this. We're having a good time. I don't want you to go."

"Your sister doesn't want me to stay."

"Don't worry about her. She'll cool down." He watched as Jessica looked around to make sure she had everything. He placed a gentle hand on her shoulder and lowered his voice. "I'm sorry she grabbed you, okay? I'll get her to apologize."

"Right after you?"

"Maybe you should apologize for showing your ass!"

"You know what? Never mind. I need to get out of here." She pulled the suitcase off the bench and headed for the door.

"How do you expect to get to the airport?"

"The same way I came."

"The car service? No. I won't be a part of your childlike tantrum, helping you take off just because you didn't get your way."

"Fine. I'll catch a cab."

He beat her to the door. "Jessica, don't do this."

"The only way I'll stay is for you to stand up for me, not your sister."

"Fine. Later, I'll have a conversation with her and let her know that her actions were not appreciated."

"No, Nathan, now. In front of the same people who saw her belittle me."

"They didn't hear what was going on."

"You think they're stupid and didn't know what was up when she all but threw the cover-up at me?"

"She didn't throw it exactly . . . babe!"

Jessica headed for the stairs, phone in hand. "Yes, can you connect me with a taxi company?"

Nathan followed her downstairs and out the door, where she sat on a bench near the circular drive. "I can't believe you're acting like this."

"And I can't believe how you're acting." Her call was connected. "Yes, hold one minute. Can you please give me the address here?"

"Jessica, hang up the—"

"Just give me the damn address!"

Nathan rattled it off, even as he wondered where his sweet Jessica had gone and who was this witch who'd slipped into her skin. She repeated it to the operator. "You realize that you're making a big mistake, right?"

"Oh, I've made the mistake? I'm not the one who threw you under the bus."

"You are being completely irrational! We're here with several other couples. You come out showing your ass. The wives start tripping and my sister asks you to go put on some damn clothes. You've ruined what up to now has been the perfect vacation. The fact that you don't get it makes me wonder who I've been dating the past few months, and whether or not I've ever known you at all."

A nonresponsive Jessica kept her eyes glued to her phone.

"For the last time, I'm asking you to stay. If you don't, things won't be the same when we return to Atlanta. We need to work out whatever this is, *now*."

This got her attention. "Are you breaking up with me?"

"I'm asking you not to leave. I'm asking you to stop acting like a . . . to stop being so angry and come back inside. We can change out of our swimsuits and rejoin the group. I'll apologize for both of us and all will be well. I hear they've organized a fabulous fireworks display for New Year's Eve. When I view it, I'd like you to be beside me."

"Why don't you go in there, pack your bags, and be beside me when I head for the airport. We can have our own special New Year's celebration . . . just the two of us."

"So now you want me to leave, too?"

"If you want us to be together to welcome the New Year."

"What can I say to get you to stay here with me?"

"Nothing. I don't want to be here."

"All right, then. Good-bye, Jessica."

She didn't answer, just watched his retreating form—broad shoulders, straight back, strong legs—taking him away from her.

Her pride refused to obey her heart and call him back, say she was sorry and ask him to forgive her. Instead she watched him go, as so many others had in her life, and allowed it to fuel the anger she'd need to help Sissy.

An enraged Jessica Bolton was not a good thing. Soon, a few very specific people were going to find this out.

CHAPTER 13

"What the hell just happened?" Randall saw his brother-in-law returning to the beach and headed his way.

Nathan huffed, still so angry he didn't know what to do. "Besides Jessica showing her ass, literally and figuratively?"

"Good Lord, man. Your girl definitely has assets . . ." Nathan gave Randall a look. "Hey, I'm just saying she looked good. But to wear that in a group setting? What in the heck was she thinking?"

"We didn't know about the other couples joining us and even if she had, Jessica doesn't worry too much about other people's opinions. Underneath her quietness is a free spirit who probably didn't think two seconds about her outfit being a problem. What I can't understand is why she was so stubborn about changing clothes."

"Sounds like you had to do some convincing."

"I tried. Didn't work though."

"So she isn't going to rejoin us?"

"She left."

"Where'd she go? It's New Year's Eve. Most of the businesses are going to be closed."

"Not the airport."

Randall's eyes widened. "She's going home?"

"Yes. Sherri told her to either go change or go pack."

"Oh man."

"She chose the latter."

"I'm sorry, Nate. I know she was angry but Sherri shouldn't have said that. Maybe there's still time to catch her at the airport. I'll go with you and apologize on my wife's behalf."

"Unfortunately, Sherri isn't the only reason for her anger. She feels I sided with my sister instead of taking up for her when all I wanted was for the fight to end. If we did find her and bring her back, I can't guarantee that another one wouldn't break out."

"Wow."

"I'm going to talk with Sherri, though. Jessica told her she was overreacting and while I didn't cosign at the time, I think she's right. She shouldn't have approached her with so much attitude."

"Well, that's probably because of the way one of the wives reacted after seeing her husband's response. He looked at your woman and licked his lips like she was a pork chop. Ha!"

Nate gave Randall a sober stare.

"Yeah, his wife didn't find anything funny, either. When they get home, I bet she and the mister are going to have a conversation."

"I'm sorry about all this, Ran."

Randall slapped him on the back. "Don't worry about it. I spiked the fruit punch, so everyone will be feeling better in no time. Come on. Let's get back to the company."

Nathan hung out with the couples but his heart wasn't in it. His head either, for that matter. He was still trying to wrap his mind around why Jessica went off the way she did. Sherri could have approached her differently, but two wrongs didn't make a right. And in Nathan's opinion, Jessica's leaving him was just as bad or worse than his sister's actions. By the time he put on a casual white linen suit for the New Year's Eve bash, he was not in the party mood.

He was the only one. When he arrived with Sherri and Randall, the party was in full swing. His normally conservative brother-in-law had gotten island fever, sporting a colorful shirt with a casual suit. Almost immediately, they spotted the neighbors who'd earlier joined them on the beach. Nathan said hello and continued to the bar. To get through tonight, he'd need help.

He found an empty bar stool and waited for the busy bartender. *Jessica would have loved this atmosphere.* The music was thumping. The place was crowded. Handsome men and beautiful women abounded. The main woman he wished was in the room, however, was not there. He put an elbow on the bar and rubbed his brow in weary frustration.

A soothing voice with a lovely, lilting accent drifted into his ear. "The night is too festive for sad faces."

Slowly, he lifted his head and turned toward the sound. The woman was as pleasing as her voice: tall, slender, with creamy skin and big brown eyes. Clunky, colorful jewelry graced her neck and wrists. Nathan imagined she'd been poured into the halter-style white maxi she wore.

"Who says I'm sad?"

She slid into the seat next to him. "Are you telling me you're not?"

"No, I'm not."

The bartender reached them, rapidly toweling down the bar. "What can I get you?"

"Double shot of Hennessy," Nathan said. "Water back, lots of ice."

Her laughter was lyrical. "Not much?" She spoke to the bartender. "I'll have a Goombay Smash . . . light on the rum."

The bartender nodded and left.

"What's that?"

"A Goombay Smash? Some call it the official drink of the

Bahamas, though that's mainly tourist talk. Henry makes his with rum, of course, an apricot liqueur, coconut, and pineapple. Goombay is a goatskin-covered drum. It is also a type of music native to our country, similar to calypso."

"Rum and liqueur in the same drink? What memory are you drowning?"

"Oh no." She waved perfectly manicured fingers boasting fire-engine-red polish. "My life is good and filled with blessings. I'm drinking to celebrate the coming of a brand-new year!" Her exuberance lifted Nathan's spirits. "I do believe that was a smile. The night may not be lost after all. By the way, my name is Develia Nixon. Most call me Dev."

He shook her extended hand. "Nice to meet you, Dev. I'm Nate Carver."

"It's very nice to meet you."

The bartender brought their drinks. Dev held hers up. "Let's toast to new friends and the New Year."

"Sounds good to me."

They toasted.

"So . . . what's a handsome man like you doing drowning his sorrows at the bar on one of the most celebratory nights of the year?"

"You're the one who's determined I'm sad. I told you that wasn't the case."

"Perhaps, but the face I saw as I walked up told me otherwise." She took a sip of her festive tropical drink that had been topped off with Maraschino cherries and orange slices. "Was it a fight with the missus?"

"Why, are you a counselor?"

"I'm a woman who doesn't like to see a man in pain. And by your answer, I believe my instincts are correct."

"I'm not married." He took a drink.

"Did she end up being a runaway bride?"

Another drink. "No. She just ended up running away."

"Do you want to talk about it?"

The band switched from island-flavored sounds to an R & B groove. "No," he said, standing and throwing back the rest of his Hennessy. "I want to dance."

And that's what they did until fireworks lit up the sky, announcing the New Year. At one a.m., Dev pulled Nathan from the club, led him to her two-seater Mercedes, and drove them to a side street near Bay Street in Nassau.

Nathan looked around, surprised at the large crowd gathered at that hour. "What's going on?"

"Junkanoo!" Dev merrily shouted, reaching behind her to pull out bells, shakers, colorful beads, and a red feather boa. She leaned over and placed the beads over Nathan's head.

He looked down, then up at her, shrugged, and opened the car door. Within minutes they were caught up in the crowd's celebratory atmosphere: dancing, playing their instruments, and hugging complete strangers as though lifelong friends.

Just before dawn, Dev pulled into the circular driveway of Château Sherri. "Thank God I know this island. Your directions were horrific!" The laughter that followed showed no hard feelings existed.

"I don't know what the heck Jugaboo is—"

"June. Kah. New. A Bahamian celebration."

"Yeah . . . right. Well, thanks to you, and Junkanoo, this night ended much better than it began." He leaned over. His lips brushed her cheeks. "Thank you."

Dev eyed him for a long moment before leaning over and pressing her lips against his. "You're welcome. Take care of yourself. She's a lucky girl."

Nathan frowned. "That reminds me. You never answered my question from earlier."

"Which was?"

"Why a lady as lovely as yourself was at the club alone."

"It is too early and too peaceful of a morning to recite such a sad tale." She reached into her handbag and pulled out a card. "If you really want to know . . . keep in touch."

CHAPTER 14

Leaving had been a mistake. Jessica had realized that about halfway to the airport, once anger receded and good sense returned. But going back had not been an option. At least that's what she'd thought. Not with Sherri angry, Nathan upset, and Miss Elaine worried about fisticuffs. So she'd continued on to the airport, paid a king's ransom to change the ticket, waited two hours to catch the flight, and six hours later opened the door to her home.

Her New Year's Eve celebration: a bottle of wine, a tasteless frozen pizza, watching the ball drop in Times Square, and staying awake until dawn wondering how her dream vacation became a nightmare. *And over a swimsuit? Really?*

When she awoke, sun was streaming through the blinds. She threw her arm over her eyes, not ready for the day. Minutes later, her phone rang. Hoping it was Nathan, she quickly checked the caller ID. Unknown number. Jessica closed her eyes. The ringing stopped but immediately started again. She checked the missed call—same unknown number. She never answered those. But when the phone rang for a third time with the same unknown ID, she huffed, reached over and answered the call.

"Hello?"

"Whew, glad you finally answered."

"Sissy?"

"Yes." She laughed. "I knew you'd be surprised at not hearing the automated system."

"Where are you calling from?"

"I got a cell phone."

"You can have cell phones there?"

"Not legally. But I needed to be able to speak freely, without being recorded. If you've got enough money in here you can get just about anything you want. It also helps that I'm sleeping with one of the guards."

"Oh. My. Goodness."

"Hey, don't knock it until you've gone without for months. Did you get yours?"

"My what?"

"Burner phone, a throwaway. I told you to get one in the last letter I wrote. Sounds like you didn't read it."

"I just got home."

"Right, the trip. I forgot. Wait. Aren't you back early?"

"Uh-huh." Said through a yawn.

"Big party last night?"

"Huge. A party of one."

"Where's Nate?"

"Bahamas."

"Then why are you home?"

"We had a fight."

"About what?"

"I don't feel like talking about it. But what I do need is for you to explain this favor so that I understand."

"I will, as soon as you buy a temporary phone so we can't be traced. Take my number and call me back."

An hour later, Jessica called Sissy from her new burner phone. "Okay, we're both untraceable," she said by way of greeting. "So help me understand what you've asked me to do."

"You read the code. I buried it in the story about—"

"—your fake friend, Bobby, who I drove myself crazy trying to remember until I figured out this was where you'd hid the code. Of course I read it. Countless times." The whole paragraph, but particularly the sentences that contained the message within the message, were burned into her memory.

> *. . . remember when I had to help our skittish neighbor catch and kill that snake? Remember the one who got blamed? Bobby caught and put it on the porch, blamed me, then lied. "She put it here!" I wanted to slap him. So full of it. Didn't matter. I adored him anyway. So hot! Can still see him sweat and get dirty playing with his cousin out behind the old coot's yard!*

The message within the message, every sixth word:
HELP KILL WHO PUT ME HERE SO I CAN GET OUT.

"I got the message. I just don't understand it. Nathan isn't why you were arrested and are now serving time."

"No, but his sister is. To go after her is too obvious. I'd be the first one she blamed. An indirect infliction of punishment can sometimes hurt far worse than direct pain. Getting her dear baby brother would be just like getting her." Sissy recounted what she'd piecemealed to Jessica through several letters, how she'd landed in prison and who was at fault. "If she'd divorced him, just walked away so Randall and I could be happy, no one would have . . . suffered." When Jessica remained silent, Sissy continued. "I know I'm asking a lot."

"You're asking me to take a life!"

"Like they've taken mine! Yes, *they*. Don't think for one second that when it came to me going to prison Nathan wasn't fully on his sister's side. I'll make it well worth your while."

"There are things more important than money . . . like the

freedom you so desperately want. What if *I* get caught and end up in prison?"

"There's no way that can happen! I've researched and analyzed this plan to the nth degree. It is foolproof. But it does require that you and Nathan be together. So whatever the reason you're home instead of still on the island . . . you need to fix it."

"What if it isn't up to me?" Her sister's laughter only riled her further.

"You're a woman, little sister. When it comes to men, we can fix anything."

"Spoken by the expert whose actions to fix it put her behind bars." Silence. "That wasn't called for . . . sorry."

"It's okay. I guess our not seeing each other for such a long time makes it easier for you to screw the man and befriend the woman who got me locked up."

"That's hardly the case. In fact, she's the reason I came back early."

"All the more reason that getting back with her brother shouldn't be a problem."

Jessica wandered from the bedroom to the kitchen, thinking back to how she'd been treated yesterday, and how to fix it. She remembered Sherri's uppity judgmental attitude and Nathan's complicity. They were partying on an island while her sister's heels cooled in prison. Some of her anger returned.

"Exactly what part did he play in your being there?" A sigh blew through the phone. "Listen, for what you've asked me to do, I deserve to know everything."

"You're right." A pause, and then, "He encouraged his sister against me, okay? Trust me, I'd rather end her breathing. But like I said, it would be too risky. Getting her darling brother is the next best thing. They're *very* close."

"Like I wish we could have been."

"No more than I do. When I saw that our jerk of a dad was getting ready to do the same thing to you that he'd done to me

for two years, I couldn't take it. You were the best thing that
had happened to me in that hellhole. I couldn't let him hurt you."

"So you—"

"—made sure he couldn't hurt you. I did what needed to
be done. Now I'm asking you to do the same."

"We'll see what happens when he returns," she finally offered. "If we get back together, I'll make sure things get handled."

"Not *if* you get back together," her sister softly chided,
"But *when*."

Jessica had taken off until the fifth but didn't want to sit
around the house. Too much time to think. The law firm had
brought on a temporary receptionist, but thankfully her boss
had texted his okay for her to return early from vacation and
catch up on administrative tasks. After chatting briefly with the
temp, she grabbed a large stack of papers, folders, and tags, and
headed to the smaller conference room to sort and file.

Perfect, she thought as she stepped inside and closed the
door. *Work to keep me busy and a door for privacy!*

Or not.

Ten minutes into sorting papers to be filed, the door
opened. "So I heard correctly. You're back."

She looked up to see the only person in the law firm, perhaps the world, who today would not get on her nerves, so she
swallowed the curt greeting on the tip of her tongue and offered a brief smile instead. "Hey, Vincent."

His brow immediately creased in concern as he closed the
door and approached the table. "Wow, that's not the mood I
expected of someone just back from paradise."

"We don't always get what we expect."

"Are we talking about me or you?"

Jessica gave him a look, then went back to sorting.

"Whatever he didn't do, I can do it, and whatever he did, I
can take the pain away. KnowhatI'msayin'?"

His expression was such a perfect mixture of jive and sincerity that Jessica had to laugh. "You are so silly. How you got through law school is beyond me."

"Hard work and a smile, baby girl." He sat at the table and lowered his voice. "I thought you were away until the fifth?"

"Plans changed."

"Folks don't usually return early from vacation, especially when they're going to the Caribbean."

Jessica frowned. "I don't want to talk about my vacation. How were your holidays?"

Vincent shrugged. "They were all right. Went back to Michigan, saw the fam."

"And . . . ?"

"That's it." Vincent sexily swiped his tongue across his cupid-shaped lips and looked down to hide the twinkle in his eye.

"You're so full of it!" They both laughed. "Don't tell me you partied with your baby's mama."

"I shouldn't have."

"And y'all had sex again."

"I shouldn't have done that, either."

Jessica shook her head as she placed stacked groups of files into folders. "Your daughter is what? Nine years old? Keep on playing with fire and end up with a newborn."

"It wasn't that deep, just a little get-together for old time's sake. It's all your fault, anyway."

"How do you figure?"

"Because you're who I wanted to be with. She was just there."

"Don't do that."

"What?"

"Feed me bullshit like I'm stupid, the way my ex used to do. You need to stop messing with that girl's feelings."

Vincent stood, eyed Jessica through his curly lashes. "Will you let me mess with you?"

She looked up to find Vincent watching her intently. She felt the electricity between them and not for the first time thought that if there was any part of her heart that didn't belong to Nathan, she'd give it to him. "Don't you have work to do? A case to win, a client to call . . . something?"

Vincent looked at his watch. "Actually, yes, in about five minutes." He walked to the door. "What's up for lunch?"

"You're taking me to Georgia's. I want gumbo."

"If I give you what you want, will you give me what—"

"Bye, Vincent."

Vincent smiled and opened the door. "Meet you downstairs at one."

She met him downstairs for lunch and the next night at the sports bar for dinner. Her guard slipped under two glasses of wine. His tongue slipped into her mouth in the parking lot. The kiss was volcanic. It felt good. He felt good. The only reason that they didn't slide back to either his house or her house and slide into bed was because as angry as she still was with Nathan . . . sliding with him felt better.

CHAPTER 15

One rarely feels worse after returning from paradise than before they left. Nathan did. During the nonstop flight from Nassau he replayed the week's events in his mind, from the time he arrived with Jessica until he boarded the return flight alone. Meeting Dev had been the lone bright spot following Jessica's departure and saved him from ringing in the New Year pissed off and alone. Still, in 20/20 hindsight, he felt bad about how he'd handled the incident between Jessica and his sister. Had he done things differently, the situation may have been defused and she may not have left. But he didn't and she did. As he left the airport parking lot and merged onto the highway, he realized that to regret something that couldn't be changed wasn't productive. *No, what will be productive is fixing the mess I now find myself in.* He tapped his steering wheel and called Jessica.

Voice mail. *Not a good sign.* Still, he waited for the beep. "Jessica, it's me, Nate. I just got back and am on my way home from the airport. Was hoping you'd pick up and were home so that I could stop by. I don't like how things went down on the island, and want to make it up to you. Call me as soon as you get a chance."

★ ★ ★

Three days later, and Jessica still hadn't got that chance. He'd called a couple more times, had even thought about calling her job. But he knew she'd taken off until today, which is why earlier he'd driven by her condo. When he didn't see her car in its slot, he'd kept it moving. Obviously her anger hadn't worn off. Deducing she needed more time away from him to get over what happened, he tapped the wheel and engaged his phone.

"Broderick!"

"Mr. Caribbean is back?"

"Absolutely."

"Happy New Year, man."

"Same to you." On a whim, Nathan made a turn and headed toward Buckhead. "How'd the year end, Broderick? We do okay?"

"Thanks to you, we did better than that. Our profits were the highest they've been in five years. Employees are happy. Clients are satisfied. I couldn't be more pleased. In fact, I want to talk with you about something."

"Shoot."

"No, it can wait until Monday. I'd rather discuss this face-to-face."

"In that case, do you have plans tonight? I'm headed to the sports bar."

"As a matter of fact, no. The wife's sister is in town. They're going to a play. What time are you planning to be there?"

"I'm headed there now."

"Perfect. I'll see you soon."

Jessica listened to Nathan's message for a third time before deleting it. Seeing that he'd called a few more times without leaving messages, she knew he must be wondering why his calls weren't returned and probably assumed she was still upset. She wished the reason was something so normal, instead of the truth. How did one talk to a man one planned to murder?

The message indicator pinged. She picked up her phone to see a text from Vincent.

Can't wait to see you. Picking you up at seven still good?

She replied that it was fine and then walked to the closet to find something to wear. She knew it was risky to flame the fires of this friendship, but being in his carefree company allowed her mind to focus on something other than Sissy's impossible request. When her sister had proposed meeting Nathan to help with something she'd explain later, Jessica had immediately agreed, no questions asked. Coming from the one who'd saved her life, almost no favor would have been refused. Then she'd gotten to know him, and developed feelings. And now the help her sister needed had been explained. The whole situation was one, big, impossible mess. Her mind was too muddled to think about fashion. So after laying out a pair of brown leather pants and a multi-colored turtle neck, she jumped in the shower. Almost an hour later, she and Vincent walked up to the entrance of the sports bar, and stepped inside.

At first, he thought he was mistaken. The bar was packed and he'd only glimpsed a side view from across the room. But now that they were seated, her face was clearly visible. The woman who hadn't returned his calls was here. At their favorite hangout. With another man.

Broderick followed his colleague's line of sight. "Whoa. That's awkward."

"Oh, you see that, too?"

"It's not my business but . . . something happen on your vacation?"

"We had a disagreement. I was giving her space to cool down. Might have given her too much."

"Look, man, if you want to handle that . . ."

Nathan gave Broderick his full attention. "No, I'm good. I'd much rather get back to what we were discussing. A VP position, huh?"

"Yes. Cecil's attention has been torn ever since his father fell ill. He'd have retired a year ago if not for the fact he thought the business would suffer. But with you on board and business booming, he's ready to step down. If you want it, the position is yours."

"I really appreciate this, Broderick. Didn't see it coming, but this type of validation is right on time."

"You've earned it." He lifted his beer mug. Nathan followed suit. "To greater success."

"Indeed."

The men clinked glassed. As Nathan drained his glass, his eyes met Jessica's, which were on him intently. He gave a look with this message: "What?" She averted her eyes. The man she was with looked at him, and then wrapped his arms around Jessica and whispered something in her ear.

Nathan's jaw clenched, and he gripped the now empty beer mug.

Broderick saw it. "Do we need to leave?"

"No, I'm cool. If that's who she wants to be with, that's where she should be."

"But ya'll seemed happy at the Christmas party. What happened?"

"Like I said, just a little misunderstanding. We can't always predict life, you know?"

"Don't I know it. This weekend, my daughter hit me with some news that rocked me on my haunches."

"She pregnant?"

"No, that would have sent me to my grave!" Nathan chuckled. "No, she joined the Peace Corps."

"That *is* news. She's never hinted at something like this be-fore?"

"Never, and even more than that, she leaves for Ecuador in six weeks."

"Wow."

They continued talking. Anyone looking on would have pegged Nathan as being totally engaged in his conversation with Broderick. But he knew the minute, the second, when Jessica and her date got up from the table and left the building.

He knew, because a part of his heart went with her.

CHAPTER 16

If you've moved on, don't bother responding to this text. If not, we need to talk. Today.

Jessica eyed Nathan's message with mixed emotions. She'd missed him terribly, had even tried to tell herself that she preferred Vincent's company. Her coworker wasn't a bad guy. In fact, some woman would be lucky to have him. At the end of the day, Vincent had nothing to do with her not wanting to return Nathan's call. When she did, a plan with dire consequences would be put in motion. Loyalty to her sister or to the man she loved? During the days without him, she'd admitted this truth. She loved Nathan Carver. How could she take his life?

Because he and his sister had effectively taken Sissy's life, that's how.

Her sister had saved her. A debt was owed. By repaying it, she hoped to have the type of bond with her sibling that she'd seen between Nathan and Sherri. *The bond you're going to destroy.* Yes, but she couldn't think about that now.

Do you want to come over?

Six words, short yet pivotal; the answer to this question would change many lives. With a sigh and almost a prayer that he wouldn't respond . . . she pressed Send.

He responded. Immediately.

I'm on my way.

Her heart dropped. It was only a little after noon, but Jessica went to her fridge, found a half bottle of Moscato, poured it into a drinking glass, and downed it like water. For her, one thing was sure: Committing murder would not come naturally.

When the doorbell rang less than ten minutes later, she jumped. For a split second she thought about not answering it, about letting Nathan think she'd stepped out unexpectedly, or changed her mind. The invisible hand of her sister pushed her toward the door. It was too late to turn back now.

"Hey." Her greeting was rushed and way too breathy. But it was the best she could do.

Nathan eyed her curiously, and was slow to respond. "Hello."

"You got here quickly."

"I live two blocks away. Are you all right?"

"Sure." She ran a nervous hand through her hair. "Come on in."

An awkward silence filled the space where a hug would usually happen.

"Can I get you something to drink?"

Nathan nodded toward the kitchen. "Is that what you're drinking?"

Damn! She'd meant to throw the empty wine bottle away. "No, that's from last night," she lied.

"With you and what's-his-name?"

Jessica sighed. "Let's sit down."

They did, with more space between them than since they began dating.

"First question," Nathan began. "Is he why you haven't returned my calls?"

"I didn't call you because . . ."

"Because you're still mad about what happened." She nodded, refusing to meet his eyes. "Are you sleeping with him?"

"No."

"He looked pretty comfortable with you."

"Vincent is comfortable with everybody. I've known him for a while. We work together, remember?"

"Right, the attorney who helped with your passport." She nodded. "Look, Jessica. I'm sorry for how I handled things on the island. I talked with my sister and let her know she dealt with you wrongly as well. She should have quietly pulled you to the side, explained the situation, and asked you to change. Demanding you obey her as if you were a child was wrong."

"You demanded, too."

"And I was wrong as well."

"I probably could have given more thought to my choice of swimsuits. My sole thought was on looking good for you and pleasing you."

"Believe me, I was pleased."

Pregnant pauses had rarely existed in their conversation. It was almost as if two strangers were trying to get to know one another.

I never knew my house could be so quiet. When she was home alone, either the television, stereo, or iPod usually kept her company.

Nathan shifted to look at her more fully. "So where do we go from here?"

By staying with me, you'll go to the morgue. "Where do you want us to go?"

"Back to where we were before the vacation—being together, enjoying each other."

But I'm planning something you will not enjoy. "I'd . . . like that, too."

"Why'd you hesitate?"

Because getting back with me is a death sentence. "Because what happened at your sister's house really hurt me. How can we have a future when your family hates me?" *Like my sister hates your family!*

"That's not true, baby. My sister stopped short of apologizing, but she did admit that she'd come on rather strong. Mom likes you, and was disappointed you'd gone home early."

"She said that?" Nathan nodded. "I like Miss Elaine. She's the type of mother I always wanted but never had."

"Stick with me and you might get what you desire . . . and more."

Sadly . . . you won't. "I don't know, Nathan. I've missed you and want us to get back together. But it's scary to put your heart out there and not know if the person holding it will crush it or caress it. Maybe we should spend some time apart and make sure that we're what each other wants."

"Are you sure you're not sleeping with Vincent?"

Jessica's eyes narrowed. "Are you sure you haven't slept with someone? Usually when someone keeps accusing you of something, they're the guilty one."

"I told you why I asked; he was all over you and you weren't pulling away. Had you already ended us in your mind?"

"Vincent makes me laugh, something that hadn't happened since I got off the plane. We are friends. He asked me out. I said yes. All I did was go out and try and have a good time." She crossed her arms, anger growing at the continued insinuations. "Besides, until you put a ring on it, you have no ownership of what's sitting over here."

Nathan nodded slowly. "I see." He stood. "I guess on that note, I'll head on out, and give you the time apart that you say you need. I had some news to share, but it can wait." They walked to the door. "When you feel like you're ready, give me a call. And if I'm still available when that happens . . . we'll go from there."

The air crackled with tension as they stood there. Finally, Nathan reached over and pulled Jessica into his arms. The hug was heartfelt by both of them. He kissed the top of her head. "Take care of yourself."

She watched him walk to the steps, listened to his booted footsteps as he went down them and out to street parking. Slowly she closed her door and leaned against it. To say she was between a rock and a hard place was an understatement. Did she gain the love of her sister by taking the life of her man?

Blood is thicker than water. You remember that!

For the rest of the afternoon, her sister's words echoed in her mind. "It killed me to watch you leave, Nate," she whispered, as tears fell. "But if you come back . . . I'll have to kill you."

CHAPTER 17

"What's up, player?"

Nathan smiled and turned down the volume on his phone. The voice of his sister's loudmouthed friend was bouncing off his loft walls. "As if you don't know."

"Who, *moi*?"

"Keep your day job, Renee. I know you've talked to Sherri and know everything that happened over the holidays."

"Yes, I can't lie. She told me."

"I figured as much."

"What I can't figure out is how either you or she could have thought for one second that showing her ass was okay!"

"Sounds like you're under the mistaken impression that I care what you think."

"Ouch!"

"I've already been down this road with Sherri. I'm not going to pull punches with you."

"She told me that you think she overreacted. But really, Nate. Your girl is going to come down to a family function in a thong?!"

"It wasn't a family function. She didn't know neighbors would be there and I didn't' know what she'd wear. What we both knew was that it was an adult outing and we were in the Caribbean. Contrary to our prudish views in America, the rest of the world views their bodies differently. They're not as uptight as we are."

"You see my butt switching by with a piece of floss between these cheeks, you'd change your tune."

"Ha! Damn, Nay. That's TMI."

"No, it's TMA—too much ass!"

They laughed. "So is harassing me the only reason that you called?"

"It's the main reason. But the other is to follow up on what you asked me a few weeks ago. Over the holidays I checked out the club scene—"

"I bet you did . . ."

"—and also talked with a couple club owners who are also friends of mine."

"Did you share my client's plans?"

"Contrary to your low opinion of my running mouth, I can be discreet. No, I said nothing of what your guy is doing in Atlanta. I just asked what types of clubs are hot now, and if they'd heard about any new clubs opening up this year."

"Had they?"

"No. But I'd suggest you advise your client to get on this quickly and if possible, hook up with one of the new hotels being built right now. These establishments are always trying to set themselves apart and a novel entertainment concept would be enticing. I sent an e-mail with information I thought you'd find useful. Oh, and I'll e-mail the invoice for this consultation."

"Ha! Fair enough."

"So when are you coming to Vegas to check things out?"

"Probably in the next couple months. I need to talk to my client, and there's been a development at work."

"What?"

"It just happened and I've not shared it with my family, so

you can't say anything." When she remained silent, he added, "I'm going to need your word on this."

"Okay. I won't say a word."

"I've been promoted to VP of the firm."

"Congratulations! Nate, that's exciting news!"

"And totally unexpected, but due to personal matters, the current man in that role stepped down."

"Look at Mr. Nitpicky!"

"Girl, you need to quit with that teenage nonsense."

"I think it fits you more now than ever."

"Thank goodness you're the only one." He checked his watch. "It's the weekend. Why are you on the phone with me and not on a date?"

"I'm three hours behind you, darling, and meeting my date in a couple hours."

"You're getting too old for the dating game. Better make a decision soon."

"Haven't you heard? Forty is the new twenty, and I'm a year away from that."

"But don't you get tired of going through the whole intro/start-up situation over and again?"

"I'd marry in a minute if I met the right man."

"Describe this right man."

"Fine, packing, confident, successful . . . someone like you."

"You're a perpetual flirt."

"Hey, it's in the genes."

"The ones in your blood or the ones you have on?"

"Both!"

"You're something else, Nay. I'd better get off here and call my family before you share my good news."

"I told you I'd keep quiet."

"Forgive me if I don't believe it. In all the years I've known you, I've not seen that before."

Renee adopted her sexy voice. "There's a lot you haven't seen."

"You're a trip, Renee. Good-bye." Laughing, he dialed his sister.

"Hey, Nathan."

"What's wrong?"

"I have a case of pre-teen disease."

"What?"

"Ask one of your coworkers with kids to explain it. Right now, I'm too tired."

"Then I've called just in time, with some good news to cheer you up."

"Okay."

"I got promoted."

"Really, Nate? That's wonderful!"

"Yes." He told her what had happened. "It'll be a lot of late hours for the next six months, until I get a handle on everything. But I'm thankful for the opportunity."

"You've always had that leader quality. You'll be great." She paused a moment. "I'm sure Jessica is excited."

"She will be once I tell her."

"I'm the first to know? What an honor."

"Actually your BFF Renee is the first one I told."

"What?"

Nathan chuckled. "She called me right before I called you."

"When did you and Renee get so cozy?"

"We reconnected over Thanksgiving, and now that one of my clients is thinking of expanding to Vegas, I've kept in touch."

"That's nice. Renee is good people."

"Yes, and crazy as hell."

"That, too."

The siblings talked for another thirty minutes. Then Nathan met some of his friends for a game of basketball. Not since he'd begun dating Jessica had a Saturday night left him without plans. There were several places he could go, and friends he could call. But he wasn't feeling a night out at the club. So he drove toward a deli for takeout. A block away from a Reuben sandwich, his phone rang.

One look at the caller ID and his face lit up. He tapped his steering wheel. "Stephen? I don't believe this! When did you break out of jail?"

"Okay, man. I guess I deserve that."

"Heck, yeah, you deserve it. I haven't heard from you in weeks. What's her name?"

"Don't I wish. I've been back home, helping my mom take care of my dad."

"What's wrong with your father?"

"He had cancer. No one knew. I just saw him in October and he looked fine. A week later Mom calls and said he had four weeks to live. He lasted five just to be ornery."

"Aw, man, Steve. I'm sorry to hear that. My condolences, man."

"Yes, these past few weeks have been crazy. I've felt emotions I didn't even know existed. His passing so quickly taught me one thing—to live every day to the fullest, and not take one thing for granted. So that's one reason I'm calling you, Nate. This girl I met right before leaving to help care for him has invited me to a private party. Her cousin is in town and she's asked me to hook her up. I really like this girl so I can't ask a hardhead who'll get in there and act a fool. So how about it, man? You down for some fun on a Friday night?"

"I don't know, Stephen. It's been a busy week with a lot going on. I was just getting ready to grab a bite and head home to chill."

"Stop acting like an old man. Just an hour or so, and if you and the cousin aren't vibing then call it a night. Plus, Ralph will be there."

"Ralph's back in Atlanta? I heard he joined the police force in Cleveland."

"That was years ago. He got married and moved back here; working as a detective now."

"All right. I'll go. Never pegged you for one needing help getting a woman but . . ."

"You know that's not true. She's just trying to show her cousin a good time."

"It would be good to see Ralph again. Give me the address. I'll see you in an hour."

Nathan arrived at a sprawling mansion in suburban Atlanta. He stepped into a home where socializing was in full swing. People stood in groups of two or three, music played and conversation flowed. After chatting with a few familiar faces, he found Stephen and met his love interest's cousin, Olivia. He could immediately see why his friend had wanted them to meet. Smart, sophisticated, with several letters behind her name, at one time she would have been just the type of woman he'd prefer. But after thirty minutes of feeling he was in a competition rather than a conversation with a woman who was as aggressive as she was attractive, he thanked her for her company, exchanged business cards, and went to find Ralph.

On the drive home, he found himself comparing women like Olivia to Jessica. Where Olivia had been understandably confident and assertive, Jessica was initially shy, reserved. Olivia was fiercely independent; Jessica deferred to Nathan, made him feel needed. He'd always thought he wanted a woman with his same drive, ambitions, education, and money as a partner. Tonight was glaring proof that he'd been wrong. He admired women like Olivia. Even with her sometimes annoying behavior, he wanted to marry someone like Jessica. One day, he'd let her know.

CHAPTER 18

Jessica rolled her eyes, wishing she'd not bothered to answer the call. "What do you mean, why not? I told you earlier that I didn't want to go. What made you think I'd changed my mind between the office and my house?"

While Vincent continued his drivel, Jessica walked across the room, picked up the remote, and turned on the TV. She muted the sound and flipped through the channels, hoping something good would be on tonight. It had been a long, lonely week. She usually enjoyed Vincent's flirtations, often responded with some game of her own. But today he was getting on her nerves and bearing the brunt of a frustrating week spent without her man. She placed the call on speaker and laid it on the bar counter in front of her.

"What's got you in such a foul mood tonight?"

"Who says I'm in a foul mood?"

He laughed. "Really? Oh, wait a minute. It isn't *what* but *who* has you in a mood. Where's your boy?"

"I don't know."

"That's why you're mad. Any sistah who doesn't know where her man is on a Friday night will have an attitude." Silence. "Y'all have a fight or something?"

"Why aren't you out chasing instead of bugging me?"

"Is that what I'm doing?"

"No. I'm just not in the mood for conversation."

"All right, then. I'll let you go. But if you change your mind and want to feel better, give me a call. I'll come over and help you get a few things off your mind."

"Ha! I just bet you will. Bye, Vincent."

Shaking her head, she ended the call, moved to the couch, and turned up the TV volume. At least Vincent put a smile on her face, something that had been lacking most of the week. She'd kept her vow to herself to not call Nathan. A herculean task that had almost required cutting off her fingers, but she'd left him alone. She missed him almost as much as she'd missed her sister all those years. Still, she prayed he'd leave her alone, forget she existed. Then she could walk away from this crazy promise and truthfully tell Sissy that he'd broken things off and her plan wouldn't work. That she'd tried and failed. She and her sister had been apart for years, and while there would be anger and disappointment at first, Jessica knew her sister loved her and in time would forget about this plot of revenge. She'd get out of prison, they'd find a place together, and make up for lost time.

Her message indicator pinged. She looked down. *Sissy.* They texted and talked often now that Sissy had a cell phone and Jessica had purchased her untraceable burner.

Has he called?

Jessica spoke to the walls as she picked up the phone. "You've got a one-track mind, girl." Her thumb tapped a quick reply: **No.**

You call him?

No. Jessica rubbed her thumb across the screen, waiting for Sissy's answer.

What?!?! Why not?

Tricky question.

Because I don't want to do this.

Her thumb hovered over the Send button as she contemplated Sissy's likely response. They'd already been around the world and back on this subject. She owed Sissy, and had given her word.
Delete.

Don't want to look too obvious.

She waited. No response. She continued.

Like you said, let him chase me.

She imagined Sissy pacing and pondering. Always pragmatic, her sister planned with precision. And once she made a decision, there was no turning back.
Her phone pinged.

Start plan ASAP. New trial in murder case. May revoke chance for parole. This needs to happen before Sherri and Nathan lock me in her 4ever!

Jessica heaved a heavy sigh. **Okay.**

You have everything?

No.

☹ **Get prepared! Gotta go. Luv u.**

Luv u 2.

She'd been bored, wanting something to do. Shopping for arsenic and antifreeze along with beverages and foods to mask them wasn't exactly what she'd had in mind.

Following her sister's advice, Jessica drove to a library across town. To bypass the need for a library card, she bribed a teenager who was already online with fifty bucks for his time on the public computer. Using the fake ID and stolen credit card info that Sissy had provided via text, Jessica ordered two bottles of arsenic trichloride for overnight delivery. After that, she researched and printed out an easy recipe for making soup. Not much of a cook, Jessica hoped her sudden channeling of Rachael Ray wouldn't seem suspicious. Then again, as sick as Nathan would be from her sneaky concoctions, he probably wouldn't even notice.

Next stop: an auto store. Several gallons of antifreeze. *Check*. A short time later, she stood at the back of her car in a grocery store parking lot. Orange juice. *Check*. Soda. *Check*. Ice cream. *Check*. Soup mix and frozen veggies. *Check*. These along with a few personal items for her went into the trunk. Heading home, she battled mixed emotions. A measure of happiness for finally being able to do something for the sister who'd done so much for her. Sadness at what this obligation would cost her. Fear of breaking the law. An eerie, inappropriate excitement over carrying out this clandestine plan.

The burner phone rang. She reached for it and tapped the speaker button. "Hey, Sissy."

"Hello, Jessie. Sorry about earlier. This dike guard's an asshole, had to hide the phone. She can't stand the fact that I shut down her bitch advances. But since I'm in with the warden's son who's a guard here, she knows I can't be touched without consequences. Women like her will never be able to compete with women like me."

"It's got to be tough in there."

"I always say it's not what happens to you but how you handle it. Ever since I snagged his namesake and only child for a boy toy, the warden has been on my side. Of course, this was my plan all along. I've been living as high a life as one can while inside. Plus, with this new attorney working to get my earlier conviction thrown out, I'm close to a new trial . . . feeling better than I have felt in a long time."

"When is all of this happening?"

"He's working on it right now, which is why it's so important to handle this other piece of business pronto."

"I ordered the . . . vitamins . . . and am just coming back from the grocery store."

"Vitamins . . . I like that! So you called him?"

"Not yet. But I'm ready."

"Cool. Don't forget the instructions. Go slow. This has to look like an accident, a medical anomaly that can't be explained."

"Okay."

"Can you believe it, Jessie? After all these years, we're back in regular communication!"

She smiled. "Yes, it's nice."

"And in a year or so we'll finally be together and get to live those dreams we talked about in those letters! Where should we buy a house? I was thinking either California or Florida; somewhere with pristine beaches and hard-bodied men!"

"My ex is in California, so not feeling that. Florida sounds nice."

"Then that's our first trip: house hunting in Miami. Ocean view with a pool, modern kitchen, marble floors, vaulted ceilings, and dual master suites. As soon as I get sprung from this joint, we'll head there to scope out the scene."

After a few more minutes, Jessica ended the call. During the rest of the short drive home and while unpacking her car, she thought about her sister's grandiose plans. Bouncing from one foster home to another, these rare but promise-filled talks with her sister had kept her alive. Then Sissy left the system, Jessica moved, and they lost contact. Just before her twenty-first birthday, Jessica tracked down Sissy, helped by foster family she lived with while dating Edwin. The reunion was short-lived. When he broke into her e-mail account and found out about it, her controlling husband put an end to their communication. Jessica defied Edwin and the sisters reconnected through Facebook. Sissy helped her leave the abusive marriage—both emotionally and financially. Shortly after that, she'd had a favor to ask.

Later that evening, her regular phone rang. Jessica cringed, eyes closed, hoping it was Vincent and not Nate. She checked the caller ID. "Hello?"

"Hello, beautiful. How are you?"

It was not Vincent. "I'm all right."

"Would you like to go out, hear some jazz or have a drink?"

"No, I don't feel like going out."

"Can I come over?"

Two seconds passed.

Five more.

"I don't think that's a good idea."

"Why? Jessica, is this over?"

Say yes! Keep him away from you and the deadly promise you made! "Shouldn't it be?"

"If I thought so I wouldn't be calling. Now, do you want to see me or not?"

"I want to see you but—"

"Good. I'm on my way."

Jessica smiled as she ended the call. *Tonight everything changes.*

CHAPTER 19

Nathan bopped up the steps, humming a tune. Dressed nice, smelling good, gifts in hand. He was more than ready for him and Jessica to get back in the groove.

The door opened. "Hello."

"Hello, Jessica." He held out a large bouquet. "These are for you."

She stepped back. "Come on in. You smell nice. These are nice, too." Closing the door, she took the flowers and inhaled their fragrance. "You didn't have to buy me flowers."

"I know. I wanted to. The week we've been apart and not talked, two weeks really, has seemed like forever."

His expression was sincere as he gave her an appreciative once-over. His eyes said what his voice did not. *A shame for a woman to make jeans and a tee look so good.* She stared back. He saw the hesitation and vulnerability in her eyes, and vowed to change that.

"Let me get a vase for these flowers." Walking toward the kitchen, she spoke over her shoulder. "Would you like something to drink?"

He followed her. "Sure. What do you have?"

She gave him a list of choices.

"What are you having?"

"Orange juice. I uh . . . hear colds and flu are up this year. So I'm trying to stay healthy."

"Then fix me that, too. But add a shot of Hennessy."

"Okay. While I'm fixing our drinks, would you mind finding something on the iPod?"

"Not at all. What are you in the mood for?"

"I don't know. Pick something."

He walked out. Jessica quickly reached under the cabinet. *Darn it. I should have put this in another container.* She made a mental note to pour the antifreeze into one of the plastic bottles in her recycle bin. A gallon jug of it next to the orange juice on the counter was not a good look. She poured a small amount into a glass. Drake's silky vocals oozed from the speakers. Footsteps quickened across the hardwood floor.

"What about something with a party groove?" The words came out in a rush as shaky hands worked to replace the cap on the antifreeze and put the container back out of sight. A brief moment of silence then Prince began jamming about a rock and roll love affair.

"How's that?"

"Um . . . let me hear a little bit." Jessica quickly dropped several ice cubes into the glass with the antifreeze, followed by a generous splash of Hennessy. She sniffed. The odor was pungent and sickly sweet. *Not too bad.* "That sounds good." After pouring the orange juice, she quickly stirred the concoction until the liquid in the glass looked creamy orange.

A gasp flew out as Nathan's arms came around her waist. "Nate! I didn't hear your footsteps."

"I wanted to surprise you. Wasn't sure if I asked that I'd get a hug."

She turned around, working on a calm, nonchalant look. But just in case fear filled her eyes, she stepped into his arms and laid her head on his shoulder.

He kissed the top of her head. "I missed you."

"I missed you, too."

"Wow, baby. Your heart is beating so fast."

"Is it?" An innocently asked question when the answer was banging out a staccato rhythm against her rib cage. Save for sheer determination and muscle control, her legs would be shaking like bamboo in the wind.

Nathan rubbed his hands across her back, neck, and shoulders. "You're tight, too." He gently set her away from him, looked deep into her eyes. "Is everything okay?"

Willing herself to meet his eyes, she answered. "Why wouldn't it be?"

"I don't know." He stared into her eyes, kneaded her shoulders. Stared for another long moment during which time Jessica's legs almost began shaking again.

She broke their embrace, turned and placed ice cubes and fresh orange juice into a glass, then gave him his drink. "Here you go."

"Thank you." He took a sip. "Damn, baby!"

"What?" *Can he taste it? I've been busted so soon?* Eyes grew wide, stomach dropped, heart felt it would beat out of her chest.

"Are you trying to get me drunk?"

Her shoulders sagged in relief. "I'm sorry, didn't taste it. Is it too strong?"

"I guess it's all right. Especially since you're trying to weaken my defenses and take advantage of me."

"Filling you with liquor, that's what it takes?"

"You know better than that. Stone-cold sober and I'll be all over you. I want that right now. I want us to be us again. But it's not just my decision. Where we go from here is up to both of us."

Jessica took his hand and headed into the living room. They sat on the couch. She nestled against his chest. He placed an arm around her. Sipping and serenading filled the next moments as a myriad of thoughts and inner dialogue plagued both of their minds.

The song ended. Another, slower one began. A jazzy instrumental with a haunting, provocative beat. "I want us again," she said softly.

A gentle squeeze from his strong arm was her reply. She ran a lazy finger up and down his forearm, tracing the strong vein that ran down it, feeling the soft skin and fine hair against her fingers. "For the most part, my life has been filled with uncertainty. I've been alone, and have had to survive largely on my own. It's hard for me to open up, very hard to trust. Something about you made it easier. I felt secure, you know?

"Down on the island, when you sided with Sherri, I once again felt isolated and on my own. Anger is a defense, a way to cover hurt and fear. So I lashed out. Once back here, I closed up. Harder to get your heart broken with a wall around it. So that's why I suggested time apart. To build up that wall."

A plaintive saxophone mirrored her words, bass guitar and cymbals riding the notes. Nathan reached for his glass. She heard him take a long, slow drink, and then another one. "It's been a long time since I've mixed Hennessy. I usually drink it straight. But this is growing on me."

"It doesn't seem so strong now?"

"The more I drink, the less I taste the alcohol. Of course, that's probably because I'm getting drunk." He set down the glass. "A couple guys in my office have gotten sick. I'll have to get some orange juice."

"I have an extra carton you can have if you want."

"You do?"

She sat up, her legs crossed beneath her. "There was a two-for-one sale. I'll give you one."

"I don't want to take the extra one you bought to stay healthy."

"Fine. I'll give you the one that's opened and partly gone. How about that?"

"I guess that's all right."

"Good. I want to keep you healthy, too."

"Careful. You're about to sound like you care for me."

Their eyes met. "I do."

He reached for her hand and began rubbing it, his thumbs gliding up and down her palm. He looked down, tracing her fingers with his own, interlocking their hands, then releasing. His touch caused goose bumps and squiggles. Her thighs clenched. This time her legs were trembling for a totally different reason.

"I've apologized for what happened at Christmas. Given the chance, I would handle things differently. But what has already happened can't be taken back. I can only say I'm sorry, which I am, and work to next time be a better man."

His words were tear-worthy. Heartfelt and sincere. Sissy swore there was a side of Nathan he kept well hidden; a cold, heartless soul that could flip emotions at will. She said Nathan and Sherri were closer than twins, and that no other woman would trump her place in his heart.

"No matter what he tells you," she'd warned, "no matter how good it feels, you'll never, *ever* be number one in his life. His sister, Sherri, will always stand between you and that hope. You may be his girlfriend, but you'll never mean more to him than his family."

Dispirited, she reached for her juice.

"So has this been enough?"

"What?" Her voice was low and breathy as she became intoxicated without one drop of cognac. No. Her high came courtesy of Nathan Carver: his scent, touch, voice, presence. Whatever else happened, Jessica knew that this two-week stint of celibacy was about to be over.

"This time apart. You say you've missed me. Has it been long enough for you to know for sure that you want us back together?"

She nodded.

"I didn't hear that."

"Yes, Nathan." Her expression was part smile, part smirk, and part something else that Nathan couldn't quite name. "I've already said as much. I want us back together."

Once again, he pulled her into his arms. "That's just what I wanted to hear. Especially now that I'm a part of my company's executive arm."

"What's that mean?"

"I got promoted to vice president."

"Really? Baby, that's . . . great . . . really."

His look became curious. "You sure about that?"

"Of course I am. Congratulations."

She wrapped her arms around his neck and leaned in. The kiss soon became caressing, which quickly turned to groping hands and shedding clothes. They moved to the bedroom and made slow, hot love, reacquainting their bodies with each other—licking, kissing, stroking, thrusting—filling the room with the scent of their longing. Once, and again, they loved. That night and the next morning they again satisfied one another.

After heading out for a hearty breakfast Nathan returned Jessica to her home, French-kissed her good-bye, and left smiling and happy . . . with his carton of juice.

CHAPTER 20

Food poisoning? It had to be. That's the only explanation Nathan could fathom for stomach cramps, excessive thirst, and regurgitating everything he'd eaten in the past five hours.

It started last night, at Jessica's house. He didn't say anything. That would have ruined the mood. After their first round of lovemaking, he'd asked Jessica for another drink—straight orange juice this time. Later, his stomach felt queasy, a rarity. He chalked it up to that strong first drink on a near-empty stomach. Before leaving for breakfast, Jessica made tea. Her domestic gestures were as appreciated as they were unusual. A tad too sweet for his liking, but aware of her good intentions he drank it right down. A subtle rumbling after breakfast, but it soon went away. For lunch, he'd met his friend Stephen for barbecue and beer. With plans to meet Jessica for a late dinner and movie, he'd fixed a turkey sandwich with tomato and mayo and downed it with a tall, cold glass of orange juice. Less than an hour later and he was praying to the porcelain god.

After waiting a moment, making sure he was done, he slowly got off the floor, rinsed his mouth, brushed his teeth, and covered his face with a cold, wet towel. He couldn't believe how bad he'd felt before stumbling into the bathroom. *I haven't been sick in years!* Placing a hand on his stomach, he took a deep breath and waited. Yes, he felt better now. Maybe the worse was over. He sank onto the couch, gave himself a few more minutes to regroup, then reached for the phone.

"Hey, babe. It's me."

"Nate? What's the matter?" The concern in Jessica's voice came through the phone. "You don't sound good."

"I've felt better."

"What happened?"

"Food poisoning, I think. Have you felt sick today?"

"Come to think of it, I did feel something earlier. But it went away."

"Maybe I shouldn't have eaten sausage for breakfast and ribs at lunch."

"I've heard too much pork is not good for you."

"Hey, I like pig. Have eaten it all my life and this never happened before. So earlier, you felt nauseous?"

"Just a little."

"Maybe it was the ribs. But I think this started coming on last night."

"While you were here?"

"Yes."

"Why didn't you say something?"

"Because I didn't want to worry you. Plus, it went away."

"It might be stomach flu. A couple of my coworkers have been sick with that or bad colds. That's why I started drinking more orange juice and tea. I hope I don't have the bug and passed it to you."

"If you had whatever I've got, you'd know it. Just threw up my insides. Thought my intestines were going to come out."

"Eww."

"Too much information? Sorry about that. At least I feel better. Not up to going out though. I hope you understand."

"Nate, don't apologize for being sick. Of course I understand. More than that, I sympathize."

He heard a rattling noise in the background. "What are
you doing?"

"Getting up, and closing the magazine I was reading. I'm
coming over."

"Jessica, you don't have to do that. I'm okay."

"I know I don't have to. But I want to. Give me an hour or
so. I'll call you when I'm on my way."

Jessica nibbled her bottom lip as she paced the floor.
Nathan was sick. The antifreeze had definitely worked and the
arsenic poured into the container she gave him probably led to
today's vomiting episode. *Should I give him more or back off for
now?* Decisions, decisions. She retrieved the burner phone
from inside her purse and sent a quick text. Hopefully her sister would reply.

Day 1. It's working. More now or wait?

She waited about a minute, then tossed the phone on the
couch and headed to the kitchen. Placing the recipe she'd
printed out on the counter, she went to the fridge and pulled
out the frozen vegetables and the roasted chicken breast she'd
purchased at the store. From the cabinets came canned tomatoes,
chicken broth, a package of noodles, and the soup mix seasoning.
She placed everything on the counter and rechecked the list of
ingredients.

Forgot to buy an onion and garlic. Oh, well. She'd have to make
do with what she had and hope it tasted good. For her, going
to the grocery was in itself an alien experience and walking
the produce aisle like a trip to the moon.

"Okay," she murmured, scrolling down the screen for instructions. "Cook meat until tender." She looked at the perfectly roasted chicken breast. "That's already done. What's next?

Add tomatoes, vegetables, noodles, and seasoning. Bring to a boil. Simmer for ten minutes." She took a breath. Sounded easy enough. Time for execution.

As the concoction simmered, her burner phone rang. She rushed to answer it. "Sissy?"

"Who else?" was the dry reply.

"I know." Jessica breathed a sigh of relief. "I'm just glad you called back. I don't know what to do next. And I'm trying to make this soup but don't know if I'm doing it right. I forgot the garlic and onions and it tastes kind of bland. I don't think—"

"Good. Don't think. Just listen. Take small steps, every few days. The vitamins will build up over time. Understand?"

"So I shouldn't do any more tonight?"

"Just a little, but not too much. We want to keep his . . . energy . . . at a certain level, but we don't want him to become overly alarmed. Got it?"

"I guess so."

"You sure? I want you to feel confident, so if you have questions, ask."

"How long until, you know, it happens?"

"I'm thinking a couple months."

"That long? How can I watch him suffer all that time?"

"By remembering how much time I've got in here. Toughen up, Jessie. We're in this together. I've got your back. And once we're together again, it will have all been worth it. Anything for the sistership."

Jessica smiled at the word Sissy had once used to describe their bond. She straightened her back and repeated, "Anything for the sistership."

"Now, about that soup . . ."

A short time later Jessica rang Nathan's bell. He was slow to answer, and when he did it was with bloodshot eyes and a wrinkled shirt. "Hey, baby." His voice was hoarse and gravelly. "I fell asleep." He stepped back for her to enter, looking at the tote she carried. "What's all that?"

"Stuff to make you feel better," she replied, passing his living room and continuing on to the kitchen.

He followed. "When did you become Miss Suzy Homemaker?"

"Ha! That's a stretch. But I do like the thought of being able to care for you. Plus, one morning in the Bahamas, I came downstairs early to find your mom in the kitchen. She was fixing something, oatmeal I think or . . ."

"Probably grits."

"Yes! I think that's it. She looked so peaceful stirring at the stove. I asked her if she liked cooking. She said she loved it; told me it sometimes relieved her stress and gave her time to think. What she said that I liked most was that cooking was a way to show love. So that's what I'm doing."

"Really?" Nate walked toward her, backing her up against the counter. "You love me now?"

She nodded.

"I can't hear that."

"Yes."

"Yes, what?"

She looked at him through lowered lashes, her head tilted shyly. "Yes . . . I do."

Nathan chuckled. "Trying not to pass those three little words through your lips, huh?" He walked over to where the tote sat on the island. "That's okay. This shows you love me." He reached inside. "Ow! This is hot!"

Jessica strolled over and gave him a look. "That's what you get for being nosy." She reached for a dish towel and carefully pulled out the plastic container.

"Is that soup?" Nate's face looked as surprised as his voice sounded.

"Yes, Nate, chicken noodle and vegetable soup." She took off the lid. Steam carried the scent to Nathan's nose.

He inhaled. "And you made it?" Incredulity took his voice up an octave.

"Geez, don't act so shocked."

"I am shocked." They laughed.

She pulled out the remaining items. "Between all of this and my TLC, you're going to get better."

Nathan pulled her into his arms and kissed her soundly. "Jessica Bolton, I might get used to this."

"Is that so," she purred.

"It is. And if that happens, I just might have to make things official to keep you around."

Again, he enveloped her in his arms, squeezed her tight, and kissed her temple. Jessica was glad he'd made that move. Not good for him to see her cry. She swiped away a single tear, and hugged him back.

CHAPTER 21

Monday morning, Nathan was thankful to wake up feeling like his old self. Jessica's remedies must have worked after all. The soup she'd made was tasty and the soda had calmed his stomach. Though he'd experienced a few cramping sensations throughout the night, he hadn't thrown up. Believing the worse was behind him, he grabbed his briefcase and headed to work.

Broderick entered his office minutes after he arrived. "Morning, Nate. How was your weekend?"

"Not bad. You?"

Broderick shrugged. "Pretty good. Hung out with the family, watched TV. That's about it."

"Sounds relaxing, just like mine."

"I was glad for the downtime. And a good thing, too."

Nathan looked up from checking e-mails. "Why, what's going on?"

Broderick shut the door and took a seat. "We need to get you up to speed ASAP. Clyde isn't going to stay through his thirty-day notice. He's leaving next week."

Nathan grimaced.

"Sorry, brother. This probably wasn't how you expected to start your week."

"No, it's not that. Over the weekend, I dealt with food poisoning or the flu, something that upset my stomach."

"Are you feeling better? I'd hate for you to stay and spread a bug through the office. But I also can't afford to have you sick right now. I don't need to tell you that this is a very crucial time."

"No, Broderick. I'm all right. Just a little cramp, that's all. What happened for Clyde to have changed his plans?"

"We changed them, me and the board. Found out that Clyde has been talking to a couple longtime clients about continuing with him once he leaves the firm. It appears he plans to do a little consulting in between golf games, handling one or two clients. Unfortunately for him, one of the men he talked to has been a loyal client of this company for fifteen years and immediately called to tell me about it."

"Wow, I'm shocked."

"No more than we were. Clyde and I have been business partners for more than twenty years. If he'd been up front about his plans, we could have worked something out. But his underhandedness has caused us to question what else he might be planning. So we feel it best to get him out of the office."

"How long before I take over his position?"

Broderick's steely dark brown eyes bore into Nate. "One week. Can you handle that?"

"I'll give it my best." Nate offered his hand and Broderick shook it. "Thanks for this opportunity, Broderick. I don't plan to disappoint."

Several blocks away, in another office building, Jessica felt sick. Her illness was not of the stomach but of the heart. Yesterday, guilt-ridden, she'd put only a small amount of arsenic into Nathan's "feel better" soup. They were together until after midnight. He complained of a headache but otherwise seemed fine. Hurting him was hurting her. And she'd just gotten started.

Between her and Sissy, she'd always been the more sensitive one. For her sister, the ends always justified the means. Jessica loved Sissy more than life. But she was beginning to seriously doubt if she had the stomach to carry out her sister's request. Looking at her watch, she saw that duty called. She hurriedly prepared the tea to take to her desk.

"Hey, pretty lady. Why the sad face?"

"Good morning, Vincent." Jessica reached for the sugar packets and added two to her cup. He didn't deserve her continued attitude but once again, she didn't feel like talking.

"No smile for me this morning?"

"Dude . . . I don't even have one for myself." She left the break room.

He followed her. "How about I take you to lunch, make you feel better."

"No, thanks."

"Come on now, Jess—"

"Look! I said no!" She immediately regretted the outburst. Vincent was being who he'd always been. She was the one who'd changed. On Friday she'd been upset because Nathan was out of her life. Today she was agitated because he was back in it.

"I'm sorry, Vincent." Her eyes were sincere as she placed a hand on his arm. "Maybe hanging out with you is exactly what I need to stop stressing out."

Jessica didn't know whether the moon was full or what, but by the time one o'clock came she was ready to run out of the firm. She'd been lied to ("I'm sure I left a message with you last week"), snapped at ("You'll put this call through and you'll do it now!"), and threatened ("Are you being short with me? I can have you fired!"). She met Vincent in the lobby.

He winked, and fell in beside her. "We're going to have to stop meeting like this."

"Probably."

"I'm just kidding, Jessica."

"I'm not. I think my boss's secretary has been eavesdropping, trying to get some business because her lonely ass has none. When I was standing at the elevator, she asked if I knew where you were."

"She's just jealous of you, baby."

"Story of my life," she mumbled.

"Huh?"

"Never mind."

"I'm sure there are those at the firm who've seen how we click. If your boy was out of the picture I'd be after you in a heartbeat."

"What about that girl you were seeing before the holidays?"

"Too needy. There's nothing more unattractive to a brothah than a sistah who acts desperate to be with you."

Jessica gave him a look. "Does that mean you didn't sleep with her?"

"Babe, just because a man isn't interested in a relationship doesn't mean he won't have sex with a woman who offers it up."

They reached the bustling restaurant and took a table near the back. After placing their orders, Vincent got right down to business.

"I let you dodge the question on Friday, but today I want answers. What's going on with you?"

Jessica reached for her water, scanning the room as she sipped.

"You know I'm your friend, right?" She nodded. He reached for her hand. "I'm concerned about you, babe. What's wrong? Are you and Nate having problems?"

"I guess you could say that."

"Is he cheating on you?"

"Not that I know of. Why would that be your first guess?"

He shrugged. "It's a common relationship problem." The

waiter set down their drinks and appetizers. "Is he still tripping over seeing us together in Buckhead that night?"

"I told him we worked together and were just hanging out as friends."

"Then what is it?" Vincent's phone rang. "Excuse me, babe," he said, standing. "Important client. I need to get this real quick."

She nodded her okay, glad for the break from Vincent's probing with the determined focus of the shrewd litigator he was.

Reaching for her cell phone to surf the Web, she thought of Vincent's comment about infidelity being a common relationship issue. Considering the reality, Jessica would give almost anything for another woman to be their problem right about now.

For the rest of the day, Nathan worked hard on getting his clients' needs streamlined and clearing his plate for the added duties to come. Not an easy feat, considering the fogginess inside his head. For a man who'd rarely been sick a day in his life, the past two days had been highly disconcerting. If this rash of symptoms continued, he'd have do the unthinkable—go to the doctor and get checked out.

Eight thirty, and he was still at the office. He wasn't surprised to see Jessica's name on the caller ID. "Good evening, sweetheart."

"Hello, Nate. I'm calling to check on you."

"That's very nice, baby, but you needn't worry. I feel fine."

"No more nausea?"

"None."

"The headache's gone?"

"Completely." A slight dizziness had overcome him when he stood up abruptly, but he'd chalked that up to not much food or sleep. Nothing to worry Jessica's pretty head about. "How was your day?"

"Just another day at the office."

"That exciting, huh?"

"I wish. Have you eaten yet? I could grab us a bite and come over. Or we could go out."

"Unfortunately, I can do neither right now. I'm still at work." He explained why. "For the next month or so, this is my life. I'll probably spend more time here than in my home."

"I'm happy for your promotion, but concerned there's so much work."

"It'll smooth out eventually. It's only during the transition that I'll be busy like this."

"Will I get to see you?"

"Of course."

"When?"

"Good question. Not tonight; I'm crashing early. By Wednesday, I should have a handle on what all needs to happen, and a schedule for how we'll operate going forth. So I'll call you."

"Okay. Take care of yourself."

"No doubt. Between working here and loving you, I've got to stay healthy."

"What's that mean?"

"Three times in one night? You figure it out."

"Oh. That."

They laughed. "Look, babe, I want to finish up here."

"Of course. We'll talk later."

Just before ten p.m., a weary Nathan trudged into his loft, stripped off his clothes and took a hot shower. He then went downstairs for a large glass of juice.

An hour later, the first cramp hit him. His illness was not over yet.

CHAPTER 22

It was the slowest week of her life. Or so it seemed. With Nathan working ten- to twelve-hour days, Jessica was left with too much time on her hands. Being alone had never bothered her before. For the most part, this had been her life—rejected, alone, isolated—even while married.

Not so in the beginning. When Jessica met Edwin she thought her luck had changed. During their one-year courtship he was courteous, generous, patient, and kind. She'd had two prior boyfriends. Edwin showed her the difference between a boy and a man. He had a big house and fancy cars, and always looked amazing. But it was his actions that won her heart. He was so concerned about her welfare.

A few months into dating, he bought her first cell phone. Sometimes he'd call two or three times a day, just to know where she was and how she was doing. If she went out, he asked that she call before leaving the foster home, then at her destination, and again when she returned. Most days, he'd pick her up from school, wanting to know all about the people she hung out with, especially boys. "To make sure you're safe," he'd told her. "It's a mean world out here." So caring were these actions to someone like Jessica, someone who'd never felt a parent's love. When he proposed not long after her eighteenth birthday, she excitedly said yes.

The honeymoon period ended during the honeymoon, when she was introduced to Edwin's other side: possessive, controlling, angry, mean. On the way to dinner a man complimented her appearance. Edwin accused her of flirting. She'd donned a cute bikini to join him poolside. He called her a whore and made her change, one reason Sherri and Nathan's Bahamas berating had stung so bad. The next to last night of that trip, Edwin wanted anal. Jessica didn't; even cringed at the thought. That was the first time he slapped her. Then he took what he wanted without her consent.

Afterwards he was full of apologies, accompanied by cards and gifts. Post-abuse good behavior usually lasted several weeks. Then she'd get hit again. And the cycle continued. Jessica learned to hide her emotions better than the bruises, to judge his moods and play the required role appropriately. How abusive was he? By the end of their marriage, Jessica had enough diamonds, jewelry, bags, and shoes to open a consignment store. When the divorce came through, she walked away from it all.

Is that what you'd do, Nathan, if things were different and we got married? Show the ugly side of you that Sissy swears is there? Except for that single moment at the beach, it hardly seemed likely. Of course she hadn't thought Edwin to be violent either. Abusers rarely came with a warning label.

Jessica walked from her couch to the window, to the dining room and back again. Plopping down, she reached for the remote. The idea of watching TV was short-lived. Eight o'clock on a Friday and Nathan was still working. The only good that had come from his long hours is that she'd spent more time with her sister. She and Sissy had talked every night. One conversation was particularly memorable. In quiet moments, it replayed in her head.

★ ★ ★

"I'm so sorry, Jessie. Will you ever forgive me?"

"What for?"

It was late night, almost two a.m. Jessica just happened to bring the burner phone upstairs to charge. Normally she didn't. That it was on her nightstand is the only reason she'd heard it ring. Her sister couldn't sleep.

"For not being there."

"Why blame yourself? You were only ten years old!"

"Doesn't matter. You were my responsibility. I failed you."

"You saved my life!"

"I kept you from dying. I didn't save your life. You went through hell, from foster homes to a jail of a marriage. Maybe what I'm asking is too much after all."

Jessica became indignant. "From what you've shared, your life was tough, too! Abused as a child and again at the orphanage, homelessness, lying boyfriends, scratching to survive. I hate what Nathan's family did to you! Helped send you to prison based on a lie."

"That's not unusual for people like them. People of privilege are used to getting their way. They take what they want and then we're tossed out like garbage. While they get to continue living their perfect, happy lives."

"We deserve happiness, too."

"Being a real family, enjoying what others take for granted."

"I can't even imagine. That sounds like a dream. Other than pictures, I haven't seen you in over fifteen years."

"That makes me very sad." Sissy's voice abruptly changed, became upbeat. "All of life will be a celebration, to make up for that lost time. Starting with July fifth, a most important occasion."

"My birthday! You remember." She paused, deep in thought. "I don't remember yours."

"Doesn't matter. Soon we'll have all the time in the world

to get reacquainted." She yawned. "I think I can sleep now. Sorry for keeping you up late. I know you have to work."

"It's okay. Sleep well, Sis."

"I love you, Jessie."

"I love you, too."

Sissy loves me! Jessica lay down wondering why three simple words could make her feel so many things at once, happiness highest among them. And then it hit her. Aside from men, most of whom didn't mean them, it's the first time she could recall those words ever being said to her.

A ringing cell phone startled Jessica out of her thoughts. She pressed the speaker button. "Hey, babe."

"Hey, you. I'm finally leaving the office. Thought I'd stop by. Are you hungry?"

"No, I ate earlier. But feel free to bring something over."

"I'll make a stop on the way."

"Sounds perfect. I'll be waiting with a hot cup of tea."

CHAPTER 23

Nathan checked himself in the mirror. He didn't feel good. Was it the long hours at the office? The stress from being promoted? Lack of sleep, lack of loving, or all of the above? He'd missed time with Jessica, but she'd been so sweet. She'd brought over juice and soda and more of her soup. Still, some type of bug persisted. But it didn't matter. Tonight was special. And day after tomorrow his promotion would be announced. Life-changing occasions. And nothing, not even sickness, could spoil his mood.

Halfway from his en suite bathroom to the walk-in closet, his phone rang. One look at the caller ID and he grimaced, then answered. "Sherri, don't start. I know you're angry. I was supposed to call you back."

"Oh, that's okay," was the sarcastically cheerful response. "It's only been a week."

"Yeah, well, I've been on the grind. Long days, short nights. It'll slow down soon."

"No complaining, Mr. Vice President. That's what happens when you join the big leagues."

"Tell me about it. Oh, happy Valentine's Day."

"Back at you, Brother."

He checked his watch. "I'm surprised you're calling. You and Randall didn't do anything special?"

"He got called to London as a last minute replacement for a conference speaker. He promised to make it up to me this weekend."

"Why didn't you go with him? That would have been a nice trip." Nathan selected a suit, then matched up shirt, shoes, and tie.

"You forget I've rejoined the workforce? It's only part-time, but I take my teaching obligation seriously."

"Of course you do. It's been so long since you've held a job, I forget. So it's still going well."

"Most days are very rewarding. But other days I look at these kids with no role models, incompetent parents, bad neighborhoods, and so much more to deal with. They all need saving. It makes me sad."

"What was that saying? Each one, teach one? You can't save everybody, Sherri. Just do what you can." He walked back into the bathroom and reached into a drawer.

"That's what I tell myself. Much harder to put into practice."

"You can do it," he mumbled.

"What are you doing?"

"Shaving, getting ready for a big date."

"You and what's-her-name hitting the town?"

He stopped mid-stroke. "Her name is Jessica."

"I was only kidding. Geez, don't get worked up."

"Well, don't play like that. Jessica is very special to me."

"Dang, if I didn't know better I'd think you were about to propose. You almost bit my head off."

"It's been a long week. My patience is short. But I know you mean well. Listen, tell the kids that Uncle said hi. Let's talk this weekend when I have more time."

"No problem. Enjoy yourself tonight. Don't do anything foolish! But have a good time."

Nathan dressed quickly. He double-checked to make sure he had everything he needed, then headed out the door. On the drive over to Jessica's, he thought about what his sister had said. Sherri's subtle warning, delivered probably because she knew him so well. To her, what he had planned might be considered foolish. For him, it was simply the right thing to do.

She fussed with her hair, straightened her dress, rethought her shoe choice. Nothing was working. *I look like crap!* Thirty minutes later, she'd changed three times—only to go back to her original choice.

And then the bell rang.

Her heart jumped. Placing a hand on her stomach, she took a deep, calming breath. Recalling the conversation from earlier today, she muttered, "You can do this, Jessie. Just like Sissy said."

She walked to the door. "Hello, handsome."

Nathan stood there, transfixed, drinking her in like a rare Perrier-Jouët.

His blatant scrutiny was unnerving.

"Do I look okay?"

"You are the most beautiful creature I've ever seen."

The resolve for follow-through faltered. She almost believed him. "You're just saying that." *Like Edwin did.* "Come on in."

He stepped in, still staring. "These aren't just words. Have you looked in the mirror? You look stunning."

"I look different because I rarely wear my hair up like this."

"The beauty I see is about much more than hair." He took a step toward her. Then another, his eyes skimming her body as though a rare treat.

Suddenly nervous around a man she'd known for months, Jessica chattered. "What time are our reservations? Would you like to sit down? I can get us some orange juice, or tea?"

He stopped in front of her. "Jessica Bolton. All I want is you."

The kiss was soft, delicate, restrained. She knew he held back. The bulge slowly growing against her dress was proof. His tongue whipped across her lips once, and again, before he pulled back, still holding her. So much emotion in such a small act. Such intensity was powerful, taking her breath.

"I ruined your lipstick."

"I have more."

"We'd better go. Five more minutes like this and the only place we'll be headed is to bed."

They arrived at Chops Lobster Bar just before eight and were promptly seated in a cozy booth. Nathan ordered a bottle of wine. Jessica tried to look calm, as if she belonged. She placed the linen napkin on her lap.

Nathan followed suit. "Have you been here before?"

She shook her head. "Heard about it, though. Some of the partners come here for lunch. They've raved about the food. What about you?"

"A couple times for business meetings. Always said when I met the right woman, I'd bring her here. The food is great and the service, superb."

As if underscoring his point, the waiter arrived and uncorked their bottle. After Nathan's faint nod of approval, he poured their wine, set the bottle on the table, then bowed and departed.

Nathan picked up his glass. "To the most beautiful woman in the room."

Jessica smiled, her glass lifted, too. "Happy Valentine's Day."

She took a healthy swig, and then another.

"Slow down, now. Or you'll be tipsy before the entrée."

"It's good."

"Yes. As wines go, this is just about the only wine I like."

Another sip. "What kind is it?"

"Nebbiolo."

"Never heard of it."

"It's not in many regular liquor stores." Nathan watched Jes-

sica fiddle with her napkin, her eyes darting around the room.
"You look nervous. Is everything okay?"

"I guess I am, a little." She smiled, unconsciously biting her
bottom lip. "I'm not used to this fancy stuff. Plus, I'm worried
about you."

"Why?"

"You look tired."

"I am. Things are going well at the office. It'll slow down."
He reached for her hand. "But I don't want to talk about work
tonight. I want to look at this menu, because thankfully my appetite has returned. And I want to talk about us."

"Okay." She perused her menu as well. "Have you had the
lobster tail?"

Nathan nodded. "Delicious."

They continued discussing the menu. After deciding on
Kobe strip steak and Chilean sea bass, Nathan replenished their
glasses.

"Oh, I forgot . . ." Jessica murmured to herself, looking
around the room.

"What, babe?"

"I wish I'd remembered to request lemons and a straw for
my water."

"I can find the waiter, have him bring what you need."

"That's okay. I'll wait until he comes back."

"No need to wait. I was going to wash my hands anyway."

"Thank you, Nate."

He stood and placed a quick kiss on her brow. "Be right
back."

As soon as his back was turned, she reached for her purse.
She moved without thought or feeling, just focused intent.
After returning his wineglass to its position and quickly using
her compact to apply powder and a small dab of gloss, she
closed her purse and reached for her wineglass.

Nathan rounded the corner, saucer in hand. "Lemons for
the lady."

"Thanks again, babe."

"I'm happy we're back in a comfortable groove. Every couple goes through their ups and downs. I can tell right now that with you, I want to experience more of the former."

"Disagreements are bound to happen."

"Did you and your ex-husband argue much?"

"I learned it was safer to just go along."

Nathan's brow creased. "Why, to not get hit?"

Her eyes were downcast as she answered. "I'd rather not talk about him. Like you said, tonight's about us."

"Fair enough." He took a drink of wine. "I have a question. If you could take a dream vacation, go anywhere in the world, where would that be?"

"Hmm. Good question. Let's see . . . somewhere really different and far away: Fiji, or Tahiti . . . someplace like that."

"Maybe we'll go. I've not been to either of those places." He took another sip of wine, held the glass up by the light to inspect the color. "This is a really good vintage. Great selection, I must say." He took another long sip.

Jessica gave him a look. "Now who's getting tipsy?"

"Touché." He set down the glass. "So I see you like islands."

"Yes. They're so beautiful, makes me feel like I'm in paradise."

Conversation flowed easier than it had in a while. While both slowed down, they continued drinking through the first three courses, and pondered ordering a second bottle as their entrées arrived.

"Ooh, this sauce smells delicious. Your steak looks good, too. Baby, we just might have to share and do a little surf and—Nate? What's the matter?"

Having clutched his stomach, he now grimaced in pain. His hand gripped the table as if for dear life.

"Babe! What's the matter?"

"My stomach," he panted, continuing to bend over until his head touched the table.

Jessica looked around, frantic. *Where is the waiter?* She'd poured more of the arsenic into his glass than intended but hadn't expected a reaction like this. She leapt from her seat. At the same time, Nathan straightened up and stood.

"Wait! Where are you going?"

"Let me get to . . . the restroom. Cold towel . . . will help me."

"No, Nathan. Sit down. I'll go get it for you." She watched in amazement as large beads of sweat simultaneously popped up and ran down his face.

"No. I need air. I'll be . . . I'll be back."

He took two steps, then two more . . . and fell flat.

"Nathan!" Jessica screamed. "Someone call an ambulance!"

CHAPTER 24

Everything happened so fast. One minute she was dreaming about fantasy vacations. The next minute she was riding in the back of an ambulance with lights blazing and horns blaring.

"What's happening?" she shrieked, her arm clutching the EMT worker. "Why are his eyes rolled back like that?"

A second EMT moved her with a firm hand. "Ma'am, you've got to calm down and let us help your husband."

"He's . . ." *Not my husband. He'll never be my husband. Or anybody else's, based on how it looks right now.* She slumped against the window, looking out the window and not seeing a thing. If he died it would be mission accomplished. But a part of her would die, too.

At the hospital, it was even more hectic. He was placed on a gurney and rushed into emergency while she ran alongside in her five-inch heels, then whisked through a door that she could not enter.

Heart pounding, she raced to the nurse's station. "My . . . he's . . . ," she eked out, pointing. "They wouldn't let me go back there. But I have to be in there. I have to know what's going on!"

"Ma'am, please." An older nurse with the face of one who'd handled a crisis or two, came around the counter and took her hand. "What's your name, dear?" Jessica told her. "I know it's scary. But you've got to calm down. The doctors are going to do all they can to save your husband."

"But I don't know what's happening." No need for fake crying. The tears were real.

"Right now, they're getting him stabilized so they can determine what's wrong. I understand that you're worried. But he's in good hands. Why don't you go have a seat and try to relax. Think happy thoughts. It will help you be okay."

Jessica looked into sincere blue eyes the color of sky. So compassionate was the nurse's countenance that she wanted to be wrapped in her arms and held like a baby. "Thank you." Those words were all she managed to whisper before running to the restroom for a good old cry.

After tears, and toilet tissue to blow her nose, she opened her purse. Too late she remembered. No burner phone. More than ever, she needed Sissy's advice. He was supposed to get sick, not end up in emergency. This was not part of the blueprint. *What am I supposed to do?* Deciding that nothing would come of her hiding in stallville, she washed her hands, splashed water on her face, and headed to the waiting room.

An hour later she understood more than ever how the room got its name. Waiting was as torturous as the hard, straight-back chairs. Finally, she looked up to see the nurse with the kind blue eyes pointing her way, and then a doctor walked toward her. She was up and out of her seat before he'd taken two more steps.

"Doctor? Is he . . . dead?"

"Jessica, right?" She nodded. "Mr. Carver is alive but he's pretty sick. He's severely dehydrated, with a fever and chills."

"Do you think it's food poisoning? We were having dinner."

"Perhaps. The symptoms line up with those of a very severe case. We'll need to hold him here a couple days, run some tests and determine exactly what's going on. But right now I'm hopeful that in a few days he'll be as good as new."

"Can I see him?"

"He's still in emergency but should be transferred to a room within the hour. Someone at the nurse's station will have the correct information."

"Thank you, Doctor."

Jessica followed the doctor out of the waiting room, then turned the opposite direction and headed out the door. One hour! Enough time to catch a taxi home, grab the throwaway phone, and hopefully be back before Nathan knew she was gone.

An extra fifty encouraged the cab driver to get her home in just under fifteen minutes. She was in and out of the house in five and back to the hospital in record time. Catching her breath, and walking on sore feet from dashing in shoes not made for running, she approached the desk.

Kind Blue Eyes was still on the clock. "Excuse me. Have they transferred Nathan Carver?"

She looked at the computer. "Not yet, dear. But his room is ready. I know you're itching to see him. As soon as he gets there, I'll let you know."

Jessica nodded. "Thanks. I'll be right back. Just need to make a quick call." She stepped outside and walked until she felt a good distance away from potential eavesdropping ears. Then she dialed Sissy. "He's in the hospital!" was her greeting.

"What?"

"I did what you said and he almost died!"

"That is the plan," Sissy drawled, before the implication sank in. "But wait! The hospital? Why did you dial nine-one-one?"

Jessica told her what happened. "Even before I instinctively yelled for an ambulance, I saw no less than three people grabbing their phones."

"This is definitely a problem. The sooner we get him out, the fewer tests they can run. So let's calm down and figure out how to make this happen." There was a moment of silence before Sissy continued. "Okay, here is what we're going to do . . ."

Ten minutes later, Jessica walked back into the emergency ward and up to the desk.

"There you are!" The nurse waved her over. "He's ready to see you. Come right this way."

Jessica trailed behind the fast-walking nurse, bracing herself for what she'd see. Entering the room, she realized that there wasn't a hall long enough to prepare her. Stopping just inside the doorway, her hand flew to her mouth. Nathan looked like death warmed over. Just hours ago he'd looked healthy and robust. Now, his skin looked ashen and tubes from both arms ran to drip bags suspended on steel rods.

With tentative steps, she approached the bed. "Nathan?" she whispered. She cleared her voice and spoke a little louder. "Babe?"

His eyes fluttered open. "Hey." His voice was raspy, his lips dry.

Her shaky hand covered his. "Hey."

"What . . ." He cleared his throat and swallowed with effort. "What happened?"

"You passed out."

His eyes closed, and for several seconds, she watched his even breathing. When they reopened, his stare was searching, curious. "At the restaurant. Felt ill . . ."

Jessica nodded. "You stood to go to the restroom, took two steps and fell."

"I got dizzy," he recalled, eyes narrowing in thought. "Felt light-headed and those cramps. . . What the hell is going on with me?"

"They want to keep you for a few days . . . to run some tests."

He slowly shook his head. "No. I can't be here that long. Too much going on at work."

"I agree." His eyes quickly shifted from the ceiling back to her. "I mean, I understand how busy you are right now, uh, with the promotion and everything. I'll do anything I can to help you, take off work, stay at your place to help you get well. Whatever you need."

He looked at her intensely before slowly nodding. "Thank you. See if you can find the doctor so I can get released. Where are my clothes?"

Jessica looked around. "Probably here." She walked over to a closet and opened it. "Yes, everything's here, Nathan."

He lifted his head in her direction. "Good." His head wearily fell against the pillow. That small move alone had expended considerable energy. "Get the doctor."

Ten minutes later a scowling ER doctor peered down at Nathan. "I strongly advise against your checking out, Mr. Carver. In order to pinpoint the cause of your collapse, several tests must be run. Assuming this was a case of the flu or food poisoning or something simple, is not wise. Hopefully, this ailment is something that can be cured easily. But if not, we need to identify it and treat it in these early stages."

"I appreciate your concern, Doc." Nathan winced as he moved his hand, causing the needle connected to the intravenous feeding bag to wiggle. "I'll make an appointment to see my physician this weekend."

"That's fine, but the equipment for the types of tests we need to run is here, in the hospital, not a doctor's office."

"I want to be released." Clipped words delivered through tight jaws.

"First thing tomorrow; that's the best I can do. At the very least, your body needs fluid." Nathan's lips thinned into a resolute line. The doctor crossed his arms. "One night for observation." He leaned toward his patient. "This is your life."

"Fine. One night. And then I'm out of here."

"I'll be right back." Jessica followed the doctor out of the room. "Is he going to be okay, Doctor?"

"I hope so. But as I've stated, the only way to know for sure what is happening is to run a battery of tests. Without that, there is no way to provide a correct diagnosis."

"Is there something I can do?"

"Keep him hydrated. Record what he eats. There's a small

chance he's developed an allergy to something and is unaware of it. Encourage plenty of rest, and persuade him to let us test him."

"Thank you." A quick nod, and the doctor walked off. Jessica watched his brisk steps down the hall, thinking about what he'd told her to do to make Nathan better and knowing that to carry out her sister's plans she was going to make him feel much, much worse.

Nathan's eyes were on her as soon as she reentered the room. She winced as a toe expressed its displeasure at still being in heels. "What is it, Jessica?"

She sat down and removed her shoes. "I've been in these heels too long."

"Why don't you go change?"

"And leave you?"

This brought a smile. "I can live without you for a little while."

"Okay. I would like to change into something else, and bring you clean clothes, too." He nodded. She replaced her shoes and walked to the closet. Suit, shirt, and tie in hand, she returned to his bedside for a quick kiss on his dry lips. "Okay, I'll see you in a bit."

His eyelids drooped. "No, you won't."

"Why not?"

"Because I need rest and so do you. I also need for you to pick up the car."

"It's still at the restaurant! I'd totally forgotten."

"Can you do that, and come back in the morning?"

"Of course."

"Will taking the morning off from your job be okay? I don't want to get you in trouble."

"Don't worry about me. I'll be here."

"Jessica!" The loud voice in Nathan's head was a mere whisper in the room. *Hopefully she won't feel the box.* He was still frowning when moments later sleep claimed him. Jessica, oblivious to Nathan's attempt to stop her, continued to the door.

She barely remembered the taxi ride to the restaurant or after retrieving his vehicle the ride to his house. Jumbled thoughts competed for dominance. Feelings were all over the place. She reached his loft and stepped inside. After removing her shoes, she headed for the closet in his master suite.

It felt different being in his home alone. Intrusive somehow, though he was aware. Seeing a pair of house shoes, she slipped them on, knowing if she tried those heels again there'd be a toe revolt. This was her first time in his closet. It smelled like him—musky and manly. Still clutching the suit in one hand, she ran the other over his wardrobe, all neatly organized. Suits, slacks, shirts, casual wear, shoes, and accessories all had their place. Several bottles of cologne lined the top of a dresser. She spotted the clothes hamper and walked over, double-checking pockets before throwing in the items. Just before tossing them she felt something in his suit coat, reached in and pulled out a small blue box.

"No!" The word exploded from her mouth through a gust of air. Mouth open, eyes wide, she stared at her hand as though it held a foreign object. *No!* Repeated in her mind, over and over. *It can't be.*

She opened the box. It most certainly was. Taunting her from its silk-lined case was an engagement ring: sparkly round diamond of at least two carats in a platinum setting, with smaller, colored diamonds down the side. Its beauty brought tears to her eyes. The impossibility of it all made her cry harder. Funny, because in years gone by, tears were rarely shed. As one foster parent had asked her, "What's the use?" Those stored-up tears fell like a Seattle storm. Sinking to the floor, there in his walk-in closet, she cried for many things: never really knowing her parents, losing her sister for so many years, unhappy foster homes, a miserable marriage. But most of all Jessica wept because it appeared that tonight the man she had sworn to kill had planned to propose.

CHAPTER 25

A little after eleven a.m. the next day, Nate was back in his loft. "It's good to see this place," he told Jessica. "I hate hospitals!"

"I'm not a big fan of them either. How are you feeling?"

"Are you going to ask me that every five minutes?"

"Maybe."

He chuckled.

"I'm just—"

"Concerned. I know." He held her face between his hands and kissed her lips. "I'm a little weak, but otherwise, I feel okay. It's nice to have a woman to take care of me. But you didn't have to take off work."

"The Christmas trip was the first vacation for me in a while and I went back to work early. I've got a bunch of vacation days. Besides," she said, wrapping her arms around him, "I like taking care of you." They kissed.

"Oh, really." They kissed again. "In that case, I'll avail you of every possible opportunity. But first, I need a shower. My body will feel better after that."

"And food, right? Did they feed you this morning?"

"You can't call what they serve patients *food*. But I'm not hungry."

"The doctor said you had to eat, and drink liquids. While you shower, I'm going to run and get a few things. If you need anything, call me. Okay?"

"Yes, Doctor."

"Ooh"—she wriggled her eyebrows in a seductive walk toward him—"I've got some medicine to give you when you . . . get back your strength."

"Baby, I'll be more than ready for that prescription. Oh, and here." He reached into the nightstand drawer. "Take this spare key. When you return, I might be asleep."

As soon as Jessica left, Nathan walked straight to his closet. After a quick scan through his suits, he moved to the clothes hamper. Inside was his suit jacket. He pulled it out, immediately tapping the inside pocket for a little blue box. It was there. A sigh of relief escaped his lips. *Good. She didn't see it.* The weight of this relief coupled with the fatigue of illness hit him full force. He swayed. The wall caught him. After a quick shower, he brought a bottle of water up to the bedroom, grabbed his cell phone and laptop, and crawled into bed. He had true gratitude for a boss like Broderick, who'd suggested they postpone the promotion announcement until he was feeling better. Nathan wouldn't hear of it. "I'll see you tomorrow, boss, bright and early," he'd told him earlier that morning. Nathan looked forward to wearing the title *vice president*.

Once situated, he checked e-mails and returned calls that had come in to the office. After relaying to Kenneth the latest information on the Vegas club possibility, he dialed Sherri.

"Hey, Sis. I was on another call."

"It's okay. I was just touching base. And just in time, I see. What is wrong with you?"

"What do you mean?"

"Boy, don't try to kid a kidder. I've known you all of your

life and mine, and can tell when something's wrong. Your date last night went that badly?"

"Sent me to the hospital."

"What?"

It was a weak laugh, but her humorous reaction was duly noted. He told her what happened.

"I don't know, Nate. You're trying to downplay the situation, but passing out sounds serious to me. You need to take those tests."

"I will . . . eventually."

"No, Nate. Now. After the VP promotion hoopla, take a couple days to focus on your health. Remember, a dead VP can't make much money."

"You're right, Sis. I'll take care."

"Make sure you do."

Jessica stood at her kitchen counter, carefully mixing Nathan's special OJ blend. She sighed, and mixed in a little more "vitamins." "He's got that big meeting tomorrow," she mumbled to herself, replacing the cap on the soda. "If he doesn't show up, that will look very suspicious. Just a little will do for now."

She placed these and other items in a box and set it by the front door. Next up was placing an order at one of Nathan's favorite delis to pick up soup and sandwiches. She'd purchased items for another pot of homemade soup. But she'd wait until the weekend to serve up this special concoction, when his becoming ill would go unnoticed by everyone but her.

"Do I have everything?" She'd placed the call to the restaurant and now double-checked to see that she had what she needed for a four-night stay at Nathan's place. *Sissy's phone.* "Right." She headed toward the bedroom where the phone had been charging but midway stopped in her tracks. *Maybe I shouldn't take it. What if Nathan sees it? How will I explain having two phones?* After another second, she continued to the room.

That phone was her only connection to Sissy. No way could she leave it. So she scooped it up along with her other items and headed to the restaurant on her way to Nathan's house.

She was almost to his door when the burner phone rang. *Yikes! I forgot to silence the ringer!* Quickly backing away from his door she set down the box of beverages and reached for the phone. "Oh my God, Sissy, that was close."

"What happened?"

"I was just about to walk into Nathan's house!"

"Why not just leave the phone at home?"

Jessica told her.

"Maybe in the four days that you're there you can finish the job."

"What happened to going slowly to not arouse suspicion?"

"Because of what my attorney told me this morning. Nathan's sister's attorney has sent another letter to the judge about denying my parole 'for their safety.'"

"How can they even do that?"

"I don't know. Their attorney probably told them I could someday get out. So of course those assholes go running to the judge with their sanctimonious bullshit! Losing her brother will rock their perfect little world. Then she'll know how it feels to have someone you love taken away from you."

Jessica's regular cell phone rang. She retrieved it from her purse. "Sissy, it's Nate calling. I've got to go."

"Speed it up."

"Okay. Bye."

Instead of answering Nathan's call, she walked to the door and let herself in. "I'm here, babe!" After setting down the box in the kitchen, she walked upstairs to the master suite and sat on the bed. "What do you need?"

"I was going to ask you to stop by the deli on your way here. Never mind, though. I'll order from one of the delivery menus."

"I'm way ahead of you," she beamed, leaning over for a kiss before standing. "One turkey breast sandwich and a bowl of soup, coming up!"

"You already went by the deli?"

She nodded. "See how in sync we are?"

"I do see, and I like it."

She fixed two trays, pouring both of their glasses of soda from the uncontaminated container. They ate and then lounged in his king-size bed. Throughout the afternoon, Nathan alternated between work and sleep. By evening he was feeling much better. He enjoyed a good night's sleep with Jessica snuggled in his arms.

The next morning, he kissed Jessica good-bye and drove to his future as a top executive of a leading consulting firm.

After celebrating his promotion at a dinner with his colleagues, Nathan spent a quiet evening at home with his sweetheart. Friday morning he almost felt back to his old self. Friday night he and Jessica went to dinner and a movie, unwinding at home with his new preferred drink: OJ, with a small amount of Hennessy. Unfortunately for him, alcohol was not the only small thing that added to this mix, a fact that by early Saturday morning, had Nathan rethinking his decision to argue with the ER doctor last weekend and demand an early release.

CHAPTER 26

"Hey, Sis." Nathan hadn't the strength to hold the phone, so after pushing the speaker button, he laid it on his chest.

"Are you sick again?" Panicked concern was evident in Sherri's voice.

"Looks like it."

"But we just talked Thursday, after your promotion. You sounded fine."

"I felt good, too. Same thing yesterday morning, and when Jessica and I went out last night. It was all good. Then about two o'clock this morning . . . stomach cramps again."

"Interesting how Jessica's always involved when you get sick. Maybe you're allergic to her."

"Look, don't start, okay? She's probably why I'm not even more ill. She's taking very good care of me."

Topics then switched from Jessica and Nate to Sherri and Randall and life in Virginia. Nathan promised his sister that he'd keep her updated on his mysterious health situation and then ended the call. He went downstairs and found Jessica sitting in the living room with an iPad on her lap. "Hey, you."

As soon as Jessica saw Nathan pass through the living room

on the way to the kitchen, she jumped up. "What can I get you, babe?"

An amused expression crossed his face as he stopped and turned around. "You're too good to me. Relax. I'm just getting a glass of juice, and will try to hang out down here awhile. I'm going stir-crazy in the bedroom."

Jessica acted as though he hadn't spoken. Quick steps closed the distance between them. "You need your rest, Nate. Let me get it."

Nathan gently yet firmly took her hands in his. "No." He kissed the tip of her nose. "You've already done more than enough. In fact, would you like some juice? It's time I served you for a minute."

"Uh, no. I'm good."

"Cool. Then go back to what you're doing. I'll join you in a sec." He walked straight to the fridge, opened the door, and looked inside. "Babe."

"Huh?"

"Why are their two bottles of juice opened?"

"Oh. I, uh, thought I'd grabbed the one that was open and accidentally opened the wrong one."

"Do you want a glass?"

Jessica barely succeeded in not reacting to the thought of drinking her own poison. "No, babe. I'm good."

He poured a drink and then walked to the couch and sat down beside her. "What are you doing?"

"Just surfing the Web."

"Sounds exciting."

"About as exciting as you sleeping half the day." She closed the window she'd been viewing and turned to him. "Are you feeling better?"

"I don't know, to tell you the truth. One day I'm fine. The next, I feel like I'm about to meet Jesus. I feel a little weak now but . . . I'm all right, I guess." He ran a hand up her arm. "Good enough to give you the loving that I haven't been able to since Valentine's Day."

An image of the beautiful engagement ring Jessica had placed back in the suit coat pocket flashed in her mind. *Give me loving, but not the ring!* It was hard enough to murder a man who was mostly kind and had made love to her better than any other in life. She doubted even her sister's heart would be hard enough to murder a fiancé.

She ran a hand over his groin. "Is this what you're talking about?"

"Absolutely."

Thank goodness! "Well . . . let's get this party started!"

That's all the encouragement Nathan needed. He wrapped his arms around her and seared her with a kiss that stole her breath. His hands began to roam, scorching her body wherever they touched: buttocks, waist, nipples fondled and tweaked into hardened peaks. She could have sworn there was a cord between her nipples and her nana. Wetness was immediate, and her nub vied for equal opportunity attention. Usually Nathan was the aggressor, but today it was Jessica who hurriedly ripped off her tee and unzipped his pants and pulled down her sweats. With no foreplay or protection, she slid down on his rock-hard shaft, riding, grinding, pumping, until . . . the flag began to fly at half-mast.

What?

She hurriedly rescued the bullet that had eased out of her firearm and tried to reignite the heat. Nothing doing. The soldier was no longer at attention. The steel rod was now a flaccid noodle. In short, the thrill had gone.

"I'm sorry—"

"It's okay—"

They both spoke at once as good manners tried to cover up embarrassment and shame.

"Damn." Nathan fell back against the couch as Jessica scurried off his lap.

"Baby, you're sick." A statement that was well-intentioned, but considering the circumstances was woefully inadequate. She cuddled against him. "But no less amazing."

The next thing Jessica knew she'd been lifted from the couch and placed on the ottoman. Before she could recover from this surprise move, Nathan had spread her legs and buried his head in her heat, his mouth finding her pearl with the precision of a heat-seeking missile. The assault was as intoxicating as it was surprising. His tongue slid along the crease of her folds—slowly, thoroughly lapping her nectar. The sensations were unlike anything she'd felt before; her body squirmed to get away lest she die from pleasure. At the same time, her hands held this torturer's head firmly in place.

The orgasm started in her big toe and spiraled straight up to her scalp. Whimpers followed screams as another ripped through her, and then one more. She lay breathless on the ottoman, her body limp and spent and satisfied.

"The way you look now makes me feel amazing," Nathan said, kissing her softly as he stood. "My stomach is acting up again. I think I'll go lie down."

He held the smile until he was behind her, then allowed the worry he felt to cover his face. He slowly climbed the stairs. Never before had his soldier failed to snap to attention at the sign of a romp. *What the hell is going on?*

Jessica held her head in her hands, trying to contain her tears. Her silent cry was anguished. *I can't, Sissy. I just can't . . . do . . . this.* But she had to; it was the only way she could have what she'd always wanted and never experienced—a close familial relationship. She stood, her legs still a little shaky from Nathan's orally induced seismic orgasm. Pacing from the couch to the window to the dining room and back, thoughts continued. *Why is this the only choice? Why does the man my sister wants dead have to be the most amazing one I've ever met? "Don't think for one second that when it came to me going to prison Nathan wasn't fully on his sister's side,"* her sister had said. Jessica knew firsthand that this was true. He'd apologized, but if made to choose sides again between her and Sherri, did Jessica really believe he'd choose her? "No!" Jessica heard Sissy's voice scream in her mind. If it was a matter of her life, he'd definitely choose Sherri. It was a matter of Sissy's life right now.

She angrily wiped away the tears that had escaped despite her resolve not to cry. "Just stop it," she scolded herself through gritted teeth. "Just do what you have to do." *The sooner I finish this, the sooner this pain will go away. I can only hope that someday I'll meet another man who is half as good to me as Nathan.* With that, she walked into the kitchen, and then up to the bedroom.

"Here, babe. I brought some tea to help you sleep."

Nathan sat up. "How'd you know I was still awake?"

"Just figured you might be." She handed him the cup.

"I really appreciate you." He sipped the steamy brew. Love-filled eyes drank in Jessica's beauty . . . and something else. "What's the matter, Jessica?"

"Nothing. Why?"

"I detect sadness behind your smile."

"Oh. I, uh, am just worried about you, babe. I want you to get better."

"Me too." The arsenic worked quickly, and this time she'd added a crushed up pain pill to try and lessen the painful cramps. Nathan was out and snoring before he finished the tea. Jessica took the cup back down to the kitchen, washed it thoroughly, and then reached for her iPad. Hopefully there was something on Netflix that would take her mind off the hell of a drama otherwise known as her life.

The movie she watched hadn't done it. Thoughts of Nate left little room for any other topic to pierce her mind. She went up to check on him. He was no longer snoring, hardly seemed to breathe. She called his name, shook him roughly, and still he slept. *Is he . . . ?* She placed a shaky finger under his nose and almost fainted with relief. She'd felt his breath! Hearing her phone, she rushed downstairs to answer it. The call was from an unknown phone number, one she wouldn't have answered had she not been so discombobulated.

"Hello?"

"Hi, Jessica. This is Sherri Atwater. I hope you don't mind but after his health scare, I requested your number from Nate in case of another emergency."

"Oh, um, of course."

"Are you at his house?"

"Yes."

"Thank goodness. Can you please put him on the phone?"

Jessica took a deep breath before answering. The last thing she needed was a suspicious Sherri hounding her with questions, but she wondered if even an explosion in the middle of the bed would wake Nathan right now. "He's asleep."

"At four in the afternoon?"

"He didn't sleep well last night." When Sherri didn't immediately respond, Jessica laughed and added, "And he got up really early this morning . . . to work from here."

More silence. When Sherri spoke again, the very thing Jessica hoped to not raise—suspicion—laced each word. "That's interesting. Because I spoke with him this morning, and he sounded too sick to work."

Dang it, I wish I'd known they talked! "I know, but since his promotion that job has been everything."

"Tell Nathan I'm getting ready to call and to answer his phone."

"He's asleep, Sherri. I'll tell him to call you when he wakes up. But don't worry about him, okay? I'm taking real good care of your brother."

"I appreciate that, but I am worried about him and so is Mom. He's almost never sick. I won't talk long, but I promised Mom I'd speak to him before calling her back."

"Again, when he wakes up"—*please let him wake up*—"he'll call you."

An hour later, her phone rang again. "Hi, Sherri."

"Jessica, he's still not answering his phone."

"He's still asleep."

"Please wake him up. I am very concerned and need to speak with him."

"And he needs his rest. If you have a message for him, I'll be glad to pass it on. But I'm not going to pass my phone to him and I'm not going to turn on his ringer."

"You turned his ringer off? How are you going to block calls to my brother? I'm sure you're doing this out of your concern for him, but can you understand that I'm worrying, too?"

"But you shouldn't. Other than this flu bug or whatever that must be going around his office . . . he's fine."

"Don't you think it's odd that he's sleeping so much?"

"Not for someone with the flu. And it's his work, too. Like I said, he hasn't been sleeping much, which is why I am *not* going to wake him up."

"Excuse me?"

"Girl, bye."

Jessica hung up quickly, before saying something that she'd later regret. Giving orders and making demands. Who did Sherri think she was talking to? *I told her he was fine. Hell, what else does she need to know?*

Nathan woke up shortly thereafter. Jessica chose not to tell Nathan about his sister's call. Instead, when he finally expressed a desire to eat, she fed him arsenic-laced soup that he washed down with antifreeze-laden orange juice. The sooner this whole sordid deed was done, the sooner she could try and put this horror behind her.

Two hour later, he was puking like a dog.

Thirty minutes after that, the doorbell rang.

Nathan's brow creased as he looked over his shoulder from his kneeling position in front of the toilet.

Jessica hurriedly stood and headed for the stairs. "I'll get rid of whoever it is." Heart pounding, she raced down the stairs. Now was not the time for an unannounced visit from one of Nathan's friends.

At the bottom step she paused to catch her breath, then tiptoed to the front door. A cautious eye glimpsed the view beyond the peephole. *Shit!* Jessica leaned against the door, her hand covering a heart that now beat furiously. No way could she let this visitor in. *Please, just go away.*

As if in answer, the doorbell rang again.

"Who is it?" An ashen-faced Nathan appeared at the top of the stairs, clutching his stomach.

"Don't worry about it, babe. I'll handle it."

Ding. Dong.

"Jessica, why don't you just—" Another heave and a race to the bathroom.

"We don't want what you're selling. Stop ringing the damn bell!"

"Open this door!"

"That sounds like . . . is that my sister?" Nathan's voice was a mixture of sickness and surprise.

"No, babe. Just somebody with magazines, probably a Jehovah's Witness. Go lie down!"

The toilet flushed.

Ding. Dong. Pause. *Ding. Dong.* A fervent knocking. *Dingdongdingdongdingdong.*

Nathan began slowly making his way downstairs.

"Babe, don't! I said I'd handle this!"

"Not as good as they're handling that doorbell."

Jessica rushed to meet him before his foot touched the bottom step. "Let's just ignore them," she suggested, firmly turning him around with a hand on his waist. "Whoever it is will eventually get tired and go away."

They were almost to the top of the stairs when both heard

a key being placed in the lock. Their heads whipped around in time to see the knob turning and the door opening.

"What the hell?" Nathan pushed Jessica behind him and hurried down the stairs.

The door flung open. "Nathan, it's me!"

"Sherri?" They fell into each other's arms for a quick hug. "Sis, I was getting ready to lay out a burglar." Something between a cough and a laugh flew out of his mouth. "What are you doing here?"

"I came because—"

Nathan turned, tripped, and fell.

"Baby!" *Oh, no.* Jessica rushed down the stairs to his side.

CHAPTER 27

"Nathan!" Sherri rushed toward him.

She was fast, but Jessica was faster. Effectively blocking Sherri's approach, she grabbed his shoulders and helped him up. "Come on, babe. Let's get you back upstairs."

"Move out of my way!" Words underscored by a forceful push that sent Jessica tumbling to the spot Nathan had recently occupied. "Brother, are you all right?"

"Ow!"

Nathan angrily jerked his arm from Sherri's grasp. "Sis, what is wrong with you?" He rushed over to where Jessica sat rubbing a barely bruised shoulder. Her ego had taken the brunt of the fall. "Baby, are you okay?" And then again, to his sister, "What in the hell is this about?"

"It's about Jessica refusing to let me talk to you repeatedly, and then hanging up in my face."

The ever-ready tears appeared. Jessica thankfully let them fall. This was war, and she needed all possible ammunition. "You needed your rest! I told her you'd call when you woke up."

"Are you hurt?" Nathan examined her arm.

"I was just trying to take care of you, baby." Her voice was a heart-melting cross between a whine and a coo as she exaggerated a wince.

"I called all afternoon," Sherri tried to calmly explain, even though she was almost shaking with anger. "Mom called, too. I told her this, expressed our concerns, and promised to talk for just a minute."

Jessica stumbled to her feet, then reached for Nathan. "Babe, let's go upstairs."

"No wait, Jessica." Nathan looked at Sherri. "Mom called?"

"Yes, twice. After finding out you weren't at work she called me, very concerned. You know how Mom is. That's when I called and talked with her for the *second* time, trying to reach you."

Nate stepped toward his sister and turned to Jessica. "Why didn't you wake me up?"

Jessica looked at Nathan standing by Sherri's side. "Come upstairs with me and I'll explain." She walked over and took his arm.

Sherri pulled him in her direction. "You'll explain later. I had to get on a plane to do it but I *will* talk to my brother and it's happening right now, understand?"

Jessica reached across Nathan to slap Sherri's arm away from his. "Come on, babe."

Sherri blocked their path. "Girl, you are really trying me. You need to go have several seats before things get ugly." Once again, she started up the stairs with Nathan.

"I'm not going anywhere!" Jessica came up the stairs and squeezed herself on the other side of Nathan, an act that pushed Sherri into the wall.

Reaction trumped thought. Sherri reached around Nathan and yanked Jessica's ponytail so hard girlfriend's neck almost snapped. Jessica tumbled backward, hit the floor and came up in fighter mode. Sherri was just a second short of pulling out a can of South Side Chicago herself. Before she could rush Sherri, Jessica found herself pinned against the wall with an arm across her throat. "I'm not going to tell you again," Sherri and Jessica were nose to nose as she spoke through gritted teeth. " Back. Off. Okay?"

"Get your hands off me!" Jessica squirmed but her slight frame was no match for Sherri's anger.

Nathan stepped between them. "Both of you . . . stop!" The energy to shout these four words caused his head to spin. His chest heaved, and he struggled for breath while looking from one woman to the other with narrowed eyes. "Jessica, Sherri's the big sis used to taking care of me. Let her play that role for a minute, okay?"

"I'm your woman, Nate. *I* should play that role." She crossed her arms in a huff, eyes glistening yet again as she waited for Nathan to choose Sherri's side. Again.

"Then you come up t—"

"Actually, Nathan, I need to speak to you alone."

"So you can make up a lie for why you pushed me down the stairs?"

Nathan placed an arm around Sherri. "Come on, Sister." Sherri tossed Jessica a side-eye and a smile.

Jessica turned to leave. He'd made his choice. He grabbed her hand, stopping her. "Come on, babe. I want you here." Jessica reciprocated with a smirk and eye roll.

The three clumsily trudged upstairs to the master suite. Sherri placed her arm around Nathan's waist. "Come on, Brother. Lean on me."

"I'm sick," Nathan said, with a weak chuckle. "Not an invalid." He gently took her arm from around his waist and went into the bathroom to brush his teeth. He came out and quickly climbed into bed. "Baby, can you please get me a glass of water?"

"Sure, baby." Jessica hurried downstairs.

As soon as her footsteps receded, both Nate and Sherri started talking at once, their voices low and hurried.

"Sherri, what—"

"Nate, your girl's about to—" He nodded for her to continue. "That girl is out of line. I was imagining all kinds of scenarios for what might be going on here. You need to let her know how our family operates."

"I understand your frustration. She meant well."

"Please . . ."

"That's just her way of taking care of me. I was asleep."

"Which is why I'm so concerned. It's not like you to sleep all day, and I can't remember the last time you've been this sick. I think you should go back to the doctor, have him take those tests that he recommended."

"It's just a case of stomach flu, or something like that." Nathan lay against the cushioned headboard, propping a pillow behind him. "I can't believe you hopped on a plane just because I couldn't be reached for a few hours." His gaze was contemplative. "What's really going on? Problems with you and Randall?"

"Randall and I are fine."

"Aaron or Albany?"

"No problems with your niece or nephew either. The only problem I have right now is with Jessica. She's someone I find very hard to like."

"You've always been hard on my girlfriends. I doubt anybody will totally measure up."

This brought a half smile to Sherri's face. "Perhaps." She pulled the cover to his chest, and patted it smooth. "But I'm telling you, Nate. My intuition says there was more to Jessica's blocking my calls than concern for you. For whatever reason, she did not want us to have a conversation. Why not? What is she hiding?"

"I'm not hiding anything." Jessica, who'd climbed the steps quieter than a cat burglar, now calmly walked back into the room. She handed Nathan the glass before crawling into bed beside him. She placed a hand against his slightly warm neck, then took the folded towel she'd wetted with cold water and dabbed his face. "You still have a little fever." She kissed his cheek. "I think the sleep did you good."

Sherri placed her hand on his forehead and neck. "You need to have those tests run, Nate, just to be on the safe side."

"He's getting better, Sherri. What he needs is rest, and lots of it." Jessica dabbed Nathan's chest with the cool, wet towel. "I'm sorry if over the phone I came off harshly. It wasn't intentional. It was because Nate is what's most important to me. Like you, I'm worried about him, and for the very reasons you stated. It's not like him to sleep a lot, or get sick."

"What . . . you were out there eavesdropping?"

"I know you don't like me," she continued, totally ignoring Sherri's accurate quip. "For the record, I'm not too fond of you either. But"—she held up her hand to stop Sherri's comeback—"you're my man's sister. I don't plan on going anywhere. So from here on out, I'm going to try and get along. I apologize if you think I was rude."

Both she and Nathan looked at Sherri.

"What? Oh, here is where I'm supposed to be sorry, too? Here is where I forget how just moments ago you tried to keep me out of my own brother's house?"

"Your head was turned. I didn't recognize you."

"You're a liar. I saw the peephole darken, showing that someone looked out. That someone had to look dead in my face."

Jessica turned to Nathan. "Is she always this jealous of the women who love you?"

Sherri's mouth gaped in astonishment. "Jealous of you? Seriously? Your refusing to let me talk to Nathan is what brought me here, and blatant falsehoods coming out of your mouth is why I called you a liar."

"I don't know why she's doing this, Nathan." The message was delivered near his ear in a whisper, as Jessica ran her fingers up and down his arm.

Nathan looked at Sherri, his loyalties clearly torn. "I wish you'd called before coming all the way down here."

"Are you not listening?" Sherri crossed her arms. "I did."

"Then I wish you'd waited to talk to me before making the trip. I'm a bit under the weather but really, Sis, Jessica is taking care of me."

"I just bet she is. All the same since I'm here, I'd like to spend the night."

"No problem at all. Babe, can you make sure the guest room is ready?"

"Never mind, Jessica. I know my way around Nathan's house." Sherri left the room.

For the rest of the evening, Jessica rarely left Nathan's side. She wisely served him nonpoisonous food and drink, aware that Sherri watched her every move. The next morning, after taking care of him the way he'd cared for her on the ottoman the day before, Jessica felt safe enough to leave sis and bro alone for a quick trip home.

As soon as Sherri heard the front door close, she left the guest room and walked into the master. "Nathan?" She looked around, then heard the shower running. While waiting for him to finish, she idly walked around the room, looking here and there, thinking this and that. After a while, she heard the water turn off. "Nathan, I'm in here," she warned. Sherri knew her brother was known for walking around in the buff.

He came out wearing a pair of sweatpants.

"You're looking better."

"I feel better. Told you Jessica was taking care of me. I love that girl, Sherri. You need to back off."

"Maybe I do. Watching how she took care of you last night made it appear that she loves you, too. That still doesn't explain why she tried to block our communication."

"Have you ever considered that the conclusion you jumped to might be because of your paranoia and dislike for her, rather than her actions?"

"Look, you can think what you want, but I know what happened. With you, she hides the bitch and brings out Mother Teresa."

"Aw, come on now, Sis . . ."

"That being said, I may have let my feelings get in the way of good judgment. Not that I'm ever going to apologize for caring about you, or coming to visit, either. But what happened to us last year has left me suspicious and paranoid."

"I appreciate that you care about me. But you might throw out a 'sorry' for pushing Jessica down the stairs."

"I didn't push her." She turned to see Nathan's teasing, twinkling eyes.

"Ha! Yes, you did. You went straight gangster on my girl."

"She pushed me into the wall. I returned the favor. A bigger sistah gets better results so her ass ended up on the floor. For that I won't apologize because I don't feel sorry."

"I haven't seen you fight since, when, junior high school?"

"You didn't see me fight tonight, though I'll admit that her accusation that I'm jealous of her threatened to bring out my uncultured side." Sherri followed Nathan downstairs. "Since it appears you'll live, and you want your girlfriend to do the same, I'll fly back tonight. But I'd feel better if you ran those tests. At the very least, talk to Randall or maybe his doctor friend, James. I'd hate for us to later find out that what you think is the flu is something more serious."

Nathan reached his back door and climbed the short staircase to his rooftop oasis. "Ah, this fresh air feels good!"

Sherri looked around. "I've always loved it up here. This amazing patio is my favorite thing about this place. Now, stop trying to change the subject. I want you to get checked out."

"I'm going to call my doctor and schedule an appointment for a physical."

"You need more than an ordinary physical, Nate. You need blood work, X-rays."

"All right, Sherri, dang. I'll get checked out. Promise."

Jessica returned. Sherri found her in the kitchen. "You got a minute?"

"Not really."

"Nate's feeling better. He says I have you to thank for that." Clearly annoyed, Jessica ignored her and continued preparing tea. "Listen, Jessica. I know we don't see eye to eye, but in watching you take care of my brother, it's clear that you care about him."

"That's right. I do."

"But never more than his family does. Trust me on that. So when we call and ask to speak to him, it needs to happen. But because of how Nathan feels, I'm willing to give you the benefit of the doubt and believe your actions were out of concern for his welfare. I do feel better knowing someone is here." She turned to leave, then stopped. "Earlier, I didn't mean to push you. It was a reaction to being shoved."

"To keep from being trampled!"

"We obviously see things differently. I'm usually not the violent type, but when it comes to my baby brother I'm his number one protector."

"Seems like being number one anything is a place for his wife."

"Once he's married, perhaps I'll step aside. Nathan . . . has special feelings for you. Because of that, I'm hoping we can get along. We might never be friends, but for the sake of peace, I'll try and be friendlier."

Jessica placed items on a tray "Thank you, Sherri. Me too. Where is he?"

"Up on the patio. A cup of tea sounds good. I'll make myself one and then join you guys."

After a slightly strained yet relatively peaceful afternoon for the three of them, hugs were exchanged before Sherri left to catch her flight. What she did to her sister notwithstanding, Nate's sister could be pleasant to be around. Earlier, during their argument, Nathan had initially taken Sherri's side. But he'd made it clear that he wanted her there, and didn't let Jessica leave. That night, it was harder than ever for her to poison Nathan's drink. So she didn't. After all, there was always tomorrow.

CHAPTER 28

"Glad you're back, man. You feel all right?"

"Morning, Broderick. I'm a lot better." Nathan joined his boss in the sitting area that anchored the large corner office. He reared back and placed his hands behind his head. "It's a beautiful Monday morning and I'm ready to work."

"Glad to hear that. Hope you don't mind putting in some extra hours these first few months."

"Had already planned on it."

"Good, because that'll continue for awhile, including tonight. Dinner meeting with the board."

"No problem."

"My assistant will forward the details and also bring over the remaining files from Cecil's office so that you can pass those clients to the appropriate staff. I know we're putting quite a bit on you, so feel free to hire a temp if you need to until we get through this transition period."

"By the end of the week I'll have a better handle on everything, and can tell you then whether or not that will be necessary."

Broderick looked at his watch. "All right, then. Time for my ten o'clock meeting. I'll see you tonight."

Nathan returned to his office and closed the door behind him. He then placed a long overdue call to someone who shortly after Valentine's Day had left a message. Being sick had made him forget to return the call. He walked to the window and eyed downtown Atlanta as he waited for the call to be answered. "Develia!" He put the call on speaker and returned to the desk to multitask. "It's Nathan Carver."

"Nathan! I'd given up on hearing from you."

"My apologies. I'd meant to call earlier. It's been a very busy year." He gave a brief rundown on the promotion that greatly increased his schedule, and the mystery illness trying to slow him down. "I'm hoping the worst is over," he finished. "But if it continues, I'll definitely have to get checked out."

"My goodness. I can't believe all that's happened in such a short time Here I was thinking you've been ignoring me, when with your hectic schedule I'm amazed you're calling now. And thrilled. I had a fabulous time on New Year's Eve."

"You made all the difference that night. I don't know when I've had so much fun. When I meet good people, I like to stay in touch."

"Your timing is perfect. One of the reasons you'd crossed my mind is because a dear friend who lives in Atlanta is having her first child. I'll be visiting in the next month or so."

"Please let me know the dates you'll be here. I'd love to share some of Atlanta the way you showed me your island."

"It's a deal. I'll be in touch."

The day passed quickly. Nathan barely noticed the time. Most men would feel overwhelmed at the increased workload, but for this organized multitasker it was an adrenaline rush. By six o'clock he'd perused the additional files, reassigned the clients, handled time-sensitive in-box matters, made important phone calls, and had his assistant order new office furniture and business cards. Once the order arrived, he'd move from his adequate space into the roomy office that came with the VP title. After wrapping up a call to Kenneth with plans to visit Vegas in the next couple weeks, he freshened up and headed out to the dinner meeting.

Halfway there, his phone rang. "What's up, Randall? No, let me guess. Sherri."

"You know your overprotective sister."

"Yes, I do. Having you call to check up, treating me like a kid instead of a grown man."

"Well, I was going to holler at you anyway . . ."

"Sure you were."

"Okay, she prodded me a bit. Is quite concerned with all this health stuff lately, and I have to agree that this isn't the norm. I mean, you're Mr. Invincible."

"I was until a little bug bit me. But it's been going around."

"What are your symptoms?" Nathan told him. "I'm no doctor, and it sounds like for the most part those could be flu related. But it probably wouldn't hurt to get a few tests done, just to be on the safe side."

"It's about time for my annual physical anyway. I'll have my assistant schedule one for next week. Not sure about getting a lot of tests run, though, especially if they're time consuming. I just got this promotion; don't want to cause speculation and second-guessing by spending a lot of time away from the office."

"I understand. Tell you what—let me give you James's number. If your physical comes back clean but you keep feeling bad, run your symptoms past him. He's a top-notch MD and will likely recognize what I'd miss. Plus, I've got pull and might even get him to do a house call."

The two talked until Nathan reached the restaurant. There, along with a succulent filet mignon and vintage cabernet, he enjoyed laying out his plans for the company's continued success. By the time he headed home after a nonstop, productive twelve-plus-hour day, Nathan was counting his blessings. He had more than most: great family, wonderful woman, high-paying, highly satisfying career, and every desired creature comfort. Life was good and getting ready to get better. This weekend he planned to finish what started on Valentine's Day. Finally, Jessica would get the ring.

★ ★ ★

"I got your message. Needless to say, with her sniffing around the situation, we've got to wrap it up as quickly as possible."

"I told you it's handled. She believes I care about him." Jessica sat at her dining room table, idly staring out the window as her sister's heated anger popped and sizzled through the speaker-phone. Ever since sharing the past weekend's events, she'd been on a full-blown tirade.

"Don't fool yourself. I've dealt with that bitch. She cannot be trusted! So what that she apologized and played nicey-nice in front of her brother? I'm telling you from personal experi-ence, she's not done being nosy, and we can't risk her finding out. Double, no, triple the dosages. It's time to bring this party to an end."

"Just days after she saw him feeling better? That will arouse suspicion."

"People relapse all the time, think they're well and then get worse. You said he's been promoted and is working long hours. People drop dead all the time. He'll just be one of those ques-tionable statistics."

"I don't know, Sissy . . ."

"Is this about Sherri, or is this about you? Jessie, are you trying to back out?"

"No. I'm trying to make sure I don't end up in a gated community like yours. All right?"

"That's fair. Sorry. Growing up like I did makes it hard to trust."

"Are you forgetting that I grew up the same way?"

"I'm glad you're back in my life, Jessie. For the first time in a long time I know somebody truly has my back."

That night Jessica shed tears as she buried the fantasy of a perfect life with Nathan. The next day she made another trip to the public library with fake ID and credit card in hand. Since the doses were going to be increased, she needed more vitamins.

CHAPTER 29

He worked most of the day, but by Saturday evening Nathan felt good enough with where things stood at the office to keep the eight o'clock reservations he had for Quinones At Bacchanalia. Bobbing his head to an Anthony Hamilton tune, he tapped his steering wheel and called Jessica.

"Hello, baby."

"Hey, Nate."

"What's the matter? Are you getting sick?"

"No, just in a mood, I guess."

"No worries. What I have planned tonight will snap you right out of it."

"I don't really feel like going out. Can we just order in and watch a movie or something?"

"That sounds good for tomorrow, but we can't change tonight. The reservations have been made and our table is waiting. I'm headed home to shower and change. Think you can still be ready by seven thirty?"

"I guess."

"Dressing to impress?"

"Uh-huh."

"Good. I'll see you soon."

At the thought of what he'd planned to make his sweet-heart feel better, Nathan's smile widened. Yes, indeed. Life was good and getting ready to get a whole lot better.

She may not have felt like going anywhere but when Jessica opened her door a short time later, she looked ready to walk the red carpet. Clad simply yet stunningly in a white dress, crystal booties, and matching jewelry, she looked like a fairy princess, a shimmering goddess ready to cast her spell. Her hair was pulled tight and high, emphasizing high cheekbones, slanted, kohl-tinged eyes, and a ruby-red mouth. She eyed him with a mixture of cautious anticipation and veiled vulnerability. It broke and warmed his heart at the same time. A part of him wanted to heal all her past hurts and protect her from future ones. The other wanted to reward the anticipation he saw by making all of her dreams come true. He hoped his actions tonight would help her realize at least one of them.

After several seconds, he spoke. "Wow. I have no words."

"I look okay?"

"Are you serious? I've never seen you look better—or anyone else, for that matter."

"Would you like to come in for a drink?"

"No, babe. We have to go. Maybe later."

"Okay."

She grabbed her clutch, and thirty minutes later they arrived at one of Atlanta's premier restaurants. The prix fixe, multi-course culinary experience, offering an upscale take on traditional favorites, changed nightly and was often booked for weeks in advance. Without the help of a couple of Ben Franklins and some of his friends, Nathan wouldn't have gotten a table.

They were seated. Nathan sat back, enjoying Jessica's maiden voyage into this type of atmosphere. Her eyes sparkled with appreciation and excitement. She blessed him with a smile.

"You like?"

"Are you kidding me? This place is beautiful. Look at those chandeliers."

"They pale in comparison to you." Her head dipped shyly. His eyes lowered, too. "Seriously, baby. You look amazing, good enough to eat. And I plan to save room for dessert . . . believe that. Excuse me for one minute. I need to . . . speak with someone."

She waited for a few seconds, made sure he was gone, and then allowed the fake smile to slide off her face. She could see Nathan's joy in trying to make her happy. Little did he know, every act of kindness was excruciating, every loving gesture felt like torture inside. The admiring look on his face at her doorstep is why the poison remained in her purse right now. She'd planned to, but couldn't do it. Couldn't mix arsenic with this fancy dinner, didn't want a repeat of what happened on Valentine's Day.

"Sorry about that, babe." Nathan returned to his seat and replaced his napkin. "Now, where were we?"

"Thinking about what an amazing man you are, and wondering how I got so lucky."

"It's crazy. I was wondering that exact same thing. How about champagne tonight?"

"Sounds perfect."

Nathan got the waiter's attention and ordered a bottle of their finest bubbly. Light talk and laughter ensued as they awaited the first course, and continued through an exquisite meal that included hamachi with fennel, pork belly with clam chowder, sweetbreads with sweet potato, and smoked country ham.

"I don't think I can eat anything else," Jessica exclaimed, after polishing off her last bite of ham.

"And you thought the menu items sounded nasty."

"Whoever heard of hamachi whatever, and kimmee—"

"Kimchee—"

"With Asian pears."

"But it was good though, huh?"

"This food was delicious."

"Which is why you must have dessert, if only a little taste."

She peered through lowered lashes. "I thought dessert was later on."

"That will be our second helping."

A waiter walked through the attraction and desire crackling around the table. "Sir, your special dessert tray, by request."

"Thank you."

The waiter offered a slight bow and left.

Nathan nodded at the tray. "Go ahead. Choose which dessert you want."

"What are they?"

"Reach over and find out."

She hesitated, and then lifted the first silver dome and uncovered a beautifully plated serving of fruit. "Not too decadent looking."

"Healthy though."

"You want it?"

"No. I want something rich and sinful."

Chuckling, she raised the second dome. "What are these?" Leaning forward, she read the card. "Fried dough?"

"Looks like beignets."

"Never had them."

"You were born in New Orleans, right?"

"Yes, but not raised there." She tasted one. Her eyes closed as she moaned in pleasure.

Nathan enjoyed a helping as well before she uncovered the third treat, chocolate pecans and cream, which they also devoured.

"One more," he said.

"Just one bite of this one, though. I'm stuffed." She raised the lid. And froze.

"Babe . . ."

"Nathan!" *Oh. No.* Her voice was soft, a mere whisper as she stared at the ring. "I . . . babe . . . I don't know what to say."

"It's not your turn, yet." He picked up the diamond ring

and kneeled before her. Her hands flew to her mouth. Heads turned, faces glowed, as what was occurring became clear.

"Jessica, I know we haven't known each other long. But it's been enough time for me to figure out that you're the woman I want for a lifetime. You've taken the time to care for me and now I want to take care of you"—he reached up, gently swiped her wet cheek—"wipe away your tears, and be the reason you smile every single day. Will you marry me?"

She was too overcome with emotion to speak.

"Babe, it's your turn."

"Yes," she finally choked out on a sob. Her arms wrapped around his neck and when he stood he brought her with him. Her feet left the floor. They twirled as the patrons applauded.

"You've just made me the happiest man alive," he whispered against her ear.

Jessica cried harder, overcome with guilt and shame. She'd just said yes to a marriage that would never happen, and to a man with numbered days. Sissy was right. It was time to end this. Too much more of Nathan loving her the way he did and she'd lose two things: her nerve to kill him and her sister.

CHAPTER 30

It started from the time Jessica closed the door. Nathan: determined, focused, ready. Wrapping her in his arms, letting his actions convey what words could not, scorching her mouth with his long, stiff tongue, squeezing her plump asset as he ground his growing manhood against her silk dress. He broke the kiss long enough to unzip and pull the piece from her shoulders and down her lean frame. Taking in her black lace bra and thong, showcased against her creamy tan flesh, made him harder. He moved to the couch, taking her with him, covering her with his body as he plundered her mouth again.

"Ooh, baby. I've been wanting this all night." He quickly stripped off his clothes, then dropped to his knees to kiss another set of lips.

Jessica's scream came out hoarse and high-pitched. Something about the way he licked her through the lacy thong, causing friction on top of friction, sent her someplace else. She tried to move away from the delicious yet mind-blowing assault. Not a chance. Nathan ripped off the thong and slid along and then inside her folds. Her pearl was treated special—nipped and licked and sucked and pulled—until Jessica stopped fighting and gave in to the thrill. A strong finger found her opening, and then there were two. Still he lapped and tongued and kissed and devoured until her legs began to shake and an orgasm spiraled from the core of her being to the tips of her toes. While still in this climax's clutches, Nate plunged inside her, full and complete.

"Nate! A condom—"

"Sorry, baby," Nate moaned, a deep thrust accompanying every other word. "I couldn't. Wait. Next time. Damn. This is good. So good."

After tattooing her insides, he pulled out and placed his tip at her mouth. She readily took him in, outlining the burgeoning mushroom tip with her tongue, licking his length, tickling the vein. She opened wider, took him deeper, tried to best what he'd given. Hard to do with a man this thick and long, but she gave it a good old college try. Must have been on to something because after pulling on his dick like a hookah pipe, Nathan abruptly stopped her.

"Baby, you're going to make me come. And we've got a long ways to go before that happens."

The loving continued every place, every way. When he knocked at her back door, she let him in, or tried at least. That's something she'd sworn would never happen again, something her ex once did by force. Nathan was gentle and patient, running a finger between her nether lips as he sucked on her ear, then kissing and tonguing her starfish until tense muscles relaxed. And later, kissing every inch of her, as if she were a fragile flower and her skin was candy glass. By the time they fell into exhausted slumber, there had been no marriage ceremony. But the consummation of their red-hot love had definitely occurred.

"You're going to do what?"

Sunday morning, early afternoon actually, and the two love birds were just beginning to stir.

Jessica turned on her side to face Nathan. "I know I didn't hear you right."

"I said I was cooking breakfast."

"You can't cook!"

"You probably don't have anything down there to cook." Jessica hid her face in the pillow.

"Uh-huh, I'm right, takeout queen. You probably don't have one raw egg or a cup of flour."

"No, but I'll put my collection of takeout menus against the best of them."

"Ha!" Nathan rolled out of bed, shameless in his naked glory. He walked into the bathroom and after the necessary ablutions returned to the room. "Didn't I leave some shorts over here, or something to wear?"

"Yes. Look in that bottom drawer." She pointed.

Nathan retrieved a pair of worn khakis and a Ravens t-shirt, slipped them on, and headed out.

"Where are you going?"

"Downstairs, to raid your pantry." Jessica scrambled out of bed. Her reaction startled him. "Where are you going?"

"To help you, of course."

"No, you're not. You're going to take a long, hot shower." His mood changed as he sauntered toward her and pulled her into an embrace. "I know I worked that body last night. And I'm still not done. So go on in there, grab that funny-looking sponge and that froufrou soap you like——"

"It's not froufrou. That gel is Vera Wang."

"Then go grab Vera and get rejuvenated."

He began to pull away, but Jessica stopped him. "I'd rather you join me."

"Later. But right now, I want to do this for you. Go on, now. Let me pamper my fiancée."

She gazed at the ring. "So incredibly beautiful. I still can't believe I'm engaged."

"Well, you are. So once you're refreshed and I've prepared this amazing spread, we can head out, maybe find a park to soak of some of this beautiful sunshine and then discuss dates over brunch."

He kissed her forehead and headed out of the room. Jessica grabbed a T-shirt and was right behind him.

"What's wrong with you?"

"I . . . want us to cook together!"

"And I want to cook for you. Now be a good little wife and obey your master. Get in the shower!" His chauvinistic words left her sputtering. He cracked up. "I knew that would get you," he said, still laughing. "But seriously. Go on, now. I've got this."

He started out again. "And don't follow me."

"Okay."

"Promise?"

"Promise."

He continued down the stairs, shaking his head at his lovable lady. He'd never been this happy or felt so complete. Stopping by her iPod dock, he turned on the music. The base of the dock was loose, but the beats played. He headed toward the kitchen. A buzz sounded. *What's that?* He looked around but when it stopped he shrugged and walked to the set of cabinets.

"Man, this is pitiful," he murmured, opening up one door and then the other. Aside from the ones that held dishes, the shelves were almost bare. The refrigerator wasn't much better. He continued opening drawers and cabinet doors, familiarizing himself with where things were: silverware, an unopened box of cookware and another of ceramic bowls, magazines, a catch-all drawer, her takeout collection. His chances of finding edible product was bleak, but still he opened the cabinets beneath the sink: dishwashing liquid, scrubbing foam, and several gallons of antifreeze.

Nathan walked over to where a pair of casual loafers he'd

left on a previous visit were still sitting by the door. Car keys were on a nearby table. He grabbed them. "Babe!"

A pause and then, "Yes?"

"I'll be right back."

Once she heard the door close, Jessica raced downstairs and into the kitchen. She looked around, praying that nothing suspicious had been lying about. At first, she'd been very cognizant about immediately storing the poisons in their proper places, but during her shower an image of liquid arsenic sitting on the counter had almost caused a heart attack. Now, as she looked around, she realized the image had been created from paranoia, not fact.

Then she heard a buzz. *Damn!* She walked into the living room and pulled the vibrating burner phone from its hiding place. "Sissy, I can't talk long. Nathan will be back soon."

Minutes later, Nathan returned with a bag of groceries. He banned Jessica from the kitchen and whipped up a turkey sausage and spinach omelet served with bagels and cream cheese.

He and Jessica sat at her bar counter, music still going and TV on mute. She took several bites without stopping. "This is good."

"Told you I could cook."

"They say food always tastes good when you're starving."

"Whatever."

"Hey, you forgot drinks." She slid off the stool. "You want an orange juice spritzer?"

"What's that?"

"OJ and club soda."

He nodded. "That sounds good."

She pulled the juice container from the fridge and moved aside the Simply Cranberry and bottles of Perrier to reach the hidden and innocent-looking six-pack of club soda. One of the cans had been opened, emptied, and refilled with antifreeze. Setting the six-pack on the counter, she secured it with her right hand while lifting her left hand to gently remove the can of poison from the plastic ring that held the cans together. A ray of afternoon sun caught the diamonds on her engagement ring and caused them to sparkle. A wave of guilt assailed her. She quickly placed the soda back in the fridge, then turned to see Nathan watching her every move.

She jumped.

"Wow, you jumped like a thief caught stealing."

"You keep sneaking up on me. I didn't expect to turn around and find you leering."

"Can't a brother leer if he wants to? Your ass shouldn't be so fine."

She poured two glasses of orange juice and gave one to Nathan.

He took a sip. "This is a spritzer?"

"No, um, I forgot that the drink also calls for a splash of grenadine, which I don't have. Sorry."

"This is fine."

They walked back to the counter and sat down. Nathan immediately dug into his food. Jessica, lost in thought, pushed her food around the plate.

"Having second thoughts already?"

"Of course not." She picked up her fork and took a small bite. "I'm just a little sleepy."

"Oh, well, I'm not going to apologize for that." He gobbled down a few more bites. "By the way, it's obvious you don't use your kitchen. Might as well take out the appliances and turn it into a game room."

"You know I don't cook."

"Yes, but you should keep something on hand in case of an emergency." Nathan drank almost half the juice before placing the glass on the table. "At least a few cans of soup, or beans, a box of crackers, some PB and J. If the city got shut down and restaurants couldn't deliver, you'd starve. Your car would run okay, though."

"Huh?"

"You've got enough antifreeze in there for the next ten winters."

Silence.

"You having car problems?"

A huge bite bought time to create an answer. "No. That's been there a long time."

"Why so much?"

"Does it matter?" Never before had Jessica found lying to be so hard on her nerves.

"It does now that you're acting so defensive about it."

"A guy I dated put them there, okay? He had an old car and always used it. I'd actually forgotten about them . . . the same way I've tried to forget him."

He sat back with a sigh. "I'm sorry, baby. Didn't mean to stir up unhappy memories, especially this weekend."

She dismissed his guilt with a wave of her fork-holding fingers. "Easy to do with the life I've had. Is there any more left of that omelet?"

"The one that's only good because you're hungry?"

"It was pretty tasty."

"Yes," he said, sliding off of the stool to replenish her plate, and in the process stealing a kiss. "Just like you."

The rest of the day passed leisurely. Instead of going out they ended up making out and both the park and brunch were forgotten. Jessica fell asleep Nathan alternated from watching sports to surfing the Web on Jessica's iPad. When he decided to listen to music and the iPod dock wobbled again, he decided to fix it.

"I don't know why I'm in this empty kitchen looking for a screwdriver," he mumbled as he rummaged through a catch-all drawer. *Why do I think I'll find tools where there's not even food?* He learned more about his wife-to-be with what he did find: receipts, loose change, pens, coupons and such, all thrown together with no rhyme or reason. He casually scanned a couple of the receipts before feeling like a snoop and placing them back in the unkempt drawer. Such a mess would drive fastidious Nathan crazy. Clearly, when living together, they'd each have their own closet.

He found some interesting things, but not the screwdriver. Jessica woke up and they finally went out, ending the weekend with a spoken-word event. He went home. Given the jam-packed and significant weekend, he should have been exhausted. But sleep was elusive. An observation he'd made earlier had been bugging him all evening and no matter how he analyzed, rationalized, and dismissed it in his mind, the uncomfortable feeling would not go away.

Sleep finally came, but when the alarm clock went off, Nathan did not feel rested.

CHAPTER 31

Come Monday, both Jessica and Nathan would get a dose of reality thrown on their magical weekend. For Nathan, it rang right around noon at the office, just after he'd finished a round of phone calls and the initial research on an unexpected project.

"Morning, Sherri."

"Hey there, VP. You got a minute?"

"Absolutely, I was going to call you anyway. What's up?"

"I saw Mom this weekend."

"You went to Raleigh?"

"Yes, me and the kids."

"How's she doing?"

"Unbelievable, considering the scare she gave all of us last year. The medication created through Randall's research is really something. It's almost like she never was sick."

"I still shudder to think of what might have happened had she not started using it when she did."

"I refuse to think about it, can't imagine life without—"

"Me neither."

Clearly, Nathan could not handle the thought of his mother dying, but that's exactly what had almost happened last year.

She went from being healthy to having intense headaches, blurred vision, and memory loss. The doctors suspected a brain tumor. Sherri's husband Randall thought it might be an infection. Tests were run, biopsies were taken, and eventually a small tumor was found and removed. But, indeed, there remained an infection caused by some mysterious microorganism resistant to standard treatment. That's where Randall's company played a major role. PSI, Progressive Scientific Innovations, had been developing and perfecting a plant-based serum for brain-related diseases. Because it hadn't been approved by the Federal Drug Administration, the drug couldn't be administered by the hospital treating her. So Randall enlisted his best friend, a doctor who treated her privately. Everyone, including the doctors who were prohibited from using it, believed it was this drug that saved Elaine Carver's life.

"Have they approved that treatment yet in America?"

"No, but Canada has used it in several cases with good results. Randall hopes red tape doesn't hold up the product indefinitely because there are people who need it."

"Mom was surprised she didn't hear from you this weekend. She said you've been calling more regularly. We both appreciate that."

"Yes, well, I have this irksome sister who keeps nagging me about acting like a concerned son, as if I wasn't one."

"I'm sure Mom thinks you're the best son she's got."

"I'm the only son she's got," he deadpanned.

"A minor detail."

"Ha!"

"Being promoted was awesome, but I'm sure it's stressful."

"True, and with what happened this weekend, life will only get busier."

"What happened?"

"Hold on." Nathan shut his office door. "I got engaged."

"You did not."

"I finally popped the question, Sis. I asked Jessica to marry me." Stunned silence, as he'd expected. " 'Congratulations, Bro. I'm happy for you. Great news' . . . or anything to that effect would be appropriate."

"Of course, I'm happy if you're happy. I'm just . . ."

"Shocked."

"That word isn't nearly strong enough."

"Appalled?"

"She wouldn't be my first choice, Nate, but I don't think she's a monster."

"Whew. Good. Then there's hope for one big happy family after all."

The sarcastically delivered statement defused the tension. They laughed. Nathan relaxed.

"Does Mom know?"

"I'm calling her next."

"When's the wedding?"

"We haven't discussed that yet."

"Don't rush into this, Nathan. It's been a whirlwind from the day you met her. Now that you've put a ring on it, slow down and take the time to really get to know her. Divorce is expensive, and forever is a long time."

"You've been trying to tell me what to do since I can re-member."

"That's because I'm your big sis."

"As much as you annoy me, I usually listen."

"I hope you will this time."

"This is going to surprise you, but what you've suggested, taking my time, is exactly what I plan to do."

"Wow, what's the occasion?"

Jessica looked up as Vincent leaned against the reception desk. "Good morning."

"Good morning, gorgeous. Did I miss the announcement for a photo shoot?"

"Do you see a camera or photographer anywhere?"

"You're beautiful enough to be a model, even without makeup. So what is it? Lunch date?" He glanced around, lowered his voice, then looked at her crazy. "Job interview?"

"You nut."

"At least I made you smile."

"You always make me smile."

"How was your weekend?"

The slightest hesitation and then, "Fine. How was yours?"

"Pretty cool, actually. A buddy of mine set me up with a date, his wife's best friend. The four of us went to dinner and then to a play at the Fox Theatre. It was nice."

"Nice enough for her to get a second date?"

"Most definitely." The elevator dinged. He straightened from his laid-back posture and reached for one of several *Wall Street Journals* the firm provided. "Enjoy your day, beautiful."

Jessica watched him stroll away, immediately aware of two things. One, the delight with which Vincent had described his date had made her jealous, which considering the past weekend's event was absolutely ludicrous, and two, this jealousy was only slightly less crazy than accepting Nathan's marriage proposal.

But I did accept it. She replayed the litany of thoughts that had flowed nonstop since a dazzling diamond and heartfelt proposal blindsided her Friday night, answering phones by rote as her mind relived the dinner, engagement, mind-blowing sex, Nathan's breakfast, shared showers, and spoken-word event. Her heart fell when recalling the voice mail that had burst the bubble of the weekend's feigned happiness. The likely fallout once that call was returned is why the two-and-a-half-carat radiant diamond from Nathan sat in its case instead of on her finger, and why dark circles beneath tired eyes were hidden with rarely worn foundation.

Minutes after she got home from work, reality called.

"You were supposed to call me back."

"I was going to in a little bit. It was a very busy weekend."

"How sick is he?"

"He's not."

"You doubled the dose and he didn't get sick?"

"No."

"That's impossible. Are you sure you—"

"I didn't do it, okay?"

"Because . . ."

Jessica took a breath deep enough to push out the words that might be some of the last ones shared with her blood kin. "Because I got engaged. He proposed, Sissy."

"That's excellent, perfect! I get it now. It was smart of you to hold off after something like that, play the excited fiancée. So this week when we double the doses, he'll start puking his life out and you'll smell like a rose."

"I don't think so."

"Of course you will. You already told me that the witch was warming up to you. Now that you've snagged her brother, she'll consider you fam."

"It's not that I don't think this will work. It's that I don't think it's going to happen. I can't do this, Sissy. I thought I could, up until this very moment I knew I would. But not now, not after agreeing to become his wife! I love you more than anyone and will do anything to help you, anything but this."

"Right now, this is the only help I need."

"Why is this the only way to help you? Nathan's got money. I can ask for some and get you a good attorney."

"I've got a good attorney, an excellent attorney. What I don't have is time to keep arguing with someone who's obviously only looking out for herself."

"That's not true."

"It isn't? You're getting ready to marry the brother of the woman who put me behind bars, to sleep with my enemy and leave me to rot. Tell me, dear sister, where are my best interests in that scenario?"

"It was his sister who wronged you. She should pay, not Nate."

"Losing the brother she loves so much will be the ultimate payback."

"How do you know that?"

"Because I know how it feels right now, at the thought of losing you."

That statement gave Jessica pause. "That won't happen. I'll never again let another man come between us or keep us from talking."

"You won't have to. If you go back on your promise, I'm the one who'll end contact. There's no way I could let someone who betrayed me remain in my life."

"Sissy, can't we just—"

"No. We can't. You need to grow a backbone and decide once and for all what you're going to do. If it's to keep your word and help me, then call me back. If it's to turn against me, then we're done. Forever. Good-bye, Jessie."

Jessica sat, stunned, processing the words of her sister. How could one feel both the highest exhilaration and the lowest disappointment in the same forty-eight hours? To marry Nathan would mean to lose her sister. Help her sister and she'd lose Nathan. Blood was thicker than water. But was love thicker than blood? And did Jessica want to risk finding out?

CHAPTER 32

Everyone else had left, but Nathan was still at the office. He twirled a pen, deep in thought as he looked at the view from his corner office on the seventeenth floor. What Broderick's East Coast contact heard was true. Because of country club connections and old money clout, Nathan was in danger of losing the Morris Environmental project—a lucrative potential contract that had helped get him promoted—to an Ivy League grad several years his junior. If that happened, then not only would the company lose big money but a year's worth of research, networking and relationship-building would have all been for naught. Crazy thoughts that had troubled last night's sleep continued to plague him and today's conversation and research only deepened his concern. Instead of running from problems, Nathan usually raced toward them. The quicker he reacted the faster they got resolved. He reached for the phone and scheduled an appointment with his contact at Morris. After reconfirming the time and date, he made another call.

"Dr. Sullivan speaking."

"Dr. Sullivan, this is Nate, Randall's brother-in-law."

"Nate! Call me James, man. Randall told me you might be calling."

"I'll do just about anything to shut my sister up. She's the one who keeps hounding me to get a checkup, even though I told her that lately I've felt fine."

"I'll be glad to work with you, Nate, but I'm curious as to why you don't just go to your regular physician?"

"The main reason is I don't have time." He told James about his promotion and his hectic schedule. "I remember your treating Mom privately and since I have a business trip to New York coming up I was hoping you could do that for me. I could tell Sherri the results and shut her mouth . . . about my health, at least."

James laughed. "You have a lovely sister, Nathan. Now your brother-in-law on the other hand . . ."

"Straight hoodlum. I'd give him the shirt off my back."

"He's a good man. Now, let's talk about this appointment . . ."

Jessica frantically pushed the elevator button, hoping to escape without having to deal with Vincent. After catching Nathan still at work and finding out he couldn't come over tonight, and tomorrow was leaving on a last-minute trip, she'd stayed late to help with a large data entry and indexing project, just for something to do. Now she wished she'd left early. Being around Vincent's natural, happy-go-lucky nature seemed to illuminate the sadness of finding out she wouldn't see Nathan tonight and knowing she wouldn't hear from her sis.

"I wasn't sure you heard me, beautiful. Thanks for holding the door."

"No problem." She watched the descending numbers, her mood sinking along with them. She thought to get off and take the stairs. As she reached toward the elevator buttons, Vincent caught her arm.

"Scared to be alone with me?"

She turned to give him a smart answer and encountered eyes filled with affection and concern. To her surprise, instead of curse words a sob burst from her throat.

Vincent sprang into action, wrapping her tightly in his arms. "Hey, it's okay," he whispered as if to a child, wiping her tears and rocking softly. "I'm right here."

The breakdown ended as quickly as it had begun. Jessica pushed away from him, embarrassed and angry at herself. "Thanks, but it's nothing. I'm just . . ." She couldn't continue, couldn't think of a word or a lie or anything to say that would stop the tears that seemed intent on flowing.

They reached the parking lot. Jessica immediately recognized Vincent's BMW in its usual reserved spot. He bypassed it and continued walking with her.

"I'm not going to leave you like this. You've been on edge for weeks."

"I'll be all right."

"Maybe, but I won't." She reached her car. He stepped forward and placed his hand on the door. "I know something's bothering you. Even though you look like a movie star, I can see the pain beneath the makeup." She continued to stand there, not meeting his eyes. "A burden is lighter when shared. Do you want to meet for a drink and talk about it?"

"I just want to go home."

"That's fine. Text me your address and I'll meet you there." He began walking, then stopped and turned. "And if you don't, I will find you. Trust me on that."

Fifteen minutes later, Vincent and Jessica sat in her living room with glasses of wine.

"Thanks for bugging me until I agreed to let you come over. I need to talk to someone, but there's no one I can trust."

"You can trust me."

She looked at him, her bright doe-eyes shining with the hope this could be true. "I want to believe that. It's the only reason you're here. If you ever betray me . . ." Her words faltered as she remembered similar words being said by Sissy last night.

"My word is my bond," Vincent said. "Whatever you share will stay between us."

She took a breath and a drink, staring at but not seeing the muted TV turned to VH1. "On Friday . . . I got engaged."

"You have my sincere condolences."

Such an unexpected answer delivered in such an overtly somber tone made Jessica burst out laughing. "You're stupid."

"I'd do anything to see you smile. And I was only partly joking. Any man would be lucky to marry you, but I was hoping that man might be me."

"You just met somebody who you said you wanted to date."

"What I said is that I'd go out on a second date with her, and that's only because you aren't available. Damn, engaged? You're really off the market now. If you're happy, I guess congratulations are in order." He eyed her silent countenance. "But it doesn't look like you're happy."

"It's complicated."

"Coming from one newly engaged, that doesn't sound too promising."

"My . . . I have some . . . family members who don't want me to marry him."

"Why not?"

"They have their reasons."

"Maybe, but at the end of the day they aren't going to be married to Nathan. You are. So you need to go with how you feel."

"Even if she's . . . if they're threatening to cut me out of their lives?"

"That's a strong ultimatum. They must have a damn good reason, or at least think they do, to take a position that hard."

"I understand their position. They don't understand mine!"

"Then you have to stick with the decision that will make you happy."

"That's just it. No decision I make will be the right one. There's more to it, stuff that I can't talk about."

"Then let's not talk. Come here. Let me just hold you in my arms until you feel better."

"That sounds good, Vincent." He reached for her. She stood abruptly. "In the vulnerable state I'm in right now, it sounds too good. Thanks for listening and for coming over but . . ."

"Now that I've made you feel better, you're going to kick me out."

"I'm sorry."

"Don't be. I've told you before that I'm here for you. I mean that." He walked to the door. "I also meant what I said about keeping a confidence. I'll handle what we discussed the same as I would attorney-client privilege."

She followed him to the door. "I appreciate that."

He turned. They hugged. Jessica placed her arms around him, resting her head on his shoulder as he rubbed her back. Lower. Slower. Pulling away before his desire physically made itself known.

"Nathan's a lucky man. I hope he knows it."

Jessica waved as Vincent neared the hallway stairs, thinking that if he knew the whole story he'd realize that he, not Nathan, was the lucky one.

CHAPTER 33

Nathan multitasked, determined to keep the engagement he'd committed to this Friday night. It had been a rough week, but his trip to New York had been productive and for once he had no work on his weekend agenda.

"No, I didn't get to Broadway, or any other entertainment venue," he said, talking via speakerphone while he shaved. "It was a one-and-a-half-day trip and all business. I'm glad I didn't miss you, though. How long will you be in town?"

"A week or so, I'm thinking. Now that you've mentioned being in one of my favorite cities, I might take a weekend to see friends in New York."

"Then how does a weeknight work for meeting up? If nothing else, we can have a quick drink or light meal. Plus you can meet . . ." He stopped in mid-shave, surprised to hear his front door open and close. He looked at the clock, picked up his cell phone from off the counter, and walked to the top of the stairs just as Jessica stepped inside. "Develia, let me call you back."

"All right, darling. Don't forget. I can't wait to see you."

"Me too." He ended the call.

Jessica looked up. "Who was that?"

"Come here, babe!" He opened his arms to welcome her. "You're here early but no worries. I'm almost done."

"The errand I ran didn't take as long as I thought . . . or as long as *you* thought," she muttered, with no move toward him.

Nathan dropped his arms, shook his head, and returned to the bathroom.

Instead of defusing the situation, his dismissive gesture pissed Jessica off. Gone all week, barely called her, and the first thing she hears is him on the phone with a random? She stomped up the stairs, rushed into the en suite bathroom and shut off the water he was using to shave. "Why don't you want to answer my question? Who was that chick on the phone?"

Nathan calmly turned the water back on and placed a towel under the steaming hot stream. "I have no problem answering your question." He wrung out the water and pressed the hot towel against his face. "What I don't want to do is argue with the woman I've been missing all week, especially after fourteen-hour days, tense business meetings, and nights spent alone. What I'd like is a hug and a welcome home." Jessica continued to stand there, waiting. "No?" He shrugged. "Okay."

He reached for aftershave and splashed it on his face, followed by a special cream. Rubbing a strong hand across a smooth jawbone and satisfied with the result, he put away his shaving equipment and left the bathroom. Jessica wasn't far behind.

"The woman I was talking to is from the Bahamas. Her name is Dev." He walked into his large, custom-made closet and began to dress.

"How'd you meet her?" Her body was as stiff as the closet door she stood next to.

"At a club I went to on New Year's Eve."

"During our vacation?" She shifted her body weight and crossed her arms.

"By then our vacation had turned into my vacation."

"Didn't take you long to get over our argument, I see."

"I wasn't over what happened. But I was in the Caribbean and it was New Year's Eve."

"I brought the New Year in alone."

"That was your choice."

"No, it was yours. I asked you to leave with me."

A silent Nathan finished buttoning his shirt and walked to the tie rack.

"You must have fucked her since it's something you felt the need to hide."

"The call was on speaker and that didn't change when I saw you. Does it look like I'm hiding?" He turned his attention to tying his tie without waiting for an answer.

"Had I not walked in on your conversation would I have ever known about her?"

"As a matter of fact, yes. I would have introduced her when I took you with me to meet her for dinner and drinks. And since I'm sure you'll assume the worst, she's not in town just to see me. She has business in the area."

She looked pointedly at his groin area. "Is that what she calls it?"

"What the hell is wrong with you? Did something happen while I was gone that I need to know about? Because I don't need this type of drama tonight."

Jessica calmed her voice. "Since I haven't heard from you since Wednesday, it didn't feel good to come in and hear you talking to another woman. That's all."

"I didn't call you because I knew I'd see you in an hour. I didn't call her either." He turned and looked at her a long moment, his expression unreadable. "Let's go. We'll be late for dinner."

On the way to the restaurant, not one word was said. But their thoughts could have filled a library.

The evening did not go well. Steve was his usual affable self and Allison was warm and friendly despite the fact that there'd been no romantic spark between Nathan and Olivia, the cousin she'd tried to set up. No matter. It would have taken the heat of a five-alarm fire to thaw the chill between Nathan and Jessica, especially when a still angry Jessica spoke only when asked a direct question and even then she answered with as few words as possible. Nathan and Steve kept up a lively banter, but when Allison asked Nathan and Jessica to join them at a jazz club, Nathan declined.

He'd hidden his chagrin well while in front of company, but once in the car, Nathan exploded. "I can't believe the way you acted tonight, even after I told you about my week and made it clear that I wanted a peaceful evening. If you didn't want to come here and meet my friends, you should have let me know."

"I did meet them."

"Yes, you did, unfortunately, and acted uncivilized to a very good friend of mine and his new lady. Being rude and antisocial was uncalled for, Jessica. That type of behavior not only makes you look bad, but affects me, too."

"So I was supposed to laugh and chitchat like everything was fine between us when you didn't talk to me in the car? I'm not going to pretend just to make you look good. I'm always going to keep it real."

"Real, huh? Is that what you call it?"

"That's exactly what I call it."

"I got it. Tonight I meet the *real* Jessica Bolton."

An uneasy quiet descended as Nathan drove through the rain-soaked streets of Atlanta, as Friday night revelers filled Peachtree Boulevard, heading here and there. At the loft, Nathan bypassed the garage entrance and stopped by Jessica's car.

"Why are you stopping here?"

"Isn't it obvious?"

"You're putting me out?"

"No, you did that yourself."

"What? Because I wouldn't—"

He threw up a hand in frustration.

She flinched.

His hand came down slowly as he looked at her. "You thought I was going to hit you?"

"It wouldn't have surprised me." She got out of his car and into her own, and sped away.

Nathan watched her leave and then pulled into the garage, drained. Last weekend he proposed to a woman he hadn't known long, but thought he knew well enough to share the rest of his life with her. Tonight he felt like he'd dined with a stranger. That she was also the woman he loved and his fiancée was a major problem. Before they got married, Nathan vowed to himself, it was one that would get solved.

A part of her regretted the argument before her car left his block. Sissy hadn't returned her calls. She hadn't seen Nathan all week. Last night Jessica was glad she hadn't heard from her sister. She'd traded dreaded thoughts of poison for fantasies of passion and had counted down the hours to being in her lover's arms.

Then she'd heard the woman's voice.

Why did I get so angry? She knew the answer. The sound of a woman's voice in Nathan's house had triggered bad memories. Walking in as they conversed took her right back to many such moments during her marriage, when Edwin would talk on the phone with one of his many women. She could be sitting right beside him and he'd put the call on speaker, blatantly throwing his infidelity in her face.

Jessica and Edwin were sitting on a loveseat in their theater/game room when his cell phone rang.

"What's up, sexy?" He put the call on speaker.

"I don't know," a sickeningly sweet voice purred through the phone. "But I know what I want to get up . . . that thick, stiff piece you're working with."

She immediately recognized the caller's voice. *I can't believe he got with that NBA groupie.* She gave him a look of disgust and prepared to rise. His large hand gripped her shoulder. She couldn't move.

He shifted, spreading his legs as his dick hardened as if on command. "That can be arranged."

Again, Jessica tried to leave. This time, Edwin yanked her back by her hair.

"Name the time and the place, baby."

"Stay by your phone. I'll hollah back in ten."

"I'll be right here, wet and waiting."

He sneered at Jessica. "Yeah, get that pussy ready for me." Ending the call, he turned to Jessica. "Did I say you could go anywhere?"

"Why do you think I want to sit here while you talk to one of your whores?"

"I don't give a damn what you want. It's all about what I want."

He reached out and flicked her nipple. She shrank away from him. Wrong move. He quickly pinned her on the loveseat, ripped off the thong she wore beneath a spandex mini and once he'd pulled out his rock-hard dick, plunged it inside her. She knew better than to fight him, had no thought to voice an objection. So she did what she'd learned to do when just ten years old. She took her mind someplace else, acted as though the assault was happening to somebody else.

When he was done and finally left the house, she took a long shower, but after scrubbing for half an hour she still did not feel clean.

By the time Jessica had driven the seven minutes to her house and entered her condo, regret was receding and justification was gathering steam. Whether or not she'd overreacted, the fact remained that Nathan had been talking to a female. And not just any woman but one he met in paradise on New Year's Eve! She decided to take a shower, and while under the spray justification wavered a bit and regret gained an edge. It may not have been the best move to embarrass Nathan in front of his friends. Steve seemed like a good person, and when Allison had tried to engage Jessica, she'd appeared genuine. *While I acted like an asshole, and kept it real.* "Real stupid," she muttered, getting out of the shower and dressing for bed. She was tired of thinking: about tonight, the engagement, the assignment, the whole sordid mess. She wanted someone to come and take care of her, to protect her and tell her what to do. Someone like . . . Shutting off her mind from depressing thoughts, she climbed into bed and reached for the TV remote. Beside it was the burner phone. In spite of her resolve not to think about her, Jessica picked it up and realized the battery had died. She plugged it in, turned it on and set it back on the nightstand.

A few seconds later an indicator pinged. Again, and then a third time. Jessica snatched up the phone in disbelief. Missed calls! From Sissy. She hit Redial, feeling better already. She'd effed up with her boyfriend, but her sister had called!

CHAPTER 34

He didn't run away from a problem. He rushed right to it. First thing Saturday morning he dialed Jessica's number and was glad she answered.

"We need to talk about last night, but I don't want to fight."

"Okay."

"Want to meet for breakfast?"

Thirty minutes later, they sat in a booth. A waiter brought Nathan coffee. Jessica drank tea. The menus had not been touched.

"I need to understand what happened last night."

"I walked into your house, heard you talking to a woman, and got upset."

"Obviously, but why? I don't understand. It was a casual conversation. That I kept the call on speaker when you walked in made it obvious that it wasn't something I was trying to hide."

"Stepping into that situation triggered stuff from my past. I probably overreacted, but in that moment the anger was real."

"By that statement can I assume that your ex-husband not only physically abused you but cheated, too?"

She snorted. "Many times. After a while he didn't even bother hiding his other women, would bring them over and entertain them right in my house. When it first started he'd try and cover up, calling them casual friends, acquaintances, cousins, accountants—oh, he had all kinds of jobs for his women of choice. But I knew better. I'd listen in on the home phone, eavesdrop while he was talking on the cell. Then I'd walk into the room. In the beginning, he'd get off the phone if I came into the room, or change the direction of the conversation.

"The first time I confronted him he denied it; in fact, the first few times. Then he met someone who he really liked and basically told me that he was going to have her and me too, and there was nothing I could do about it. That's the first time I tried to leave."

"What happened?"

"He found me. After he . . . showed me how angry my leaving had made him . . . I never tried to leave again. Until I knew it was for good."

Nathan, quiet, simmered with rage. In his mind the lowest man on the planet was one who put his hands on a woman. "I'm sorry that happened to you," he finally said, wanting to touch her but also wanting to let her know his feelings went far beyond their physical connection. "No woman deserves to be mistreated, disrespected, the way he did you. Obviously he didn't have anyone around to show him what a real man looks like." She remained quiet. "Perhaps you've never seen one either."

She looked at him then—sad, vulnerable—and slowly shook her head.

"Hopefully, you'll give me the chance to show one to you, to prove that not all men are alike. I can't do anything about what's happened in your past. If I could, I would. What I can do is try and make sure ours is a positive relationship, one totally opposite from the others you've had. I can't do that if you won't let me, if anytime you see or hear something that you don't understand, you assume the worst about me. I'm not perfect. I've cheated before; not proud of it, but it happened."

"Then how do I know it won't happen with me?"

The innocent desire in her large, doe eyes caused his heart to clench, made him want to protect her from all of life's miseries, to find every man who'd ever hurt her and inflict pain on them. He took her hand, rubbed his thumb across the ring on the third finger of her left hand. "This is how you know. When I proposed to you, I was saying that from that day forward you would be my one and only. You're the only one for me, Jessica. I love you, not only as someone who'll be my wife, but also as the mother of my son."

She cocked her head. "A son, huh? And what if we have a girl?"

"I'm not trying to need a shotgun to keep jerks off a daughter. I only have boy bullets."

"Oh." She smiled.

He brushed her cheek with his finger. "I feel differently about you than all the other women I've dated. That makes all the difference."

They decided to go back to his place. As she got into her car and drove over, Jessica was more conflicted than ever. No man had ever said the things Nathan had said, the way he'd said them. So forthright and sincere. She wanted so very much to believe him, and had it not been for the conversation with Sissy last night, she probably would have scooped up his declarations and swallowed them whole.

"I don't know, Sissy. He's really mad this time."

"Doesn't matter. If a man is into what's between your legs, he's not going far. He'll call, and be sorry, and whisper all the sweet words and smooth lies he thinks you want to hear. I want you," Sissy said, lowering her voice to mimic a man. "I need you. I love you!" She took her voice even lower and drew out the words. She and Jessica laughed, a rare light moment between them. It was short-lived, as Sissy's tone turned dark. "A man will tell you anything to get your heart in the palm of his hand . . . so he can control it and you. Your ex proved that better than anyone. Give him your body, Jessie, but not your heart. Do you hear me? When he calls you with a comeback line, invites you over—and you know what for—go give him what he wants and give it to him good. Perform the blow job of your life. I've chained many a man to my heart with my mouth, and I wasn't talking. Let me give you a couple tips . . ."

She reached Nathan's condo. He'd texted her saying he was already inside. She went up and within minutes they were naked and screwing on the rooftop patio as a light rain fell. At one point she dropped to her knees, took him in, and did what Sissy suggested. In less than a minute he exploded with such force they almost fell over. Jessica smiled, confident she'd followed instructions to a tee. She couldn't wait to tell teacher what student had done. Later that night, Nathan whispered sweet words and smooth lies into her ear. Jessica listened to him but thought about Sissy. The next night was spent at her house. She went into the kitchen to fix Nathan a Hennessy and OJ, and add something extra. Before mixing it, however, with a brief spark of conscience, she took off the engagement ring.

CHAPTER 35

"Nathan, there's a Dr. Sullivan on line one for you."

"Thanks."

Nathan walked over and closed his office door before taking the call. "Good morning, James."

"Good morning, Nathan. How are you feeling?"

"Fine, and you?"

"Can't complain."

"I assume you're calling about the physical."

"I am."

"So, what's the verdict? Am I going to live?"

"That's a question for somebody with more power than me." Nathan laughed at James's impassive answer. "But going from the tests I've run so far, which are all of the common ones, I'd say you'll be around for a pretty long time."

"That's good news."

"Your blood pressure is good, cholesterol average; there was no sign of prostate cancer or tumors. The only potential cause I saw for your recurring illness was a slightly lower than normal white blood cell count, which in some cases can lessen the body's natural ability to stave off viruses and other common, highly contagious diseases."

"I really hadn't been worried about my health, all along thought it was a virus of some kind. But to get proof is definitely a relief."

"Glad I could help. I ran every test of a general physical and a couple more as well. So unless you have a recurrence of past symptoms, I'd say to take extra precaution when going out into the elements and as much as possible, get eight hours of sleep. The lack of it is another major reason why our bodies break down."

"You know, James, I would like to run one more thing by you."

"Sure."

After a soft tap, his door opened. He looked up to see Broderick entering his office, suit coat slung over his shoulder and briefcase in hand. "On second thought, let me get back to you on that."

"Or send a text."

"Even better." He ended the call. "You out of here, boss?"

"Yes. The wife has a society function, so I have to go and put on a monkey suit. How's it going?"

"A little swamped but manageable."

"That trip to New York was right on time. Hadn't been for that tip from my man up there, we may have lost the account already."

"Things are back on track, at least for the moment. I'll have to stay on top of it though, do a little hand-holding until the final decision has been made."

"It's a million-dollar hand, so rub it, pet it, even kiss that baby if you have to, but don't lose that deal!"

"Ha! I'll do my best."

"Solid experience trumps a blue-blood boost when there's money on the line. I sent you an e-mail on the junior consultant candidates that were interviewed. There's a couple I'd like to pass on to you for a second."

"Good." Nathan reared back, his eyes narrowing. Broderick seemed to sense a change in mood. "What else is going on?"

"I'm concerned about my report for the board meeting. It will be my first one as vice president, so the scrutiny will be intense."

"I'm not worried. Looks like you are, though. Don't stress about it, Nate. You'll do fine."

"Are significant others invited on this trip?" Like many businesses, this company's annual board meeting was held in a beautiful location. This year they were headed to the Enchantment Resort in Sedona, Arizona, with seventy panoramic acres of natural red rock terrain.

"The chairman is against it, of course, because he's going through a high-profile divorce and won't be able to bring his mistress."

"Good Lord . . ."

"But the treasurer just got remarried and wants to show off the trophy wife twenty years his junior. I say we stick to business and entertain our women some other time."

"I'm with you."

"But some of the wives will never go for that. So Jessica is welcome."

Broderick looked at his watch. "I have to go, man. You should, too. Wouldn't want you to get burned out within months of the job."

"No chance of that, man. See you tomorrow."

He'd planned to stay late. But following Broderick's advice, Nathan placed some materials in his briefcase, sent a text to James, and less than an hour after his boss's departure, headed out of the building.

On the way home, he phoned Jessica and asked her to meet him at his house. She was there when he arrived. He wasn't surprised to see she'd brought over dinner, this time from one of his favorite steakhouses.

"What'd you get me?" he asked, once he'd gone upstairs and changed into baggy jeans and a tee. He walked over to where she was reheating the food. "And what did you snatch up when I entered the kitchen?"

She gave him a playful push in the chest. "You are so nosy! Do something useful like pour our drinks."

He pulled two glasses from the cabinet and walked to the fridge, chuckling as she stopped and watched him pour cola for them both.

"You didn't see the orange juice in there? That cola is for me."

"I feel like switching it up tonight."

"I thought you didn't like cola."

"Usually I don't. But I'm tired of orange juice."

"Try and treat a man special and look where it gets me."

He walked over and kissed her temple. "It's gotten you a ring, baby. I'd say that's a pretty good return on your investment."

Jessica brought their plates to the table. For a few minutes, clanking silverware was the only conversation.

"This is good, baby," Nathan mumbled around a bite of steak and baked potato.

"I thought you liked creamed spinach."

"I do."

"You haven't touched it."

"Here." He scooped up a forkful. "You try it."

She moved her head away from the fork. "I don't like spinach."

"Come on. It's good for you."

"You eat it. I've got broccoli." She speared a floret and popped it into her mouth. "Yum." Pointing at his untouched spinach, she demanded, "Eat it."

He took a couple bites as she watched him.

"That's better." She walked into the kitchen to get more cola. When she came back, the spinach was gone. "Dang, that was fast."

"I don't think I've ever had their spinach and it's delicious. Besides, I told you I'd eat it."

"Good." She walked back into the kitchen and returned with a glass of orange juice. "Now, drink this, too. You've been feeling good lately. We don't want a relapse."

"I'll get to it," he said, cutting another bite of steak. "Having a woman like you around makes a man want to live for a very long time."

They retired early, made love, and went to sleep. Or tried to. Hard to do when minds were full and hearts were torn. Jessica lay waiting for the arsenic-laden spinach and antifreeze OJ to take effect and send Nathan running to the bathroom. Nathan tried not to squirm and disturb Jessica as he fought nausea and his stomach cramped. Each thought the other was sleeping, but when dawn slowly stretched her pink and orange fingers across the sky, Nathan and Jessica were both wide-awake.

Unfortunately for Nathan, the alarm clock didn't care what time he went to sleep. It still went off promptly at six a.m. Easing out of the bed so as not to wake Jessica, he headed for the shower. She sang out good-bye before he was done. He dressed quickly and by seven thirty was seated in his office.

His new executive assistant arrived shortly thereafter. "Good morning, Beverly. I need to see you for a minute."

"Certainly." Within seconds she entered his office with iPad in hand. "Good morning, Mr. Carver."

When she called him that he still had the urge to look and see if his dad was standing behind him. He'd told her to call him Nathan, but she felt it improper to not use his surname. "You're a high-level executive and my boss," she'd told him. "It's the respectful way to address you."

He held up his hand as she prepared to sit down. "I need you to run an errand for me."

"Oh, okay."

He pulled a small package from his briefcase. "I need this

sent FedEx, overnight, a.m. delivery. It's important, so make sure a signature is required."

She gave a curt nod and took the padded envelope. "Is that all?"

"Not quite. Have you had breakfast?"

"No, I haven't."

"Me either, and I'm starved. Go somewhere and find us a good breakfast sandwich. Bring mine back with a large coffee."

"I thought you preferred tea, Mr. Carver."

"Usually, but today I simply prefer to stay awake."

Beverly chuckled. "Then I'll try and get back quickly."

"I appreciate that, Beverly. You're doing a great job."

"Thank you. I'm grateful for the opportunity."

She left, and for a moment he sat deep in thought. Beverly's hadn't been the most accomplished résumé he'd received. He'd interviewed candidates from more prestigious schools and with more job experience. But something in his gut had told him Beverly was the one he should choose: good character, strong morals, loyal employee, and hard worker. His intuition didn't kick in often, but if he paid attention when it did, the actions he took were usually the correct ones.

The phone rang. Nathan turned his attention to the demands of the day, feeling good about the actions he'd taken.

CHAPTER 36

"Seriously, man . . . a weak-ass defense? That's all you've got?"

It was Thursday evening. For the first time this year, Nate had left the office at five p.m. and taken Steve up on his offer to meet at the club for a friendly game of basketball. The heavy work schedule had pushed regular exercise to the background. The detective, Ralph, and another friend had joined them. Working up a sweat felt good.

"Steve, that big mouth," Nathan countered, slowly bouncing the ball as he eased toward the net, "is that all you've got?" Before Steve could answer, Nathan faked left, moved right, and scored a layup.

"That's game." Ralph walked over to Nathan and gave him dap. "Way to play, Nate."

"I see you've still got it. A little slower maybe . . ."

Ralph toweled off and grabbed his bottle of water. "Shoot, I'm a lot slower than I was five years ago. Age is catching up with me."

"Steve fell in step beside them. "It's catching up with us all."

The men reached the parking lot and said their good-byes. Ralph and Nathan continued to walk toward their nearby cars.

"How's the detective business doing these days?"

"Booming."

"Really? That many people trying to find something out?"

"You'd be surprised."

"I was surprised when Steve told me you'd moved from police work into this line of business. What made you change careers?"

"My wife. I loved being on the force, but she thought it was too dangerous, spent her time worrying herself to death about me. While on the squad I'd dabbled a little in investigations—scoping out a criminal's whereabouts, trying to find witnesses, following up on leads by people who'd rather not get involved . . . things like that. Then one day I got a call from a friend of mine who suspected his wife was having an affair. Needless to say, this is something he didn't want anyone to know about, so he asked me to check into it. I balked at first, didn't want to get in the middle of their private lives. I suggested he search the yellow pages for a real detective. He couldn't bring himself to share his private life with a stranger. So I helped him out."

Nathan leaned against Ralph's car. "What was that like?"

"Way more exciting than I thought it would be. Didn't take me long to find out that indeed she was stepping out on her marriage, but proving she was in a relationship was a whole different game. I took pictures of her and her lover at various places but nowhere she couldn't explain away their being together. I had to hand it to his wife. She handled her business, paid attention to detail, covered her tracks. She never used a credit card or anything that could be traced back to her and this guy. They had some kind of system for when they met in hotels, never entered or left together, were never seen together even in the common areas: lobby, bar, restaurant."

"So how'd you catch her?"

"Patience, my brother, and a few detective maneuvers that

I can't disclose. Let's just say she was caught on tape with ir-refutable evidence that she'd been unfaithful."

"Man, I don't know if I could do that."

"It's hard work. My friend was devastated, wanted to hurt the wife, kill the lover . . . for a minute I thought he was going to snap! I understood, to tell you the truth. But after he calmed down and agreed that neither one of them was worth a life-time in prison, he used what I'd gathered to get a divorce, with the judge ruling totally in his favor. So at the end of the day it felt good to help him get clarity and move on, even though there was a lot of pain in the process. So if you ever need in-formation on somebody, let me know."

"I think I'm good, Ralph," Nathan said with a laugh. "But thanks for the offer."

"Hey, you never know." He reached into his car door pocket and gave Nathan the business card he retrieved. "I look at everyone as a potential client."

Nathan gave the card a quick scan. "This your cell num-ber?" Ralph nodded. "All right, then." They shared a soul-brothers handshake. "We'll have to do this again soon." Nathan turned and walked toward his car.

"I'm down for it. Just give me a call."

Nathan hadn't been in the car five minutes when his phone rang. One look at his dash and he groaned aloud. *Dev!* He'd been so excited about getting a workout in that he'd to-tally forgotten they were supposed to meet.

He tapped a button on the steering wheel. "I am so sorry and deserve whatever curses you want to hurl at me."

Her lyrical laughter floated around the car. "No curses, ever. But you have been a bad boy and deserve a spanking."

"I sincerely apologize. A friend of mine called me up for an impromptu game of basketball. It's been forever since I worked out and I jumped at the chance to get in some exercise. It's rare for me to miss an appointment. Let me make it up to you tomorrow night."

"That can only happen if you meet me in New York."

"Ah, right. So you and your friends decided to hit the city."

"Indeed."

"Will you be back?"

"I'm afraid not. On Tuesday, I'll leave Manhattan for home."

"Oh, man. I feel really bad now." Nathan stopped at the light, giving a quick nod to the woman in the lane next to him, who'd honked to get his attention. "Tell you what. I'll give you my address. You can come to my house, have a drink on the roof while I shower and change, and then we can go somewhere for a late dinner, or if you've already eaten, head to a club or a jazz spot . . . whatever you'd like. I'll call Jessica so that she can meet us. How does that sound?"

"Perfect."

Nathan rattled off his address and then called Jessica. The call went to voice mail. "Hey, baby, it's me. Listen, I want to—" He looked at the dash as another call came in. "Just call me, okay?"

He switched calls. "James! What's going on, brothah?"

"Just getting back with you regarding the text and everything. Sorry it took so long, man. I was out of town. But I got the information you wanted."

"No worries, James. I appreciate your sharing your expertise. When a project deals with science or biology, I hit up Randall. Anything medical . . . I come to you."

"Anytime, Nathan."

"What'd you find out?" James began speaking just as Nathan hit a dead zone. "Wait a minute. James?"

"Can you hear me?"

"I'm almost home. Let me call you back from a land line."

"You'll call tonight?"

At least these are the words Nathan assumed he'd said. "I'll call you back in ten minutes."

Nathan arrived home, poured a glass of juice, sat down, and picked up the phone. "James. Nate. I'm now on my landline."

"Good. So this is what I found out . . ."

James talked. Nathan listened. When Dev arrived at his house a half hour later, he was still on the phone.

CHAPTER 37

The doorbell rang twice before Nathan got up and opened the door. "Dev."

"Nathan!" She stepped in and gave him an enthusiastic hug. He returned it with a mediocre one. "Sorry I'm not dressed yet. Was on a call longer than intended."

"I'm on vacation with nothing but time." He didn't respond. Dev stepped back, brows knitted. "Are you all right?"

"Not really," he admitted. "Come on. Let's sit down."

They entered the living room and sat on the couch.

"You don't look good, Nathan."

"I don't feel good either."

"What happened? Just a little while ago, you sounded fine."

"Yes, well . . ." Nathan placed his face in his hands, taking a deep breath before rubbing his eyes and face and then allowing his hands to drop into his lap. "I've been dealing with something, a sickness that comes and goes."

"Have you seen a doctor?"

He nodded. "Just got off the phone with one, matter of fact. He ran some tests."

Dev waited. When Nathan remained quiet, she asked him, "Did he find anything?"

Nate's phone rang. He looked at it but ignored the call. "There's nothing for you to worry about, Develia Nixon, especially on your last night in Atlanta." He stood. "So let me fix you a drink, show you the roof, and jump into the shower. You helped me have a great time in Nassau. It's time for me to return the favor!"

"Are you sure?"

"Absolutely. In fact, come on in the kitchen while I mix your drink. I might need your help with something."

Five minutes later Dev went to the roof and Nathan headed for the shower. He felt better under the spray of hot water, but by the time he joined Dev a short time later, his stomach was in knots again.

Jessica was numb. Her emotions were shot. Sissy was getting more and more frustrated at her lack of progress in taking out Nathan. She'd questioned her sincerity in carrying out the plan and again threatened to cut off contact if she changed her mind or, in Sissy's words, "chose him over family." And on top of that, her stupid cell phone was deciding which calls it would answer and which ones she wouldn't receive at all. Dialing out had been a problem, too. She knew she shouldn't have listened to Sprint when she'd been tempted to switch to AT&T. She'd called to cancel and they'd transferred her to the retention department, who'd given her more features while lowering her bill by fifteen dollars. Today she was learning that it didn't matter how low your bill was if the phone didn't work. For the third time that day, she tried to reach Nate. After calling his office and being surprised with the news that he'd left work at five, she'd tried him on his cell. The next two times she'd tried to call him, her phone had other ideas. *Please go through.* She impatiently tapped her fingers on the steering wheel. *Dial tone!*

Yay! Voice mail. Crap. She tossed down the phone in frustration. Time for Plan B. *I'll just go to his house anyway. If he's not there, I'll wait.*

Thanks to light traffic it took only half an hour to get home, and that included two stops. She stood in the kitchen, checking off a mental list as she looked around. *I think I have everything.* She placed the warm plastic container of soup she'd bought from Nate's favorite deli into a recycle bag, along with yet more of his special juice and soda. Extra antifreeze was poured into an empty shampoo bottle and the arsenic was transferred from its medicinal-looking bottle into a colored travel-size plastic container. After placing these items at the bottom of an overnight bag, she threw in an outfit for work tomorrow, undies and toiletries and was out the door.

Before she left her block, the phone rang. One look at the caller ID and she immediately thought to ignore the call. *Of all the times my phone chooses to work. This is the last person I want to talk to right now.* Then, remembering what Sissy had said about keeping Sherri out of Atlanta, she pulled to the side of the road. This conversation was going to demand her full attention, and acting skills as well. She pressed the speaker button. "Hello, Sherri."

"Jessica, hi. I'm glad I caught you."

"What's going on?"

"It's Nathan. He's been hard to reach and when we do talk, our conversations are brief. He seems to rush me off the phone, and that's unusual. Have you seen him lately?"

"Not as much as I'd like. We haven't had the chance to talk much, either. He's had back-to-back out of town trips, and business meetings that last all day. I'm on my way to his house now though, and can have him call you."

"I'd appreciate that," Sherri murmured, obviously processing what Jessica said.

"He does need to slow down, and tonight that's what I

plan to help him do. I want to take his mind off work . . . if you know what I mean . . . get him to relax."

She heard Sherri's sigh of relief. "Thank you, Jessica. You know what? I owe you an apology. Nathan told me about the engagement. I should have called sooner. We've had our problems, but my brother seems happy. Congratulations."

Jessica relaxed, not knowing whether to laugh or cry at the statement's irony. "Thank you." She swallowed the sudden lump that formed in her throat, forced it away along with tears and feelings.

"So he hasn't been sick again, not since he went to emergency?"

"No." Never had it been harder to push a two-letter lie past her lips.

"That's what he told me. He said the tests James ran all checked out okay."

Jessica's eyes widened. *What kind of tests are you talking about? And who the hell is James?*

"Did he share anything more specific with you?"

"He told me the same thing. That everything is good. Except for not getting enough sleep, I think he's fine. His appetite is normal and when he was sick, he hardly ate a thing." This fact both bothered Jessica and brought relief. That's why she'd bought extra. Tonight, she wanted results!

"Thanks again, Jessica. I feel better after talking to you."

"You're welcome." *I've answered your questions. Now please say good-bye.*

"Nathan is my heart. What happened between us in the beginning was never personal. It really wasn't. I only want what's best for my brother and who's best for him. From what he's told me, and now what I'm seeing, it could be you."

Again tears threatened. She dug sharp fingernails into her palm to quell her emotions. It was easy to despise the bitchy Sherri she'd encountered on the island. The words coming from this kind, gentler version threatened to seep through the wall she'd built around her heart and more lately, her conscience. *This call must end. Now!* "Thank you. Good—"

"Nate says that after he gets settled into his new position, he might go down to the Bahamas on a mini-break. I'm sure he'll want to take you with him."

"If I can get the time off, I'll go. Look, I—"

"What do you do? I'm not being nosy, just still know so little about you, and since we're going to be sisters it's time I learn more."

The less the better, is what she thought. "At a law firm," is what she said. "Sherri, I'm at Nathan's and have bags to carry inside. I'll talk to you later. Good-bye."

She ended the call, waited ten full seconds, and burst into tears.

After returning home to wash the emotion off her face—stained cheeks, red eyes—she hurried back to the loft. He'd called. She'd missed it while running water in the bathroom sink. He hadn't sounded good at all. *Perhaps he drank all of the orange juice I left.* That carton contained both toxins, in higher doses. Trying to follow Sissy's instructions—increase the doses but keep him out of the emergency room—was a tall order for a novice, especially one who didn't really want him to die. Sherri's call only increased her stress. If the increased doses were working, then Nathan would become very ill. If Sherri learned this, she'd catch the next flight. *I'll have to think of something to keep them from talking and to keep her away.* Jessica decided to call Sissy. Her devious sister always had a plan.

Jessica rang the doorbell and then let herself in. "Nathan, it's me!"

The house was quiet. And dark. "Babe?" A chill snaked down her spine. *What if . . . no.* She called louder. "Nathan?" Still no answer. Her heart began to pound. She set down her bags near the door and looked up the stairs. "Baby, are you up there?"

She placed a foot on the first stair. The stillness became oppressive, threatened to overwhelm her. Throughout this process she'd not thought about this moment, had forced away the possibility of watching him die or finding him dead. *Stop being silly, Jessica. He just called.* But he'd sounded so weak on the message. Her knees began to shake, forcing her to stop on the third stair and grab the rail for balance. An errant thought flittered through her mind. *I've never been to a funeral before, or seen a dead body up close.* The reality of what her actions may have caused, a man's death, made her nauseous. The thought of seeing Nathan cold and lifeless created abject sadness. Tiny beads of sweat broke out on her forehead; clammy hands clutched her throat. She'd never had a panic attack but thought this might be one. She sat down and bent over so blood rushed to her head, took several breaths—deep, even—until the shaking stopped. After a moment she gritted her teeth, got up from the step, and slowly climbed the staircase.

"Nathan?"

Her voice sounded loud and hollow: an intruder to the quiet, an invader to the eerie peace.

Top of the stairs. Down the hall. She was here now. Just outside his door. Optimism flared as she processed what she saw. *Is this why he didn't hear me? Because his bedroom door is closed?*

She knocked, first softly and then louder. "Nathan!"

Silence. She almost faltered. What she'd set out to do had obviously been accomplished. *I loved you, Nathan. I'm so very sorry. I loved you so much!*

This realization brought a new set of fears. She and Sissy hadn't talked about what to do with his body. Whatever it was couldn't implicate her. Jessica had begun to reach for the doorknob, but this thought made her pull back her hand. *I shouldn't touch the doorknob. It will leave fingerprints. What am I thinking? My prints are all over this friggin' house!* There was no way she could be the one to find him. Had anyone seen her come into his place? What about the empty containers from what he'd eaten and drank? Were they in the garbage? Had his trash been picked up? So many questions, so many loose ends to secure. The sooner she confirmed her worst fears, the faster she could focus on distancing herself from this loft and his illness.

With an empty heart and steely resolution she covered her hand with a piece of her top, reached for the knob, and turned it.

CHAPTER 38

The bed was empty.

She collapsed on it with the weight of relief. The feeling was short-lived. As his scent enveloped her so did worry and fear. The shaking returned, even as she worked to calm her erratic heartbeat. He wasn't here, which led her to assume that he wasn't dead either. As horrific as finding him dead would have been, at least the nightmare would have almost been over.

Jessica was physically tired and emotionally drained. No doubt she loved Sissy, but the stress was too much! In trying to kill Nathan, she was about to die herself. She rolled to her back and stared at the ceiling. Closing her eyes, she tried to remember life before that fateful e-mail from Sissy, before moving to Atlanta, before meeting Nate.

Edwin. That had been her life before. No one could have told her that in leaving this abuser she'd be jumping out of the frying pan into the fire.

It doesn't have to be this way. You could choose Nathan, and be happy. At the mere reflection on this possibility her eyes flew open. In moments like this, it did seem possible that what Nathan had told her was true. Maybe all men were not alike. Maybe he really loved her. She'd lose Sissy, but what happened if she carried out these plans, somehow got caught, and went to prison? She would lose both of them and her life as well. Then again . . . Jessica sat up as an idea occurred . . . maybe one day Sissy would get over being angry and both she and Nathan could be in her life.

Her heartbeat slowed. The shaking stopped. Jessica laughed out loud. She wasn't the only one.

Was that another voice? Frowning, Jessica eased off the bed, cocked her head toward the hallway from where she thought the sound came. Holding her breath, she waited. Took a step. Listened. A low murmur of voices. Or did she imagine it? Soft, barely audible. *Could it be a neighbor?* Occasionally sounds would bleed through the walls, usually music though, or a loud shout. Once she and Nathan thought they heard the sounds of sex. She didn't remember ever hearing low voices, like a conversation going on just out of reach.

She eased into the hallway and walked toward the stairs that led to the roof. More murmuring. Stop. Pause. *I am definitely hearing someone talking.* At the base of the short staircase she stopped again. They were clearer now. *They, as in more than one person.* The melodic sound of happy female laughter trickled through the opening and fell on her like rain. Only instead of soothing, like water, the laughter pricked, like nails.

And here I was about to lose my mind at the thought of him dying. Jessica quietly climbed the stairs, now ready to kill him on sight.

Thoughts of a sneak attack were quickly dashed. Nathan sat on a bar stool with a direct line of sight to the rooftop entrance. He saw her right away.

"There you are!" Standing, his attempt to smile was only partly successful. "I've been trying to reach you. Did you get my message?"

"Yeah, I got it." She accepted his hug and worked hard not to glare at the woman sitting on a bar stool next to Nathan. In fact, she'd only taken a dismissive glance. The woman was beautiful, stunning, in a natural, genuine way that made Jessica want to find something sharp and pointed, and mar her face.

"You must be Jessica."

It's you. The Bahamas side piece. So much for not glaring. In that instant, her anger rose and invited jealousy and insecurity to join it.

"I'm Develia, and it's wonderful to meet you."

"Dev, baby." Nathan kept his arm around Jessica until they reached the bar stools and sat. "The woman on the phone when you came over early that day."

"Nathan has been going on and on about you and the engagement. Girl, this man is ready to marry you today!"

The woman's infectious smile and kind eyes weakened Jessica's defenses and soothed nerves already frayed by the search for a corpse. But that didn't mean she liked her. It just meant no one would be thrown from the roof. She offered a limp hand. "Hi, Dev."

Dev clasped it in both of hers. "You are so pretty, as beautiful as Nathan told me you were."

"Thanks." She turned her full attention to Nathan. "How are you, Nate? On the message, you didn't sound so good."

"I think that bug is back again."

"Oh no." She placed a hand to his forehead, and under his chin. "You don't have a fever. When did you start feeling sick?"

"I started feeling something yesterday but ignored it. Woke up this morning feeling pretty good. That continued all day until I got home, started up the stairs, and got dizzy."

"So why are you here and not lying down?"

"Being in the fresh air has made me feel better."

"Have you been drinking lots of water?"

"There was still a carton of the orange juice you brought me. I've been drinking that."

"Good, but you need water, too. I'll go get you some."

He tightened his hold on her. "No, you won't." Sliding off the stool, he sat her on it. "I'll bring us all drinks while you two get acquainted." He kissed her and left the roof.

"Nathan said you were with him in the Bahamas but left early. How did you like our little island?"

"It's nice."

"Did you get to see much of it?"

"Not really. Mostly where Nate's sister lives and the Sandals resort."

"That's a popular destination. The next time you come, I'd like to suggest a fabulous place unknown to most foreigners. It's a privately owned villa with amazing views, a private beach entrance, and modern, luxurious décor. I guarantee it will be unlike anywhere else you've ever stayed."

They continued to chat, Dev mostly. Jessica found herself in the rare position of listening to a woman with interest rather than annoyance. Dev asked questions in a way that didn't seem probing, and shared information in a way that encouraged the same. When Nathan returned, Jessica was recalling the pleasant parts of the Turks and Caicos trip. The bad times with Edwin had been so traumatic, she'd almost forgotten that sometimes they'd liked each other and even had fun.

She'd gone from high anxiety to anger to agreeable within the span of ten minutes. When she looked up and saw a tray-bearing Nathan walking toward her, she almost fell off the stool.

"Nice cold orange juice for everyone!" Nathan placed the tray on the bar counter. Along with the juice was a bowl of chips. "With all the germs floating around and these wild temperature swings, I figured we could all use a dose of vitamin C. Here you go, babe."

Jessica took the glass and placed it on the bar beside her.

"Dev."

"Thanks, Nathan." She took one small sip, another one,

and then turned up the glass. When she stopped to breathe, two-thirds of the glass's contents was gone. "I didn't know I was so thirsty," she explained. "But this is good." She looked at Nathan. "Is it fresh-squeezed?"

He turned to Jessica. "Baby?"

"Um, no," Jessica said as she shook her head. *No, not fresh at all and no, not going to drink it.*

Nathan took a healthy swig of his as well. He munched on a chip. Conversation ceased. Jessica became aware of music and wondered if it had played the whole time she was here. The wind blew, lifting the hair from her shoulders and sending a chill.

She eased off the stool. "I'm going inside. It's getting cold out here." She started toward the door.

"Baby, your juice."

"Oh, thanks."

"The temperature has dropped," Dev said, rubbing her hands along her arms. "If you don't mind, Jessica, I think I'll join you. Nathan?"

"Right behind you."

Jessica hadn't waited to hear what Dev said. As soon as she was out of their sight she raced down the stairs and into the kitchen, turning on the water even as she poured the poisonous orange mix into the sink. Seconds later, she heard Nathan and Dev coming down the stairs.

"Oww!"

The cry was one of anguish and pain. Jessica braced herself, then came around the corner. Dev was doubled over. Nathan placed his hands under her arms and gently guided her to the floor.

"Dev, what is it?"

"My stomach," she moaned. "It . . . hurts . . ."

"Hurts how? Are you cramping?" She nodded. "Nausea?"

"Yes. It happened all of a sudden, out of nowhere. Ooh . . ."
She grabbed her stomach and rolled into a fetal position.

Nathan looked at Jessica as he reached for his phone. "I think we should call nine-one-one."

"No!" She hadn't meant it to come out so forcefully, but she meant what she said. "You had these same symptoms, Nate, and I helped you. Remember?"

"Yes, but this might be different."

"Okay, let's get her to the couch and lay her down." Jessica raced into the kitchen and came back with a glass of a carbonated beverage. "Try and get her to drink as much of this as possible."

"No," Dev whimpered. "I'll throw it up."

"That's the best thing you could have happen. I'll run get a couple of cool, wet towels." She took the steps two at a time.

CHAPTER 39

Dev lay on the couch. Nathan handed her the glass. "Come on, Dev." His authoritative voice sounded loud in the silence. "Try and drink some."

Dev took a few sips and set down the glass.

Their eyes met. Something felt but unspoken flashed between them.

"Do you think you're going to be all right?"

She slowly sat up. "I think so."

"Take a rain check on that dinner I promised?"

"Absolutely." She gave him a lazy smile. Her eyes fluttered closed. He pulled her into his arms for a grateful hug.

Jessica came down the stairs to a lover's tableau.

Nathan looked up and slowly eased out of the embrace. "She's feeling better."

Dev eased her legs off the couch and turned to look at Jessica. The move scrunched her breasts together, creating a tempting cleavage. Nate noticed. Jessica noticed Nate's noticing. *Well, I'll. Be. Damned.*

"Yes, thank goodness, Jessica. The hard cramping has passed."

"I see." She quelled the urge to throw the wet towels at Nathan's head. "Would you like a cold towel?"

"No, thank you."

"Are you well enough to drive?" If veiled sarcasm had a face, it would look like Jessica.

"I think so."

"Then you should go back to your hotel, or wherever you're staying."

Nate was appalled. "Jessica, the woman just went through a painful ordeal."

"No, Nathan, it's okay." Develia stood and looked around. "Where's my purse?"

"I'll get it." Nathan hurried to retrieve the bag and handed it over. He placed a hand on her shoulder. "Dev, are you sure you're okay to drive?

"I'm sorry if my suggestion seemed rude." Jessica didn't sound sorry at all. "But you need lots of water, a hot shower, and a long, peaceful sleep. Tomorrow you'll feel better." Jessica walked over to Nate and wrapped an arm around his waist. "Right, babe?"

Nathan looked at Dev.

"She's right." Dev pulled her keys from the bag. "Jessica, I'm sorry I wasn't able to spend more time and get to know you better. I rarely get sick. In fact, I can't remember the last time I had more than a cold."

"Happens to the best of us," Jessica said, not so subtly urging Dev toward the door. "Almost everyone I know has caught some part of the bug that's been going around."

"Except you," Nathan countered. "I don't think you've gotten sick at all."

"That's because I didn't tell you. It was the week you went to New York. By the time you got back I was all better. So there was no need for you to know."

He stared.

She glared.

Dev opened the door.

"I'll walk you to your car," Nathan said.

Dev saw Jessica's reaction and spoke up quickly. "No, that's quite all right. It was good seeing you again, Nathan."

"You as well. Take care of yourself." They hugged. He kissed her cheek. "Please keep in touch and let me know how you're doing, and that you've made it home safely."

Dev waved without turning around and disappeared around the corner.

Nathan closed the door and headed toward the stairs.

"Where are you going?"

"To lie down," he answered without turning around.

Jessica followed him. "Are you sick, too?"

"I'm not fine."

They reached the master suite. Nathan stripped down to his boxers and climbed into bed. Jessica got naked and joined him. She snuggled beside him, running her hand over his body: face, chest, thighs, manhood. "You're not hot."

No answer.

"Then again, you may be hot and I can't tell because I'm burning up." Emboldened, she slid her hand beneath the elastic band of his boxers and gripped his power. Alternating between firm grips and gentle squeezes, she rubbed her nipples against Nathan's arm, ran her tongue up from his navel to his chin, pressed her lips against his, swiped her tongue across the crease of his mouth, a strong hint for him to open it.

Nothing.

She put her attention back on the task in hand. Pull. Squeeze. Rub. Tickle the balls. Not only was the flag not at half mast, it didn't rise at all. Jessica's eyes narrowed. *There's only one way a man can lie next to a naked woman who is working his dick, and not get hard.* She slid down, positioned her mouth above his tip and—

Felt Nathan's firm grip on her shoulder. "Stop, Jessica. Not tonight."

"Why not?"

He looked at the flaccid member currently resembling a dead snake, then at her. "You have to ask?"

Jessica gave a sneaky chuckle. "If that's all it is, baby, I can take care of that real quick."

She lowered her head and again Nathan stopped her. "I guess I'm just not in the mood."

"What, you can't sex two women on the same day? My ex could run through three, maybe four women in a couple hours. You're a one-and-done kind of dude?"

Nathan turned away from her. "I'm going to act like you didn't say that and try and get some sleep. You can either lie quietly beside me, or you can turn out the lights on your way out."

"I don't want to lie here, I want to make love. Now." For a third time she groped him. This time his backside was the target.

"Damn, Jessica." He angrily sat up. "Just stop it. Okay?"

He'd actually surprised her. Even angry, Nathan rarely raised his voice. "So are you . . ." The question died on her tongue as she watched him roll away from her again, pulling the sheet around him, fluffing a pillow and nestling in for a nap.

"Fine. I got the message loud and clear."

In less than five minutes she jerked on her clothes, put her belongings together, and went downstairs. She sprinkled all the remaining arsenic she had on her onto every item in the refrigerator where it wouldn't show.

She left the house, phone in hand, and returned the call she'd earlier ignored. Vincent answered before she reached her car.

"Hello, beautiful."

At the sound of his voice, she felt better already. "What are you doing?"

"I'm over at a club where one of my partners has a band that's playing. I called earlier to see if you wanted to join me."

"I just saw the missed call."

"What are you doing now?"

"Nothing, headed home."

"You want me to come over?"

"If you want to."

"You know I do. I'd rather be with you than with a bunch of hardheads. See you in a few."

As soon as Vincent stepped into her home, he opened his arms and swept her inside them. Hugging quickly became kissing, interrupted by two glasses of wine.

"You're so tight," he said, once they'd sat on the couch and he squeezed her shoulder. Continuing to the nape of her neck and across her back, he placed down his wineglass. "I know what you need. Come on."

"Where are we going?"

"Your bedroom. I'm going to give you a massage."

"Really, Vincent? That's the oldest trick in the player playbook. Your grandfather probably used it."

"Could be how I got here. I guarantee you this. I won't do anything that you don't want me to do. Deal?"

She pulled herself off the couch. "Deal."

They went into her bedroom. She went into the bathroom, changed into shorts and a spaghetti-strap top and brought out a bottle of vanilla-scented massage oil.

Vincent took the bottle, poured a small amount into his hands and began briskly rubbing them together. "Now lie down, close your eyes, and try to relax."

His hands worked as if they'd been trained in the profession. For thirty minutes, he worked out kinks from the balls of her feet to the top of her head. Finally, he sat beside her.

"Jessica?" he whispered. "Are you asleep?"

She groaned. He chuckled.

"Do you feel better?"

"Uh-huh." She slowly turned toward him. "That felt amazing."

"Good. I could feel when you truly began to relax. I'm glad I could help you get a good night's sleep."

"I'm sure to do that," she said amid a yawn.

"That looks like my cue to get kicked out."

Jessica rolled onto her back and looked at him through hooded eyes. "Do you want to leave?"

He did that sexy half lick, half lip-chew thing that can only be pulled off by certain men with a particular swagger. "You know I don't."

"Then I won't kick you out."

Soon clothes came off, bodies rubbed together and a different kind of stroking lasted well into the night.

CHAPTER 40

Jessica braced herself for seeing Vincent in the office. He'd left during the early morning hours, told her he had a breakfast meeting and would be in around ten. It was now ten thirty and he still wasn't there. It wasn't that she cared whether or not he showed up for work. She just wanted to get this first-time-seeing-coworker-after-screwing encounter over with.

Ding.

Forcing herself not to look, she reached into her drawer for a file she didn't need.

"Good morning, beautiful."

Three words and the girl almost needed to go change her panties. Instant flashes of what he'd done, she'd done, what they'd done to each other last night. She squeezed her thighs tight and turned to address Mr. Givens the attorney, not Vincent the freak.

It would have worked had she not looked at him in time to see his hazel-green eyes darken to an earthy brown. "Hello." The word came out in a whisper, on a gust of air. As if on cue, Ms. Nosy from around the corner chose this sexually tense moment to need something from the front desk.

"Mr. Underwood is expecting a FedEx package," she said curtly, looking between Vincent and Jessica as though they were under arrest. "Has it arrived?"

"All packages are delivered immediately. I'll call as soon as it's here."

"I know the procedures around here better than you do," Ms. Nosy snarled. "And all the rules as well. So watch yourself."

They watched her stiff retreat, barely containing their laughter.

As Vincent left right after with a wink and a smile, Jessica thanked Ms. Nosy. The Ice Queen's interruption doused a fire about to burn out of control. When it came to keeping this little tryst under wraps, the two had work to do.

Jessica tried to focus on a variety of tasks, but it was difficult. From the time Vincent darkened her door until he left, she'd not given Nathan a thought. Soon after, however, came thoughts of the unfinished business for Sissy and the woman named Develia that would make said business easier to complete. Then Vincent texted her, and musing over Nathan and his island side-piece again left her mind. But today was proving to be a slow one, with rarely ringing phones and only busy work to occupy the hours. The reality of what had happened yesterday could no longer be ignored. Everything her sister had said about Nathan had proved true. He'd say that he loved her. He'd cheat. He'd lie. He'd promise to change, buy her a gift, and then do it all again.

She reached for her cell phone. There was a text message from Vincent.

Meet me here at 1. There was an address.

What restaurant is this?

Vincent's Place. ☺

She hesitated, not sure if she should be with Vincent while dealing with Nathan.

Don't say no. It's important.

She smiled, amazed at how well Vincent knew her. **All right. I'll be there.**

Ten minutes later, when she went on break, she called Nathan. The call went to voice mail so she left a message. Now it was just a waiting game to see if he'd call back.

By 12:50 she still hadn't heard from him. But her backup returned from lunch and her boss was gone, so she left a little early and headed to a gentrified area fifteen minutes south of downtown. Following her GPS, she pulled in front of a two-story bungalow house with large picture windows and a small but nicely landscaped yard. Similar homes filled the quiet block. Tall, full trees gave the neighborhood a grounded, well-established vibe. Looking around but not seeing Vincent's car, she sent a text.

Within seconds, her phone rang. "Get in here, beautiful. We don't have all day."

She laughed and hurried to the front door. It opened steps before she reached it. Vincent pulled her in and greeted her with a hot, wet kiss.

"Come in and see what I've prepared for you." He held her hand, leading her from the foyer through a long living room with a high ceiling.

Jessica took in the home as they went. "This is really nice, Vincent. I didn't think I liked old houses, but this is beautiful."

When they reached the dining room, she stopped short. Her mouth dropped open. Before her was an elaborate table setting and a four-course meal, so beautifully displayed it could have been ripped from a magazine.

She looked at him, eyes shining. "I can't believe you did

this." She stepped up and took in the menu: creamed broccoli soup; a tomato, avocado, and fresh mozzarella salad; pecan-crusted pork chops on a bed of wild rice; and sliced strawberries with whipped cream. "You've got to give me the name of the restaurant that provided this setup. Everything looks delicious. They must have an amazing chef!"

"You're looking at him."

"No way." He nodded. "How, when you had a breakfast appointment and got to work before eleven?"

"Preparing this for you was my appointment. Let's eat, my love, before the food gets cold."

She sat down and soon her taste buds were in heaven. Every bite she relished was better than the last.

Vincent barely ate, instead content to watch pure enjoyment skip across her face. "I've dreamt of this moment," he admitted. "From the first day you joined us, I imagined you here, in that chair, eating something wonderful I'd prepared."

"You really cooked all of this?"

An impish smile slowly spread across his face. "I so want to have you believe that I did. But I can't take the credit. I hired a chef."

"Just for me? That is so sweet."

"I thought you'd like it. But having lunch is only one reason why I asked you here, a very small part of the overall plan."

"What plan is that?"

"I really care about you, Jessica. I just knew that if we got together it was going to be magic. Last night proved I was right. I don't want this to be just a casual fling or a string of clandestine sexual encounters. I want you to be my woman, move into this house, meet my grandmother, build some dreams. And I want to be your man."

His words had slowed Jessica's eating, the sounds of which were almost as good as the taste of the food. She loved Nathan, but knowing he'd lied about his and Dev's relationship, saying they were just friends when Jessica knew their thing began at the New Year, had broken a huge trust. Not to mention his behavior after she'd left. He never turned down sex . . . ever, until last night. Nathan had seemed different, but less than six months in and he was just like the rest. She looked at Vincent, intelligent and handsome, looking sincere. *What's to say that you're different, that this nice home won't become my prison?* Her shoulders slumped.

Vincent did not miss the shift. "You don't believe me."

"I do. I mean I want to but . . . something happened yesterday."

"What?"

"Remember when I said Nathan and I had problems and you asked if he was cheating?" He nodded. "He was. I met her yesterday."

"What? How?"

She told him the story. "I got in my car and left," she finished. "And then I called you."

"I'm glad that you called me, Jessie, but I want to be more than a rebound lover. What, why are you looking at me that way?"

"What did you say?"

"I said I'm glad you called but—"

"No, what did you call me?"

"Oh, Jessie? I'm sorry. That's my pet name for you in my mind. Are you offended?"

"No, I like it. I like it a lot."

"Have you broken the engagement and given back the ring?" She shook her head. "Why not?"

"I was so numb when I left his house, I didn't think at all."

"Then I'll give you space to do that. I don't mind waiting. But only if I know that I'm not just wasting my time, that me and you being together is actually possible."

She pondered his question, then looked up and smiled. "Anything's possible."

★ ★ ★

Nathan stood at the office window facing his backyard. It was Friday, there were no meetings at the office, so he'd decided to work from home. With extra sleep and a slower pace he'd felt better until now, when digesting the news he'd just received, from the person answering phones where Jessica worked, turned his stomach again. She'd left for lunch almost two hours ago and still wasn't back. Vincent had left about the same time, he was told, and hadn't returned either. "Is that why you've been so paranoid, Jessica? Continually accusing me of cheating because of your duplicity?"

The ringing of his cell phone interrupted his thoughts. "Hello, Dev."

"Good afternoon, Nathan. How are you?"

"I'm okay. How are you?"

"I'm amazing. There's something about New York that lifts your spirits and energizes you. We just landed a couple hours ago and I've felt great ever since."

"I'm glad you're having a good time."

"Between shopping, eating, sightseeing, and shows, we've got almost every waking hour planned for the next three days. But I got your text and wanted to call to let you know I've arrived and I'm okay. Let's plan a long chat for next week, when I return home."

"That sounds perfect, Dev. Thanks again for being so understanding and for . . . just being you."

They ended the call. Nathan held a conference call with the Morris Environmental project and called Renee to cancel the Vegas trip. He'd expected disappointment and her usual flirting and was surprised yet pleased to learn that she had stopped trying to get her groove back and had landed a seasoned gent. "I thought the only thing I could do with fifty-five was the speed limit," she'd explained with a laugh. "I've never been treated so well in my life!" After promising to keep in touch, he let her go and refocused on work. The next time he looked up it was six o'clock. The day had flown by with no call from Jessica. So he picked up a gourmet pizza and a bottle of wine, and headed over to her condo.

He buzzed her unit, and after receiving no answer used the key she'd given to him shortly after the sickness started and he'd given her a key to his place. He placed the pizza on the kitchen counter and the wine in the fridge. Walking into the living room, he stood and looked around. It was the first time he'd come in without Jessica present and was taken by how strange it felt to be here. He pulled out his phone and shot her a quick text.

Don't stop for food. I'm at your house. Dinner's waiting.

That message sent, Nathan put his hands in his pockets and strolled around the living room. He noticed several things for the first time: a framed poem called "Cotton Candy on a Rainy Day" by Nikki Giovanni, a collection of miniature porcelain birds atop a silver branch, an old faded picture in a silver frame, of two young girls, all smiles and pigtails. He picked up the picture and studied it carefully. *Is this Jessica?* He couldn't say exactly but assumed so. *And the sister she once mentioned . . . but lately hadn't seen.* He put the framed picture back in its place and continued his casual perusal. When he heard the front door, he stepped out of her bedroom and entered the living room from the hallway as she walked inside.

They stopped and looked at each other with mixed expressions.

"Hey," he finally said.

"Hey."

"I tried reaching you today."

"Yeah, I know." She moved past him, set her things on the coffee table, and began checking her mail. "I called you, too."

She tossed the envelopes on the table. "I'm kind of surprised to see you here, Nathan. I thought you'd be with Dev."

"Is that what you thought, or what you hoped so you could be with Vincent?"

Bam.

Jessica took the bullet without flinching. "The person who gets caught tries to throw shade on the one who caught him. Very original, Nathan."

"It's not true? You're not still seeing Vincent? He looked at her hand. Is that why you're not wearing my ring?"

She plopped on the couch and picked up a magazine with a resigned sigh. "I'm not going to do this, Nathan. If you want to talk, we can talk. If you want to break up with me, I can't stop you and am honestly too tired to try. What I'm not going to do is sit here and go tit for tat about who's stepping out when according to both of us, it's both of us!"

The air crackled with tension.

Jessica looked over, then back at the magazine.

Nathan sat at the bar counter and scrolled his cell phone.

He didn't leave, for a very specific reason.

She wanted him to stay, for reasons of her own.

Jessica broke almost ten minutes of silence by offering Nathan a can of soda. Nathan thanked her and accepted it. He told Jessica that Dev was a friend, nothing more. She told him that Vincent was a co-worker, that's all. Jessica heated the pizza. They drank the wine. Jessica yawned and headed for bed. Nathan went home.

This chess game could continue for only so long. Either one or the other would call checkmate. But one thing was for sure: There was no way they could both get what they wanted.

CHAPTER 41

Things changed. Subtle shifts, slight irregularities, unusual bumps in what in the beginning had been a smooth groove. Ever since Friday night a week ago, when Nathan and Jessica had agreed to give their relationship one last try, there had been a cognitive dissonance played out in many ways. There had also been a return of nausea and cramps.

The following Monday, Nate had been awakened by a five a.m. phone call. Broderick wanted him to meet a small group at the DeKalb Peachtree Airport for a day trip to Jackson, Mississippi, where a client proposed to purchase a large acreage of real estate. It was a full schedule, from the time the corporate jet took off at seven, until it landed at five. Afterwards, the group had gone to dinner. During this time, Jessica had called several times and finally texted him a question about his health. Unusual, since she knew how hectic his days normally were, especially when out of town. Even after he'd replied saying he felt better, she called twice more. On his way home, when he could finally return her call and find out what the heck was going on, she'd simply said, "I'm worried about you."

Tuesday night, she'd gone over to Nathan's, bringing her

now staple gifts of orange juice and soda that she purchased every week. "You don't have to do that," he'd told her.

"But you were out," she'd replied, as if the answer should have been obvious.

Which led Nathan to ponder: *When did she start checking my refrigerator for supplies?*

And tonight, after a full week for Nathan and a long one for Jessica, they sat at an Atlanta Hawks basketball game intermission like virtual strangers, acting like they were enjoying themselves, when neither—for different reasons—felt joyous at all.

After watching the halftime show in silence and then feeling Nathan was more interested in checking out the jerseys hanging from the rafters than in talking to her, she tapped his arm. "What's going on with you?"

Nathan answered without looking at her. "Nothing."

"Do you still feel sick?" He nodded. "Have you been drinking the orange juice and soda?"

"Yes."

"And eating the soup I fixed?"

He looked at her. "Faithfully."

"I can't understand why you're not—I mean, with this constant illness, I'm surprised you had the strength to work all week, and then come here."

"It hasn't been easy."

"That's why you're quiet. You don't feel well."

"Yes, but I didn't feel like staying at home, keeping you cooped up."

"I wouldn't have cared."

He looked at her intently before turning his attention to the players warming up for the second half. "I probably should go back to the hospital and take those tests the doctor suggested."

"I don't think so."

This comment got his attention again. "Really? I'd think

with how worried you've been about me, getting an all clear from the doctor would be a relief."

"I was only thinking of your job, and your schedule, the reasons you haven't gone so far. But if you can spare three, four days in the hospital . . ." She shrugged and watched the cheerleaders' showy routine.

They were both glad when the game resumed and they had somewhere to legitimately place their focus other than on each other. Afterward, the colleague who'd given Nathan the choice seat tickets texted him about a VIP after-party.

He relayed the message to Jessica. "Do you want to go?"

"Do you?"

He rubbed his stomach. "Yes and no."

Watching him, Jessica didn't hesitate to answer. "Let's go home."

"Your place or mine?"

"Let's go to my house. I've got a new tea I want you to try."

On the way to her home, Jessica's phone rang. When she didn't answer, Nathan looked over. "You're not going to get that?"

She placed a hand on his thigh and squeezed. "I'm with you, babe. Everyone else can wait."

When it rang again an hour later, she silenced her phone. Nathan noticed but said nothing.

"It was Vincent."

"Why didn't you answer?"

"I didn't want to be disrespectful."

"By not answering, you come off looking suspicious."

She reached for her phone. "I'll call him back and put it on speaker."

"That's all right. If this is going to work, we've got to trust each other."

She fixed tea and a plate of snacks. He asked for water, too. Sitting side by side on the couch, they checked e-mails and social media sites. Jessica carefully watched Nathan drink his tea. It seemed to take forever, but when she'd returned from the restroom, he'd finished the cup.

Maybe that will do it, maybe now he'll get sick enough to . . . Rushing to the guest bathroom, she threw cold water on her face and took several deep breaths. Nathan cheating on her with Dev had made her angry and helped her grow the backbone Sissy had suggested. But it hadn't made the idea of killing him a comfortable one. Especially since the process had taken far longer than expected. He'd get sick and bounce back. Cramp up and feel better. Throw up and be near death one day, then back in the office greeting clients the next. In a last-ditch effort, Sissy had given her the name of another drug to try. She said it was strong enough to kill a horse. That's what was in his drink.

After watching him covertly for several seconds, she put on a smile and reentered the living room. "Feeling better?" she asked cheerfully.

Nathan grimaced. "Not really. My head started feeling woozy just now."

She sat next to him and placed a hand on his forehead. "I don't feel a fever."

"I know but I'm . . ." Doubling over, he let out a low, deep moan.

It's kicking in. Jessica swallowed the urge to panic, willed herself to be strong enough to finish this impossible task. *Looks like pouring in all of what remained in that vial is what was needed.* Rubbing his back she spoke softly. "Breathe, babe. Just breathe."

His moans grew louder. Jessica's eyes widened as he began to shake. She did too, from a thought so terrifying that it was totally possible that if Nathan started convulsing, she would, too. *What's going to happen if he dies in my house? How will I move him? What if his death is questioned? They'll come looking for me!*

"Nathan!" Spittle now dripped from his mouth to the floor. She rushed into the kitchen for paper towels to catch the drool.

"Babe, help me try and get you outside. You need fresh air, and sleep. Come on. I'll drive you home."

It took a while, thirty minutes to be exact, for Jessica to get Nathan out of the house and into her car. That's after he'd moaned about cramps, complained of a migraine, and then spent considerable time in the john.

"My car," he eked out, still doubled over.

"I'll bring it over and leave the keys on your table."

"So sick," he mumbled. "Hospital . . ."

"You'll feel better after getting a good night's sleep. I promise."

She was right. The next morning anyone looking at Nathan would have had no clue that he'd been deathly ill just twelve hours prior. They'd think he was the picture of health. Except for one thing—looks can be deceiving.

CHAPTER 42

Jessica resembled a caged tiger as she paced the length of her living room. She'd been keyed up since last night, when it looked as though Nathan might die on her floor.

"Sissy, I have never been so scared in my life as when that man keeled over and started drooling on my hardwood. I can't believe all this time I've been taking this huge chance doing this here, in my house!"

"I hear you, Jessie, but you've got to calm down. What could have happened didn't. Okay? So we just need to think about how we're going to proceed from here."

"I don't understand why it isn't over already. You said with these increased amounts it would be three weeks tops."

"Yes, if he'd had them every day. Your constant fights and petty arguments prevented that from happening. Have you talked to him today?"

"Not yet."

"Then, heck, let's think positive. Based on how he acted last night, he might be dead now."

"Since I still have to deal with the body, forgive me for not feeling particularly comforted by that thought. I won't rest until he's discovered, identified, and a ruling on his death has been made in which I'm in no way connected."

"I wish the vitamins would have worked faster. Everybody is different, Jessie. Depending on their height, weight, hereditary disposition . . . crap. You're right. This has gotten too complicated. It's the last thing we need right now. Especially since . . ."

"Since what?"

"Since finding out the prosecutor on my case currently has his hands full denying a bribe accusation. My attorney believes if we strike right now, we could score a new trial. That only leaves one person who could potentially cause trouble. With her distracted, a new trial is all but guaranteed, and I assure you there's no way I'll be convicted a second time. I'll do whatever, screw whomever, to hear 'not guilty.' If I leave here, I am *not* coming back."

"So what do we do?"

"Give me a day or so to think about it. As soon as I figure out a plan, I'll call you. Oh, and Jessie?"

"What?"

"I love you to pieces."

Tears filled her eyes. At least somebody did. "I love you too, Sissy. Can't wait until we're together again."

Nathan rested against the back of his suede accent chair that anchored a corner of the sitting room in the master suite, his feet propped up on its matching ottoman. After three months of an absolutely insane work schedule, recurring sickness, and a difficult engagement, he was finally enjoying a few evenings of downtime. Jessica still had the ring, but they'd put off setting a date. He'd reestablished regular communication with his mom, who'd practically threatened to disown him; and Sherri, who swore he was being held hostage in a cave that Jessica built and guarded. Steve was still in the honeymoon of his new relationship and didn't meet them as often as he used to, but Nathan had spent quality time catching up with Ralph. He'd met his wife and daughter and discussed possibly hooking up on a project or two. On the phone, he heard the little one who had daddy wrapped around her finger, vying for his attention in the background.

"Nate, let me catch you later, man."

"I hear Little Mama." Nathan laughed. "She's got your number. I feel for you when that child hits her teens."

"I don't even want to think about that yet."

"I'll see you on the court next week. Take care now."

He placed the home phone back in its cradle and proceeded to the bathroom. Looking in the mirror, he took in his eye color, faint crow's feet at the edges of his eyes, and the tint of his skin. *You're not the healthiest man in Atlanta, but considering what's been happening, you look okay.*

He showered, dressed, and headed out the door. After a quick call to Jessica to say he felt better and was meeting the guys for an early dinner, Nathan called Sherri.

"Sherri, what's up?"

"Nate? For the second time in one week? I feel special."

"As you should, being my sister and all. What are y'all doing?"

"Al and Aaron are out with friends. Randall and I are soaking up the peace and quiet and absolutely delighted to be doing nothing at all."

"I know the feeling."

"What about you?"

"Heading out for an early dinner with the guys."

"Where's Jessica?"

"At home, I guess."

"Hmm. I can remember a time when I could barely get to you for her blocking. Yet the last few times we've talked, I've been the one to bring her up. Is the bloom beginning to fade from this rosy love story?"

"Every couple goes through their challenges and we're no exception."

"I've suspected it for a long time, all the way back to when you first got sick and she out and out lied to me about it, and then tried to prevent me from coming in your house. That was beyond strange, and while I've tried to be supportive, Brother, I've never quite gotten over that incident."

"I understand, Sis. Had it been you and a guy I had reservations about, I'd be guarded, too. I was very protective back then and probably didn't let you know how much I appreciated your having my back. But I did, and I do."

"Hey, have you talked to your friend from the island lately?"

"Dev? Not in a month or more. I've been planning to call her though. Are you guys planning a visit soon? I was thinking about maybe taking Memorial Day and heading down there for a long, relaxing vacation."

"You're welcome to go there anytime. We'll be there over the Fourth. You can join us then too, if you'd like. By the way, I noticed you said *I*, not *we*."

"A wise woman once told me that divorce is expensive and marriage is forever, and to take my time before I make that final commitment. The last few months have been one situation after another. I need time to relax and clear my mind."

"Wow, Nathan. This woman you talked to sounds amazing. Likewise, it takes a smart and special man to heed wise counsel."

"Only a fool would ignore it."

Nathan made one more call, to his mother, and then headed out for male bonding time. By the time he reached the restaurant, he'd mentally firmed up his upcoming holiday plans. He'd head to the Bahamas and lay up at Château Sherri. And he would go alone.

★   ★   ★

A few days later, all plans in place, Jessica reached for her phone. She and Nathan had shared time the past weekend, but because of Nathan's illness it had been two weeks since they'd made love. Monday he'd worked from home, something that happened more regularly now, and that night he'd been too sick to see her. She'd used this time to grow a killer backbone, shut down all emotion, and focus on the end. That's during those moments she wasn't with Vincent, her patient knight in shining armor waiting in the wings. She hadn't told Sissy about Vincent. For just a little while longer, she wanted to believe that he was really as wonderful as he seemed right now. Her growing feelings for him had helped distance her from Nathan. Every time a shred of guilt tried to creep in over how bad he was feeling, she'd think about Dev and remember that the cheating scoundrel who'd helped send her sister to prison was getting exactly what he deserved.

She sat on a chair in the dining room, her rapidly shaking right leg the only sign of nervousness. He answered. She took a breath, and hoped this would be easy.

"Hey, lover." Sultry. Flirty. Seductive.

"Listen to you, sounding sexy."

"I am?"

Purring like a kitten getting its belly scratched. "You know it. I think absence makes your heart grow fonder."

"You might be right. How are you feeling today, babe?"

"I'm okay."

"Well, I'm not."

"What's going on?"

"I'm missing you. That's why I've decided on two things. The first is for you, a vitamin capsule filled with natural herbs that is supposed to be excellent for stomach conditions."

"What did I tell you about worrying? The stomach virus or whatever it was has rarely flared up since my stress level dropped. I feel pretty good these days."

"By taking vitamins, you'll feel even better. This isn't

something to heal you but rather to prevent any new illness from taking place in the future."

"Where'd you find this miracle pill?"

"The wife of one of the attorneys swears by them."

"I might give it a try. What's the second thing?"

"I've seen you once in the past four days. I'm coming to get you and we're hanging out."

"Jessica, I'm working."

"It's Saturday. We don't have to be out long. I won't take no for an answer. When we spend several days apart in a row, it's not good for my health." *Wait. Did he just snort?* "I'm serious! So I'm going to pick you up, and we're going to take a drive to the countryside."

"The countryside. For what?"

"To breathe in the fresh country air."

"Girl, you're tripping."

"Okay, the real reason: to check out my new storage unit. One of the attorneys at work owns the facility, and said I could use one for free."

"You know nothing's really free, right?"

"In this case, it is. He's one of the senior partners, old enough to be my grandfather."

"Grandfathers need love, too."

"Please, spare me the visual. On the way back from the storage unit, I'm treating you to lunch. Either you'll come out or I'll come in and get you. Be by in half an hour."

She hung up before Nathan could say no. If he just got into her car and took the pill, she'd be home free. Sissy said he'd be disoriented but able to walk. Once inside the space where she'd park the car, she only had to give him the shot and leave. By the time it took effect, she'd be long gone. Before the day was over . . . so would he.

CHAPTER 43

Once she left her condo's garage, she called Nathan. He was ready, and came out right away. So far, so good.

"Okay, here's the vitamin," she said, almost as soon as he'd gotten in the car.

"You want me to take it right now?"

"Absolutely. The sooner it gets in your system, the sooner you'll feel better."

"Okay."

"Here, I've got water."

"That's okay." He held up a bottle. "I brought my own."

"Oh. Um, okay." To be on the safe side, she'd added a small amount of arsenic to the water bottle she'd brought Nathan. Hopefully the pill alone was enough to do the job.

She watched carefully as Nathan popped the pill and took a long swallow of water. "Wow, I feel better already!"

"You're silly." She pulled away from the curb. He began coughing.

"Are you okay?"

"A little water went down the wrong way. That's all." He pulled out his phone.

"Who are you texting?"

"Just answering one from Steve that I read earlier." He finished the text and looked out the window. "Where are we going?"

"Just sit back and enjoy the ride. And don't worry if you get sleepy. My coworker said that because our bodies heal faster when asleep, that's a side effect."

"So why pick me up for a scenic drive, and then put me to sleep?"

"If we come to something interesting, I'll wake you up."

Jessica easily navigated the fairly light late-morning Sunday traffic and soon she'd turned onto Ponce de Leon, headed to Decatur.

"Where are we going again?"

"Good try, Nate. I didn't say. Just relax and enjoy being chauffeured."

"All right, woman. I think that vitamin you gave me is taking effect." He leaned his head against the headrest and closed his eyes.

Jessica could barely keep her eyes on the road for glancing at him. Feeling he was indeed asleep, she reached for the earbud kept in her door pocket, slipped it on her left ear, and tapped the GPS feature that would lead her to their destination. Part of her story had been true. The senior partner did own the storage facility. But he didn't give her a storage unit. After she had overheard his conversation with one of the other attorneys about empty units and she learned that a side door was always kept unlocked, the plan that Sissy had shared with her all fell into place.

The burner phone vibrated, brought along so that Jessica could call her sister as soon as the deed was done. She hesitated answering it, afraid that Nathan might wake up. At the same time, she could use her sister's support right now. So she had to take the chance.

"Hello?"

"How's it going?"

"I'm fine."

"Good to know, but I'm not talking about you. Where are we at with everything?"

"Just driving to check out a storage facility."

"Oh-h," the word drawn out with understanding. "He's with you."

"Yes."

"I wish I could be a fly on the wall when that bitch gets the news about her brother."

"Okay, I'll call you later."

"Right away. I want to know the second her beloved baby brother is dead."

It didn't take long to get to the facility in Decatur. Looking around, she found the area wasn't so much isolated as it was an industrial area with little weekend activity—perfect for Jessica's plan. She drove through the empty parking lot and continued around to the back of the building, close to the unlocked door. Parking behind the building also kept her car somewhat hidden. In hindsight, she should have driven a rental. Too late to dwell on that now, though. She was here. It was time.

"Nathan?" She watched his slow, even breathing, his face in peaceful repose. *Stop it! Stay focused.* Nothing could come from being sentimental or thinking about repercussions. This was a chance to help her sister get out of prison and avoid a life sentence. She would do whatever it took.

"Nathan!" she called louder, gently shaking his shoulder.

His eyes slowly opened. He looked around, as if disoriented. "Where are we?"

The pill is working just as Sissy said it would. "We're at the facility. Come on, let's go inside."

Rubbing his eyes, he asked her, "Where are the boxes?"

"Huh?"

"You're here to store stuff, right?"

"Uh, not today. I . . . have to look at the space first to see what will fit. It won't take long. Come on."

"I'm so tired . . ."

She opened her car door. "I'll help you."

It took some effort to get Nathan out of the car. He leaned against it as if the effort to stand had used up his energy. Jessica looked around, desperate for a way to get him inside, give him the shot, and leave him in the locked space. Just as she was about to panic, she noticed a large moving dolly.

"Wait right here!"

She ran over to get the dolly and quickly wheeled it over to where Nathan now slumped against the trunk.

"Here, sit down."

"Huh?"

"Please, babe. Just sit!"

He half sat, half fell onto the platform. It took effort wheeling two hundred pounds of deadweight, but eventually Jessica got them through the door and into an elevator. They exited on the third floor where according to what she'd over-heard were mostly empty units. Jessica noticed several doors without locks. She chose an empty end unit, the farthest away from the elevator and stairwell, hopefully less likely to be no-ticed by staff. She wheeled Nathan into the three-by-five-foot unit, against the far wall, and closed the metal door. After try-ing to catch her breath and slow her rapid heartbeat, she looked over at Nathan, again sleeping peacefully. After turning her back to him, she reached into her purse and pulled out the syringe she'd purchased at a medical supply company using the fake ID information that Sissy had provided. With her sister's help she'd already filled it with the fluid that was supposed to send Nathan into a peaceful, forever sleep. The reality of final-ity seeped through her steely resolve not to feel, and clutched her heart.

"I'm sorry, Nathan," she whispered in anguish, staring at the steel door that at least temporarily would hide her crime. "I don't want to do this. I don't! But it's the only way to help my sister. She's the only family I've got, and this is the only way to free her. If there was another way, believe me, I'd do it. But I have no choice. Hopefully someday you'll forgive me."

She wiped her tears, took a deep breath, and with needle in hand turned around. The scream that followed reverberated against the metal walls.

CHAPTER 44

"Nathan!" His name shot out of her mouth riding a blast of incredulous breath

"Surprised to see how well your *vitamin* worked?" He stood erect, legs spread, arms crossed, looking fit as a fiddle.

Scrambling to recover, she got to her knees. "Yes! I, uh, I never thought it would be so . . ."

"Ineffective? Is that the word you're looking for?"

"I-I-I just . . ." Legs wobbled as she stood, all words lost.

His eyes went from her face to the hand still clutching the syringe. She immediately recognized the mistake and put the offending appendage behind her.

Closing the distance between them, Nathan's voice was low and calm. Too calm, given the circumstances. "Why'd you do that?"

"What?"

He gave her a look that read "don't play with me" all day long.

"I was going to tell you eventually."

"Tell me what?"

"That, um, that I'm a diabetic. I shouldn't be ashamed of it, but I am."

"You know what, Jessica? You are without a doubt the best liar I've ever met. I almost don't know whether to be angry or impressed."

Jessica stood there, trembling, trying to breathe.

"How long have you been trying to poison me?"

Her mouth dropped. "What? I—"

"Stop lying!" Finally, the gasket was blown. Suddenly and without warning, he gripped her arm and forced it from behind her back.

"You're hurting me!"

"Give me the damn needle," he demanded between clenched teeth.

The struggle was brief. Nathan squeezed her wrist and took the syringe, then pushed her to the other side of the unit so that he now stood in front of the door. For several long seconds he looked at her, his intense gaze piercing her soul, his hooded eyes unreadable. Her eyes darted around, looking for a way to get by him and escape. There was none.

Nathan removed a handkerchief from his pocket, wrapped it around the syringe, and continued to hold it as he leaned against the door. His expression softened, and when he next spoke it was casual, friendly, as if shooting the breeze with a friend.

"Before meeting you, I'd rarely been sick a day in my life. Lived in Atlanta for years, and Chicago before that. Experienced my share of cold weather filled with ice, rain, and snow. But cold? Flu?" He shook his head. "Almost never. Since moving south, I honestly can't remember having to take off work for illness.

"And then all of a sudden I come down with something terrible, I mean it felt like I was going to die! You were so helpful then, so kind and loving. I thought, wow, what a woman."

His eyes flashed anger. His voice—unruffled.

"Sherri implored me to get tests taken, just like the doctor had, remember? But I, like you, felt that it was just a stomach ailment, some flu-like sickness that would soon go away. Only it didn't. It kept getting worse. I couldn't understand it, kept thinking 'what the heck is wrong with me?' Then, little by little, this impossible scenario started coming together. Of course I couldn't believe it possible. My fiancée poisoning me? Never."

"Baby, no! I would never—"

"Shut. Up! I have never hit a woman, but I swear if you deny this shit one more time, you might get knocked the fuck out."

The statement hung in the air like the noose on a gallows. Wobbly legs no longer able to hold her, Jessica plopped down on the dolly and stared at the floor.

"This nagging thought persisted. All that antifreeze you had under the sink, and stumbling onto one very interesting receipt, for antifreeze no less, when I searched for a screwdriver. You'd said it was purchased a long time ago, but the receipt showed otherwise. That's the first time it clicked in my mind that something was off. Something wasn't right. I thought, 'Why would she lie about buying something for her car?' Then, when you kept insisting I drink orange juice like water and kept bringing me large amounts of soup and soda, the thought got louder. It wouldn't go away. So at the next opportunity, I snuck a peek at your browser search history, just knowing I wouldn't find anything, right? But I'll be damned if I didn't see searches for poisons and how to poison using antifreeze, arsenic, and all kinds of other bullshit. So I called my brother-in-law the scientist, and asked a few questions. He suggested I contact his boy James, a medical doctor. I did, and afterwards sent him samples from the orange juice, the soda, and that abominable soup that I forced myself to eat just because your non-cooking ass fixed it. He confirmed what I otherwise would never have believed."

Jessica raised her head. "But if you knew, why'd you keep drinking what I gave you?"

"I made you think I was drinking it, would hold the cup or glass to my lips, but after what the doctor found out, I never took another sip or bite of anything that came from your hand. You'd leave the room, and I'd toss most of whatever was in the glass so you'd think I drank it. When in bed, I had a trash can on the far side where I'd dump everything you brought me.

"When I first found out, I was so angry and confused that I didn't know what to do. My initial thought was to confront you and then kick you out of my life. But curiosity got the best of me. Why was she doing this? That's the question that kept going around in my mind. That's why I kept up the farce, to get more information. I kept sending samples to the doctor, who said the dosages were now at dangerously lethal levels. I was like 'Got-damn, she wants my ass dead, quick!' So last week, when we were at the restaurant *making up*"—he used air quotes—"and you poured whatever that shit was into my cup, I knew it was time to stop this madness before you succeeded in actually taking me out." She hid her shock this time . . . almost. "Oh, didn't know I saw that, huh? My going to the bathroom was just an excuse to leave you alone, and watch what happened. I turned the corner but didn't keep going, which you didn't notice because, hey, you were busy yourself. You were seated and the partition is low. So it was easy to take a picture which, once I had it blown up, clearly shows some type of vial in your hand, the contents of which you poured in my drink."

Her gaze slowly moved from the floor to his face. Anger flared in her eyes. "Putting something in your drink doesn't prove anything. I say it was agave or maple syrup or something you asked me to add for you. My word against yours. So what?"

"I thought of that, which is why when I stayed behind to leave the tip, I took the cup and sent it off for testing." He spared a brief, lethal smile. "Baby, maple syrup isn't what the lab technicians found." His expression hardened. "With the doctor's reports, preserved samples and lab results, the receipt that I copied, and dated cell phone pictures of everything from your refrigerator contents to the browser history that got this party started, there's more than enough evidence for an arrest. That's why we're here."

The thought of being incarcerated reenergized Jessica, fired her up. She jumped to her feet, her face twisted in a scowl.

"Arrest? For what, some ridiculous story you've made up in your head? I didn't do any of what you're suggesting, and even if I did, there's no way you can prove it. You were angry about Vincent, and planted all of this evidence,"—she mocked him by using air quotes as he'd done earlier—"just to take me away from the man who took me from you. It would be your word against mine. So now that I know how little you think of me"—she pulled off the engagement ring and dropped it on the concrete floor—"consider us finished. You need to let me out of here and you can find another way to get back home."

"Didn't figure on having to give me a ride back, huh?"

She pulled out her phone. "If you don't let me out, I'm going to call the police."

"I've saved you the trouble. They're already here." He opened the door. His friend Ralph, along with two uniformed officers, stood just outside.

The taller and seemingly older of the two officers stepped forward and removed the handcuffs from his belt. "Jessica Bolton, you're under arrest for the attempted murder of Nathan Carver."

He reached for her arm. She jumped back, slid around them and began running down the hall. Bypassing the elevator, she entered the stairwell, taking the steps two at a time. She'd reached the second floor before the younger officer caught up with her, wrestled a kicking, biting, screaming, writhing Jessica to the floor, and threw on the handcuffs.

Nathan, Ralph, and the other officer arrived just as he was lifting her to a standing position.

"Not a good move," the older officer told her. "You've just added resisting arrest to the other charges."

"That's just it! There shouldn't be any charges! You have no right to arrest me simply based on something he said. He's lying!"

The senior officer motioned to the staircase. "Take her to the car."

Even with her hands behind her back and a steel grip on her arm, Jessica tried to wrestle free. "No! Nathan, stop them!"

Nathan did not look at her, and didn't say a word. Once they were out of earshot he pulled what looked like an ordinary pen from his pocket and gave it to Ralph. "I hope this worked as good as you promised."

Ralph took the pen, twisted the bottom for a few seconds and then clicked the cap. Jessica's screams for Nathan to stop the arrest came through loud and clear.

"Impressive." Nathan turned to the senior officer. "What happens now?"

"She'll be booked into county jail and bail will be set. On Monday, she'll go before the judge and be formally charged." The senior officer looked from Nathan to Ralph.

"Thanks, man," Ralph said, holding out his hand. They shook.

"No problem," the officer responded. "You've helped me out of many binds. Glad to be able to return the favor."

"I'll call you tomorrow."

The officer nodded at Ralph, shook Nathan's hand, and continued down the stairwell. The two men listened as his heavy shoes reverberated against the steel steps. Soon they faded and were gone.

Nathan let out a relieved sigh. Ralph placed a sympathetic hand on his shoulder. The silence was welcome, as Nathan tried to process what had just occurred. Finally, in an effort to gather himself, he ran a hand over his face and quickly rubbed his hands together.

"I see the tracking device worked."

Ralph nodded. "We set out as soon as you texted me and the app we placed on your phone led us directly to the unit's door. I'd say we were there long enough to hear at least half of the conversation between you."

"That pen recorder caught what you missed. I tell you one thing, when I heard you'd returned to Atlanta and were now a detective, I never thought I'd be needing your services."

"I told you business was booming."

"I guess you didn't lie."

"I'm just sorry that this happened."

Nathan shook his head. "I have no words."

"Why do you think she did it?"

Nathan paused as the words from Jessica's tearful confession rang in his ears, the one she uttered just before she was getting ready to give him what was probably a shot of something fatal. His eyes narrowed, and once again his countenance changed. "I don't know, Ralph. But I'm definitely going to find out."

"I'll be right here to help you, man, starting with giving you a ride back to the city. Let's go."

CHAPTER 45

For Nathan, the next twenty-four hours were a blur. On the way home, he remembered his car was at Jessica's house. Ralph dropped him off at Jessica's complex. Once back home he took a long shower, put on a pair of sweats, and went to his office. There he initiated a conference call between him, Sherri, Randall, and Renee. No way did he want to tell this story twice.

"I knew there was something about her." Throughout Nathan's narration, Sherri repeated this phrase. "Didn't I tell you? Didn't I say there was something about that girl that I didn't like? I couldn't put my finger on it, but I told you. I told you!"

Nathan let her vent. She was right, after all.

As if she and Sherri were a tag team, Renee took up the conversation where Sherri had left it. "I hate to say it, bro, but that was my initial gut feeling, too."

"Yes, Renee. I vividly remember the conversation."

"Sherri never trusted her," Randall chimed in. "Said she was sneaky, couldn't look her in the eye, but that's some straight-up drama, TV-movie shit right there. Poisoning with arsenic and antifreeze? I didn't think that happened in real life."

"And because of what?" Sherri asked. "You'd given her a ring. She was engaged to you, for goodness' sake. What the heck else did she want?"

"I don't know." Nathan's voice was laced with fatigue. "That's the confusing part."

"She never gave you a sign of anything being wrong, never mentioned something that made her uncomfortable?"

"Not uncomfortable enough to want to kill me!"

"Nathan."

"Yes, Renee?"

"What about a big argument, or fight? Maybe you pissed her off about something and didn't know how upset the sistah truly was."

"The most we've ever fought about was Dev, with whom she believed I was having sex. But she began spiking my juice long before that."

"She did leave the Bahamas early," Sherri reminded him.

"Yes, but after a few conversations when we met back up, nothing more was said about that. She even agreed with me that all of us could have handled that situation differently."

"Damn." Randall voiced everyone's feeling. "Is somebody pouring crazy in the water? Last year it was Jacqueline. Now a chick named Jessica has lost her mind."

"Maybe it's the letter J. Nathan, don't date anyone again whose name starts with that letter. Try a letter that will ensure you get someone incredible, like an R, for instance."

"Renee, I knew where you were headed!" Nate experienced his first real smile all day.

"Can't pass up an opportunity to plug myself."

"Randall, I can't believe all you knew. We need to have a serious conversation."

"Sis, please don't dog out Randall for not telling you about this. I made him swear not to tell you. I wanted proof that there was need to worry, and after I got proof, I wanted to know why she was doing it."

"And you still don't know."

"Not yet. But I will."

After an hour of discussion, Nathan was no closer to understanding Jessica's actions than when he'd first called. He thanked them for listening and promised to keep them posted.

Later that evening, Ralph called.

"Hey, Ralph. What's going on?"

"First of all, how are you holding up?"

"Hanging in there."

"Good. I do have news for you."

"I'm ready."

"As you know, Jessica's belongings were taken upon her booking into county jail. During this process, I discovered that she was in possession of two cell phones, a silver one and a black one. Were you aware of this?"

"I've never seen her with a black phone, only silver."

"Now, that in and of itself is not altogether unusual, but considering the circumstances, I felt it warranted further investigation. So I checked the call logs. The silver phone was clearly her main mode of communication. Your number appeared many times.

"There was only one number on the black phone. I wrote it down, along with a few other numbers from the silver phone. I want you to take a look at them; see if we can get to the reason behind her actions."

"Why not just call the number on the black phone?"

"And say what? That we arrested Jessica and have a few questions for them?"

"Ah, yes. That might be problematic. I guess that's why you're the detective."

"The job is harder than it looks. Do you have time to meet this evening?"

"I'll make time. What about around eight?"

"You want to meet at the sports bar?"

"Given the game that girl was running, sounds like the perfect place."

Two days later, Jessica sat on the couch in her condo, looking for her life. Still in shock from her first time ever behind bars and the fiasco leading up to being arrested, she was just trying to find normal so that she could function, even if only in the most basic way. By now, she thought this whole sordid situation would have been behind her, that she'd have given her sister the wonderful news, the motion for a new trial would have been filed, and she and Sissy would be busy planning their Miami life. Instead, she was fighting to not join her sister behind bars.

Sissy!

Being locked up for three days could change one's priorities. Her sister was not how she'd used her one allowed call. Jessica walked over to the counter, where the new burner phone was still in its package. She tore it open, knowing that her sister was by now probably out of her mind.

She got voice mail. Considering the new number, she was not surprised. "Sissy, it's me. I know you've been waiting. You're not going to like what I have to tell you, but call me anyway."

The phone rang two minutes later.

"Sis—"

"What the hell, Jessie?!"

However upset Jessica had imagined her sister would be? Sissy was madder than that.

"I can't friggin' believe you've kept me waiting for three whole days. Do you know what you've put me through? Don't answer that. I really don't care. And then leave me a cryptic message that only irked me more? I'm so angry at you right now, Jessie, you would not believe!" She finally paused to take a breath. "Just tell me that asshole is dead."

"Nathan's still alive. I just got out of jail."

Sissy was silent for a very long time. Jessica waited, preferring silence to the continued tirade.

"What happened?"

"Nathan deceived me! He sent some of the juice I'd given him to a doctor for testing, found out what was in it, and then tricked me into thinking he was still getting sick."

"How is that possible? I've never heard of someone guessing antifreeze was in their food."

Jessica closed her eyes and swallowed the truth. Telling Sissy about the antifreeze under the sink wouldn't change a thing. Instead, she mixed the facts with a bit of creative storytelling. "He just happened upon an article about it, and realized the symptoms they mentioned were all the ones he experienced. So he sent some doctor friend a sample. My goose was cooked. After Nate confronted me at the storage space, he had the police waiting outside. I'm so sorry, Sissy."

"I can't believe this. I trusted you with my life!"

"I tried my best—"

"You failed! End of story! I knew I shouldn't have trusted you to be able to come through on this. You're pathetic."

Tears flowed. Jessica didn't bother wiping them away.

"Sissy, can I come see you? Maybe together we can figure out something else to do."

"Come for a visit? You can't be serious. I asked you to do one thing and it didn't get done. Thanks to you, I might not get out of here for a very long time."

"What about me, Sissy? Because of trying to help you, I'm facing time, too!"

"No, *you're* facing time because *you* screwed up!" An expletive punched her eardrum before Sissy ended the call.

So shocked was she at the venomous good-bye, Jessica actually looked at the phone, then let it drop to the floor. It skidded across her polished hardwoods, landing against the baseboard. So shocked that her tears dried up and her mind stopped working. So shocked that she curled up on the couch, the most comfortable place she had laid her head in seventy-two hours, and fell asleep.

She awoke two hours later, hoping that the past few days had been a horrible nightmare. One look at the new burner phone on the floor brought everything back. Nathan was alive. She'd gone to jail. That was real. But what couldn't be true was what Sissy had spewed in anger. There's no way the sister who so much wanted them to be together, to live in the same house, could want to be left alone.

"She was just angry," Jessica told herself as she retrieved the phone and redialed Sissy's number. She waited until the end of the beep. "Sissy, it's me. I know you're angry and disappointed. So am I! More than that, I'm scared. Please call me back."

By the end of the day, she'd called her sister half a dozen times with no response. For the first time since reconnecting with her sister, Jessica felt bereft and utterly alone. Most of her life, it had been this way. Only now, having experienced the closeness of sisterhood and the love of her life, the loneliness felt much worse.

There was no one to talk to, no one to help her. Until an image flashed before her eyes and she sensed a lifeline. The person she had contacted with her one allowed phone call. She picked up the burner phone without hesitation. Again, the call wasn't answered, but she didn't mind.

"Vincent, it's Jessica. When you get this message, can you please call?"

CHAPTER 46

Nathan stood as Ralph approached his table, located away from the TVs in the popular bar's quieter section. "Ralph."

"Nate."

They gave each other dap.

Ralph held up his hand to get a waitress's attention. "How was your day?"

"Pretty good, all things considered. I sent off a sample of what was in the syringe. We should have the results in seven to fourteen days. What about you?"

"Interesting." Ralph pulled out a small notepad.

Nathan's brow arched. "Wow, you're old school. I didn't realize people still put pen to paper."

"Hey, man, don't look down on this lowly beginning. When the electricity and satellites fail, man can still communicate with a writing instrument and a surface."

"You've got a point."

"Plus there's something about writing things out that helps me gain perspective."

The waitress came over with a bowl of pretzels and nuts. Ralph ordered a pitcher of beer. He opened his notepad. "I spent some time today going over the numbers found in Ms.

Bolton's cell phone logs. Those on her regular cell phone were fairly easily identified: you, of course; takeout spots; utility companies; her workplace; the usual stuff. There was only one number connected to a name: Vincent Givens. Do you know him?"

Despite her efforts to kill him, the name still made him frown. "He's one of the attorneys at the law firm where she works as a receptionist. I suspect he might be more than that."

A raised brow was Ralph's only physical reaction. "Any reason to believe he has something to do with this?"

"I've never met him, don't really know much about him. But could he be involved? Sure, why not? After what I just lived through, I no longer believe anything is impossible."

Ralph jotted down a few notes, flipped the page and turned the small notebook toward Nathan. "What about this number? Do you recognize it?"

Nathan shook his head. "No, I don't. Was this on her throwaway phone?"

"Yes, and it was the only number she received calls from, and the only number she called."

"Interesting."

"I thought so. Unfortunately, the number is to a burner phone as well. I'm working with the phone company to establish the tower it was using, which will give us a location, but not the cell phone owner's identity. One thing is clear: Either Ms. Bolton or this caller wanted to keep these communications private and confidential." Ralph shook a few peanuts in his hand before tossing them into his mouth. "There's a part on the tape where she mentions a sister, near the end, in a whisper. Doing this for her sister, helping her sister . . ."

Nathan snapped his finger. "She has a sister!"

He recalled a conversation early on in their dating, the aged picture he saw in her condo and the rambling confession Jessica mumbled just before she planned to give him the shot to end his life.

Ralph flipped through the pages of his notepad, found

what he was looking for and read, "I don't want to do this. I don't! But it's the only way to help my sister. She's the only family I've got, and this is the only way to free her." He looked at Nathan. "Does that mean anything to you?"

Nathan's eyes narrowed. "No, but on the way to the storage unit, when she thought I was sleeping, someone called. I couldn't make out the words on the other end but it was definitely a female voice."

Ralph scribbled and Nathan pondered as the waitress returned with a frothing pitcher and two cold mugs. Ralph filled both of the mugs, then took a healthy swig.

"Anyone other than her sister that you can think of: friends, coworkers, neighbors she might have mentioned?"

Nathan's mug remained untouched. "Now that I think about it, there's very little about Jessica that I truly know. Other than Vincent, her ex, and this sister, she never spoke of family, friends, or past work associates. Her marriage ended badly. To my knowledge she has no contact with her ex. She was born in New Orleans but has no memories of that city, moved to Oakland when still quite young. Her parents died, and she went into the foster care system, an experience she didn't like to talk about."

Ralph nodded as he took notes.

"I can't figure it out." Nathan reached for his mug, took a thoughtful sip. "How would killing me help anybody, especially someone who I don't know and Jessica hasn't seen for years?"

"How do you know that?"

"It's what she told me. Which means it's probably not true."

"I'll check to see whether Bolton is her married or maiden name. If the latter, I'll look for Boltons wherever the person she was calling resides." Nathan let out a frustrated sigh. "It might take time to connect the dots between points A and B. But we'll get there."

Ralph placed the notepad back in his suit coat pocket, sat back and picked up his beer.

"Is she out yet?"

"Posted bail this afternoon."

Nathan felt conflicted. The woman who'd just tried to kill him was also the last woman he'd made love to, the same one he'd asked to be his wife just one month ago.

"Does she have an attorney, or is she using a public defender?"

"I don't have that information, Nathan. But I can check."

"How long before she goes to trial?"

Ralph shrugged. "Hard to say. Could be anywhere from a few months to a year or more, depending on the attorneys, the judge, and the court load. Have you secured an attorney?"

"Not yet. I hate to think this ordeal might last that long."

"It might not, but I'm giving you worst case. If that happens and this thing drags on, are you ready to stay the course and put her behind bars? You need to get a lawyer ASAP, who can tell you your options, plea deals, et cetera. I know one in particular I can recommend. He's a shark in the courtroom, with stellar credentials and an excellent record."

"Sure. Shoot me the contact information."

Ralph pulled out his phone. "I'll do that right now."

Nathan saved the information on his cell phone, still marveling that instead of looking for a preacher and honeymoon destinations, he was looking for somebody to help him lock his ex away.

"Come on, Jessica. You've got to eat."

"Quit, Vincent! I'm not hungry. Leave me alone."

It was Friday, six days after the mess at the storage unit, four days since she returned home from jail and told Vincent everything. She'd called Sissy dozens of times. Today when she phoned, a message informed her that the number she'd reached was no longer in service.

Vincent sat at the end of the couch, near where Jessica lay curled on her side. "Sweetheart, I'm worried about you. You can't survive without food."

She raised her head enough to look at him through swollen, bloodshot eyes. "Who says I want to?"

"Come on now, beautiful. Don't even joke like that."

Falling back on the pillow, she muttered, "What do I have to live for?"

"Everything! I know you're hurting now, but I'm here for you. And I'm not going to leave. We'll get through this together!"

"What's the point!" Jessica sat up as she yelled, looking like a banshee with her wrinkled clothes, uncombed hair, and a dirty look. She grabbed the pillow beside her, hugging it as she rocked back and forth. "I almost killed someone. The person I did it for, my sister, isn't speaking to me. You grew up with family around you, people who loved you. You don't know what it's like to be thrown away and passed around like yesterday's garbage. To have no friends, no one to trust except yourself. It's been that way all my life. Until my sister helped me get out of a bad situation and laid out plans where we could be together . . . her and me."

"Then if that's what you want, I'll help you find her."

"I know where she is."

"Then since she won't take your calls, we'll go to her house."

Jessica snorted. "We'll need more than an address to get in." She took in Vincent's look of confusion. "She's in prison, a women's facility in North Carolina."

"Damn. For what?"

"Nothing, to hear her tell it. Except having an affair with Randall Atwater, Sherri's husband. So they had her framed for a murder she didn't commit."

Vincent whistled. "That's a hefty charge. And she was convicted?"

"But she didn't do it!"

"I'm not saying I don't believe you. There's a lot of inno-cent people sitting in jail. How'd she get mixed up with Sherri's husband?"

"He's a scientist. She's a writer who covered that industry for magazines and stuff. They met at a conference."

"Interesting." Vincent reached for his laptop. "What's her name?"

"Jamie, but professionally she went by Jacqueline. Jacque-line Tate."

Vincent plugged the name into a search engine. Several links appeared right away, all connected to articles she'd writ-ten. He clicked on images. "Wow! Good looks run in the fam-ily. She's beautiful."

"Yes . . . she is."

"When's the last time you saw her?"

"It's been a very long time, over ten years. We haven't shared a home since I was five and Sissy—Jamie—was ten. That's why I would have done anything . . ."

Vincent set aside his computer and took Jessica in his arms. "Tell me about those early years. They had to be wonderful, for the two of you to go to the lengths you did to get back to-gether."

"I don't remember a lot of it, to tell you the truth. I wish I did."

"Why not ask your sister?"

"She doesn't like talking about our childhood, doesn't like being reminded about our parents' death."

"What about an aunt, uncle, or cousin? You've said she's all you have but are you sure? Maybe there are relatives you don't know about."

For a moment Jessica didn't move, barely breathed. Then, slowly, she turned her head to meet Vincent's eyes. "Sissy always said all we had was each other. I never questioned it, never thought to search for myself." The flicker of light in her eyes dimmed quickly. "But why would I do that now, when even if I found someone there's a good chance I won't have the freedom to visit?"

"At least you'd know. Family means the world to you. The reaction to your sister's callous disregard is proof of that. How would you feel to know there is someone else out there who might be related? Maybe a couple, maybe a dozen? What if there were other family with whom you could connect?"

Jessica changed the subject but what Vincent had suggested stayed at the forefront of her mind. So much so that early the next morning she fired up her iPad, used a variety of search engines, and two hours later completed her search. Shortly after Vincent got off work and arrived at her house she placed a call to Canada—her true birthplace.

"Please answer," she said, nervously gnawing on a fingernail. She pushed the speaker button as the phone continued to ring.

Just as she was about to end the call, someone answered. "Hello?"

"Um, yes, I'm looking for Mrs. Hurley."

"Which one?"

Nerves had made her mouth dry. "Iris," she eked out, reaching for a glass of water on the table.

"One moment."

Jessica almost spewed out the drink she'd just taken. Vincent gave her leg a reassuring squeeze. The wait was only a minute but felt like eternity.

"Hello?"

The sound of a shrill voice she barely remembered almost brought tears. "Mrs. Hurley?"

"Yes, dear. Who's this?"

"Someone from a long time ago, that you might not remember. My name is Jessie Barnes. My sister's name is Jamie. We're the ones whose parents—"

"Got killed in the fire! Of course, I remember you. Oh, my

word! This is the little one, Jessie? Lord, I can't believe this! What a wonderful surprise. I thought about you down through the years and wondered what became of you. I'd asked around but you never returned. Understandable, though. So tragic what happened, what your sister did."

Jessica frowned slightly. "Well, we survived, my sister and I, and that's sort of why I'm calling. As far as I know, Sissy is my only living blood relative—"

"Is that what she told you?"

Jessica looked at Vincent, who mouthed encouragement. *Go on.*

"Yes, but I thought maybe our parents had siblings and there may be cousins or other kin that I don't know."

"If there are, I don't know them. Your daddy pretty much kept to himself. Your mama was friendly but never talked about brothers or sisters. She told me about Jamie, though, a bad seed that one . . . very bad."

"Excuse me?" Indignant. Appalled.

"You disagree with me? After she killed your parents?"

"What?!" Jessica angrily jumped to her sister's defense. "Sissy didn't kill them. They died in a fire!"

"Yes, the one that Jamie set after she'd stabbed one to death and poisoned the other."

At the mention of poison, Jessica's jaw dropped, along with her voice. "I don't believe you."

"I've got proof, darling." Mrs. Hurley's voice was soft but steady, and laced with regret. "My family has lived in this town more than seventy-five years. There are very few people that I don't know, therefore there's very few situations that I don't know about. As I learned things about that Jamie and her cold, calculated deeds, your situation included, I gathered what I could—any kind of document, newspaper article, or such— cause I knew if I ever got the chance I'd tell what happened. And I had an idea that you wouldn't believe me."

"I know what happened!" Her voice sounded confident but her heart was unsure.

"Child, it's best you know the truth." Jessica gripped the phone. Vincent held on to Jessica. "Jamie isn't really your sister."

She yanked her arm away from Vincent and jumped to her feet. "You're lying!"

"Shortly after your dad moved here, he fell in love with a woman who was drop-dead gorgeous but as crazy as a loon and wild as a cheetah. He married her as fast as he could, only to find out a couple months later that she'd been pregnant when he did. But doing the right thing, he stayed with her and adopted the kid, Jamie. Three years later, she ran off with another man—just up and left the family without so much as a God-bless-you. Jim was distraught, started drinking, probably would have died sooner had he not met your mom. She took them both in, though she drank even more than he did. Then you came along: petite, bubbly, more beautiful. Everybody doted on you because you were the cutest, happiest baby we'd ever seen. Everyone except Jamie."

Jessica returned to the couch, and sank down on its cushion.

"She came over to my house one day, Jamie did. Couldn't have been more than six or seven years old. Said she hated you, and wished you were dead. I watched her mouth form the words before they hit my ears! I told her there was no such thing as hating your kinfolk; told her to never talk that way again. Other than that I didn't pay what she said any mind. Talking a bunch of nonsense is what children do.

"A few years later, the fire happened. Eventually, when she turned eighteen, she got a wad of insurance money from your mother's estate. Your mother, not hers. You said the two of you are in contact. Did she tell you about it? Did she give you any of the money she stole?" No answer. "I saw her a year or two ago and didn't recognize the highfalutin society woman she'd become. But she recognized me and made sure I knew who she was. Under all that makeup and fancy clothes was the still hateful little girl who got away with murder."

"If she did it, and you know she did it, how did she get away?"

"The police believe she did it, too. Couldn't prove it though, not enough to satisfy the law. She's fooling a lot of people, but not Mrs. Hurley. Designer clothes and expensive perfume can cover up a dark soul, but that don't change it. Especially when what she's enjoying rightfully belongs to you.

"Now darling, I can't begin to imagine your feelings about all I've told you. But I had to tell you, Jessie. You have a right to know. I'm sorry to have talked badly about your Jamie. Being your half-sister, she is kin. But like her mama, that girl is from the devil. The farther you stay away from her, the better off you'll be."

CHAPTER 47

She'd never been a drinker. But in the thirty-six hours since the painfully revealing conversation with Mrs. Hurley, she'd finished two bottles of wine. In the eight hours since reading the packet her old Canadian neighbor had sent, she'd drunk one more. Inebriated, devastated, and reeling from the revelations, Jessica now sat at her dining room table, fingers on her laptop keys, trying to type a letter. Any other day it would have been easy. But today, words—errant, disjointed—floated around in her head. Somewhere she knew that if put together they'd form a sentence. But for the life of her, it seemed to be the hardest thing to do.

Closing her eyes, she tried to concentrate but was quickly interrupted by her ringing cell phone. She checked the ID and closed her eyes again. His calls seemed constant since she made him leave several hours after the Hurley call. He hadn't wanted to. "I'll worry," he said. But she'd insisted. He'd called the following morning, noon, and night. And yesterday. This morning she didn't answer his call, but sent him a text saying she'd talk to him soon. *Please, Vincent, just stop calling. I told you that I needed space, that I would be all right. And I will.*

She struggled yet again to focus on the screen, and began typing.

Dear Nathan:

No, that sounds too formal.

What's up, Nate:

Delete. *That's more like what one of his boys would say.*

To My Love:

Her eyes welled with tears, amazing since she felt all cried out yesterday. "You were my love," she whispered, wiping tears. "But not anymore. Trying to take your life killed my chances of having one. And all for somebody who it turns out I never knew at all."

She decided to start the letter without a heading. The more she typed, the more her flow returned. Soon she was almost back to her regular speed, the words spilling from her mind to the page as her fingers deftly punched keys. Once done she read it, changed a few things, and read it again. Believing she'd conveyed how she felt as best she could, she placed one word in the subject line, placed her finger over the Send button . . . and pressed it.

Taking a deep breath, she sent out two more e-mails. They were shorter but no less heartfelt. After sending the last one, she fell back against the chair, as if this task had drained the last bit of her strength. Struggling from the chair, she reached for the wine bottle, poured its remaining contents into a glass, and weaved her way to the window.

It was a picture-perfect spring day in Atlanta. The sky was a vibrant blue with fluffy clouds, the new leaves bright green, the sun's rays warm on her face. For a long time she stood there, taking in the trees, flowers, cars, and other buildings in view. She watched a bird soar to a tall tree and balance its round body on a tiny branch. *That's what I am going to do . . . soar just like that bird.*

Jessica went upstairs to her bedroom. She climbed on the bed, reached for the vial on the nightstand, and poured its contents into the wineglass, which, after swirling to mix it with the wine, she drank straight down. Wiping her mouth and setting down the glass, she reached for a pillow and lay on her side. A myriad of thoughts crisscrossed her mind. The last one she remembered, however, was the one she now hoped for the most.

. . . that death comes quickly.

Nathan arrived home on Sunday night around nine p.m., tired but content after a day spent in the company of a good friend and a lovely young woman. Earlier, Ralph had called with an invitation to join him and his wife for brunch at their home. Not one to turn down the rare opportunity for a home-cooked meal, he readily accepted the invitation. Once there, Ralph's wife had got an unexpected call from a longtime friend in town for the weekend. She was invited over as well. Any trepidation about meeting a strange woman disappeared as soon as she entered the room. Thick and curvy, with naturally curly hair, bright eyes, and a warm smile, the unassuming woman was down-to-earth and so funny she could have been a comedienne. Not wanting to stop the fun begun at the dinner table, the foursome decided to go bowling—something Nathan had never done. The ladies didn't bowl much either, but Ralph was a pro. To say the results were hilarious would be an understatement. They ended the night with coffee and dessert. Nathan was thankful to have pleasant memories to cover the hellish ones of the past week.

Nathan changed into a pair of comfortable sweats, grabbed his laptop, and settled in front of the TV to catch up with sports news. He casually scrolled through his e-mails—first work, then home—to see if there was anything that needed to be addressed before morning. One particular e-mail address made him look twice: Nuts-n-Bolton@gmail.com.

One word in the subject line: GOOD-BYE. He paused, his finger set to open the e-mail, then quickly changed his mind.

"Been there, done that," he murmured, scrolling further down the page. "All the good-byes we needed happened before they hauled you away in handcuffs."

No longer caring about the contents of his inbox, Nathan closed the computer, turned off the television, and went to bed.

The next morning, Nathan had just finished a conference call and was about to head to lunch when his assistant rang the intercom. "Nathan?"

"Yes."

"Mr. Givens is here to see you."

"Who?"

He heard muffled conversation before she answered, "Mr. Vincent Givens. He says it's urgent."

It only took a second for the name to ring a bell. "Send him back in five minutes." Nathan swiveled around and looked out the window. *This should be interesting.* He fired up his laptop and put Vincent's name into the search engine. A profile came up immediately. *Attorney; Graduate, Loyola Law School at Loyola Marymount; Member, American Bar Association, Association of Corporate Counsel, National Black Business Council,* etc. He closed the screen and switched to the one containing a memo from the corporation's investors, and had just begun to read when the door opened.

After being announced, Vincent entered the office and closed the door behind him. Nathan stood, not knowing whether to expect a formal handshake or a thuggish beat-down. He could handle either.

"Vincent, what can I do for you?"

"You can't do anything for me, man. It's about Jessica."

Nathan gestured toward the chair in front of his desk before sitting down.

"No need to sit. I won't be long. I'm worried about her. She was very upset when I left her on Friday, and soon after she stopped taking my calls. I went over there, knocked, but got no answer even though her car is in its spot."

Nathan shrugged. "As I'm sure you're aware, Jessica is no longer my problem."

"Are you hearing me?!" Vincent's voice rose before, remembering where he was, he lowered it. He placed his hands on Nathan's desk and leaned in close. "I don't give a damn about what happened between y'all: what you did, what she did, or why."

Nathan's voice was cucumber cool. "You need to back up."

Vincent stood straight. "Do you have a key to Jessica's place? Something is wrong. I need to check on her."

Nathan's casual expression masked turbulent thoughts. As angry, disgusted, and done as he was with her, and as much as he believed she should go to prison for what she'd tried, Nathan just wasn't the type of man to wish serious harm on anyone. Nor did he necessarily want to turn over his spare key to Jessica's colleague. He didn't know the nature of Vincent's request. For all Nathan knew, Vincent could be using his legal contacts to help Jessica get away with trying to kill him.

"You'll have to get into her place some other way," he finally said. "Perhaps there's a management company you can call or a neighbor who can help you, because I can't." He once again closed his computer, stood, and reached for his suit jacket. "I'll see you out."

"Just remember this moment, because if she's found dead because you couldn't help me, her blood will be on your hands."

Nathan left the office and headed to a steakhouse just down the street. He tried to shake them off, but Vincent's words continued to haunt him. So much so that after placing his order he reached for his phone, tapped on the e-mail icon and scrolled to the e-mail Jessica had sent yesterday.

He started reading, and his heart fell.

I'm sorry, Nathan. For everything. So very sorry for so many things, but most of all . . . for hurting you.

I could sit here and rehash the whole sordid mess of what happened and why I did it. You may already know. If you don't, you will. Either way, what does it matter? It won't fix what I did. It won't change how you feel.

Know this: You were the BEST thing that ever happened to me. I realized that when it was too late. I could have had the family I wanted, the love that I wanted. I could have had it all. But I ruined it. And without you, I don't want to be here.

He'd read enough. Nathan threw a twenty on the table and ran the block from the restaurant to his office's parking garage and jumped in his car. Swerving through traffic, his mind racing, Nathan was hit with a sobering thought. *Why am I rushing to potentially save a woman who tried to kill me?* His foot eased off the pedal. His blood pressure dropped, and he released the race-car-driver hold he had on the steering wheel. *Chances are this is much ado about nothing; maybe a move by Jessica to get me over there. If I find out that this is some bullshit . . .* He turned up the stereo, letting TLC help him escape by chasing waterfalls.

He stopped by his house, grabbed the key that until Vincent's visit he'd forgotten he had, and then proceeded over to her condo. While parking, catching the elevator, and walking to her door, he told himself that this was more than likely a huge overreaction on the part of a brothah trying to get points by showing concern. *Good luck with it, Vincent,* he thought, reaching her door and unlocking it. *But watch your back.*

Stepping inside, the quiet gripped Nathan, producing a chill. He pressed forward.

"Jessica! Jessica, are you here?" No answer. "It's Nate. I'm dropping off your key."

Still hearing nothing, he walked to the bottom of the stairs. "Jessica! Are you up there?"

He mounted the stairs, all the while telling himself he was probably getting alarmed for nothing. Vincent may not have been able to reach her because she was with another man. If she was home and ignored him when he came to the door, then she might call the cops and have him arrested.

"Jessica?"

He reached her bedroom and stepped inside. Relief washed over him. She was here, asleep. *Or is she?* "Jessica!" No reaction. Nathan raced to the bed and attempted to wake her. After yelling and shaking her with no response, he reached for his phone and dialed 9-1-1. "Operator, I just discovered a friend who is unresponsive. We need an ambulance." He gave the address. "Please hurry."

An hour later, Nathan was still in the waiting room, hoping to hear something from the doctors. He'd tried to reach Vincent by calling the law firm, but his call went to voice mail, and considering the circumstances, Nathan didn't want to leave a message at the front desk. He also didn't want to leave without knowing whether or not Jessica survived what the paramedics believed was a suicide attempt. If she lived, he'd have an urgent, confidential note delivered to Vincent, who would no doubt be happy to take it from there.

A doctor came into the room, obviously searching for someone. Nathan stood. She walked over. "Are you the person who called the ambulance for Ms. Bolton?"

"Yes. Is she alive?"

"Thanks to you. Another hour or two max and her organs would have totally shut down. As it is, there have been varying degrees of deterioration. We won't know for another twenty-four to forty-eight hours how bad the damage is and her prognosis. Right now, it's touch-and-go. But, as you probably know, her organs are not our only concern."

"What do you mean?"

"If her organs can't be brought back to a fully functional level, and quickly, it will be hard to save the child."

If "what the hell" had a face, it would look like Nathan's did right then.

The doctor pulled off her glasses, wiping them as she studied Nathan. "I guess you didn't know. Perhaps she didn't either. Ms. Bolton is pregnant. Now, if you'll excuse me, I have to get back to trying to save that baby."

CHAPTER 48

The baby news changed everything.

After finding out that Jessica would spend the night in intensive care and not be allowed visitors, Nathan called the office and took the afternoon off. While at the hospital, he'd read the rest of Jessica's letter, which mentioned a package from someone in Canada. She'd written that he should read it. He couldn't imagine why.

Five minutes after entering her condo and scanning the packet's contents, which included a short letter that Jessica wrote, the reason became clear. And Nathan's world changed once again.

He ended up in his parking garage, but didn't remember driving. With effort he made it home to his office, collapsed in the chair, placed a phone call to Vincent, e-mailed his sister, and now waited for her call.

He'd never gone to war, but Nathan believed he now knew what it meant to be shell-shocked. In fact, after what he'd learned in the past two hours, a word had probably not yet been invented for how he felt right now. *Jessica was from Canada? Their initial meeting was a plan to set him up? Jessica was pregnant? Jessica Bolton was Jacqueline Tate's sister, only—wait for it—not really?* He placed his elbows on his legs and his head in his hands. Either he was going crazy or had entered the twilight zone.

Seriously, it was too much.

"Sherri's going to freak out," Nathan muttered, changing positions to rest his head against the back of the chair. He tried to relax. Impossible. He attempted not to think. Ridiculous. Chasing the thoughts running through his head was all he could do. He'd just jumped up to go to the roof and try and clear his head, when the phone rang.

He pushed the speaker button. "Sherri."

"I. Can't. Believe it."

He fell into the chair. "I know, right?"

"Nathan, I mean it. If this is a joke, it's not funny."

"You think I could make this shit up?"

"I'd hoped so. This is beyond crazy, it's ludicrous! What you've shared sounds like a movie script, I mean, it can't be real life!"

"Not just real life. My life."

"I have no words."

"You either?"

"All of this *and* Jessica's pregnant?"

"Yep."

"Plus, she's related to the woman that made our lives a living hell?"

"Yes and no. Did you read all of what I sent?"

"Brother, I barely made it through the first few lines before picking up the phone."

"Well, read the rest."

"I don't know if my heart can stand it." Nathan's attempted laugh sounded more like a wounded bear growling. "I mean, she tried to kill herself, she's pregnant, she's a witch's sister . . ."

"What are the chances, huh? Even though she approached me with intent, why of all women did I have to fall in love with her? With as many women as I've been with, why did I have to go and get her pregnant?"

"Considering who we're dealing with, I wouldn't jump to conclusions. Wait on the DNA."

"Yes, I guess I should but . . ."

"But what?"

"I'm pretty sure it's mine."

"Pretty sure isn't positive; DNA is."

"You're right."

"Wait, how is this going to affect the attempted murder charge against her?"

"I have no idea."

"I know you're dealing with a lot, Nathan. But don't lose sight of the fact that the girl tried to kill you, an action made even more heinous now that we know who was behind the plot! You wait until we get our hands on some evidence, just one shred of anything that can prove this is true. Jessica can join her sister and they can both rot in prison until they rot in hell!"

The room became quiet as both siblings contemplated the strange turn of events. When Sherri spoke again, her voice was soft, compassionate. "What are you going to do, Nate?"

"I don't know."

"I have a suggestion."

"What? Go to the hospital and pull out her life-sustaining apparatus?"

"Ha! But that's a way better idea than mine! Seriously, though, why don't you go down to the island, get away for a couple days, walk on the beach, breathe in fresh air, clear your head?"

"That's actually not a bad idea. These walls are closing in on me, that's for sure. For a moment, I thought I'd lost my mind."

"Anybody receiving all of this news at once would have

crossed over the insanity line right now, or at least be walking on it."

"Trust me, I'm there."

"Would you be all right down there by yourself? I'm always up for a vacation and can talk to Randall and see if he can get away for a few days."

"Maybe I'll get your girl to meet us there, too."

"Renee? She might want to join us. I could meet her new man. Do you want me to ask her?"

"I thought about her because . . . I don't know . . . she chills me out, makes me laugh. And she really cares about our family. I forgot about her new dude, she'll probably act different with him around."

"There's a reason she and I have been friends all these years. Never once did I think of you two together. Eww."

When Nathan said nothing, Sherri changed the subject. "What are you thinking?"

"About Jessica and the baby."

"I understand your thinking about the baby, but other than how long a sentence we can get that deceitful heifah, she shouldn't cross your mind! I'm sorry. If I'm this upset, I can only imagine how you feel. Have you eaten?"

"I'm not hungry."

"That's okay. Your body still needs fuel. Go get something to eat—out, in a restaurant, with people around to hopefully take your mind off all this for just a minute. And then try and get some sleep."

"That's good advice, Sis. Thanks."

"Keep me posted."

"Will do."

"I love you, Bro."

"Love you, Sis."

★ ★ ★

Jessica opened her eyes, blinking against the bright light just above her. *Is this heaven?* She tried moving her arm. It felt constrained. She tried to see what was holding it down but could move her body only so far. She squeezed her eyes shut and then opened them again. The longer her gaze, the more what she saw came into focus. The light was not a spiritual being, but a large plastic square covering fluorescent lighting, set in a low ceiling of acoustical tiles. No wonder *Sissy abandoned me. I can't do anything right . . . even kill myself.* She turned her head slightly but only saw windows and walls. *Where am I?*

The answer came within minutes, when a cheery young nurse walked up to her bed. "Good morning! Sleeping beauty is now awake! How are you feeling?"

"Bad," she croaked.

"But you're feeling. That's a good sign. Let's check a few vitals, shall we?" The nurse hummed as she went about her tasks, checking Jessica's blood pressure and vital signs, and the room's temperature.

"Where am I?"

"Emory University Hospital's intensive care ward. With continued improvement, however, we should be able to move you to a regular room in a couple days."

"How did I get here?"

"Ambulance is all I know. The doctor will be able to tell you more."

"When will he be here?"

"*She* should be making her rounds within the hour. Let me get you some water. We're feeding you intravenously, but your mouth is probably parched. Oh, now that you're awake we can loosen these restraints." The nurse quickly unfastened and removed the straps, then raised Jessica's bed before pouring a cup of water from a nearby pitcher. "Here you go. Just small sips, okay?"

Jessica hurriedly followed one sip with another.

The nurse gently held her wrist. "Slowly, okay? You and the little one have been through quite a traumatic experience. So we've got to be very gentle with the body for the next few days."

"Me and who?"

"Your baby."

Jessica's eyes widened.

"You didn't know?" Jessica shook her head. The nurse covered her mouth. "Oops, I'm sorry. It's on the chart. When the doctor tells you, act surprised and help me keep my job!"

She winked. Jessica blankly nodded.

The nurse refilled the small white cup. "Here's a little more water. Remember to drink it slowly. The doctor will be in soon."

Jessica set the water on a tray and rested her head against the pillow. *There must be a mistake. There's no way I can be pregnant.* Almost subconsciously, she ran her hand across her taut, flat stomach. *Can I?* The possibility was so daunting, so overwhelming, that all Jessica could do was cry.

Two days later, Jessica was well enough to be moved to a private room. Two large bouquets of flowers greeted her. The nurse pulled the card and handed it to her. For a split second she thought of Nathan, and the chance he might have sent them. Then she remembered the solemn truth: Nathan was out of her life.

She pulled out the card:

May these brighten your room the way you brighten my life. Love, Vincent.

"A secret admirer?" the floor nurse asked, fluffing Jessica's pillows and straightening the covers.

"A good friend."

"Smart girls marry friends like that," she answered with a wink. "You need anything, just ring your call button."

Jessica fell asleep. When she awoke, two hazel-green concerned eyes stared down at her. "Hello, Vincent."

"Hello, sweetheart." He placed a light kiss on her forehead. "I can't tell you how good it is to see you alive. I've never been so worried about someone. Please don't ever do that again."

"I'm sorry."

"I had a bad feeling when you sent me away. When you stopped answering my calls, I was beside myself."

"How did you get into the apartment to save me?"

"I didn't . . ." Vincent caught himself. "I didn't take no for an answer, from anybody. I wouldn't stop until I got to you." He enveloped her hand in his. "It's good to see your eyes."

"You saved my life." Her eyes shone with gratitude . . . and something indefinable.

"That's because you *are* my life. It's what I've been trying to get you to understand for months now. With me you won't need to worry or depend on anyone else. I'll be your family, your lover, your friend . . . whatever you need."

"I don't deserve you."

"You deserve someone much better. But no one will love you more. In fact, as soon as you're well enough, I want to . . ." His words died as Jessica's attention was obviously pulled to something behind him.

He turned as Jessica spoke. "Nathan? What are you doing here?"

"Yes." Vincent's was almost a fighting stance as he glared at his unwelcome rival walking through the door. "What are you doing here? That's what we'd *both* like to know."

EPILOGUE

The sand was warm, the water cool against his feet. The water lapped lazily, methodically, against the shore, ebbing and flowing to the same steady beat for thousands of years. Nathan focused on the contrasts, relished them, along with the hot Bahamas sun causing a thin sheen of sweat to cover his shirtless body. He reached the umbrella chair set under a small palm tree that pretended to give shade and took a drink of bottled water, allowing deep, full breaths of clean air to fill his lungs before slowly releasing.

Coming down here was the best idea.

Walking the beach, swimming, reading, eating, and sleeping. These activities had pretty much been his life since arriving at Sherri and Randall's vacation home three days ago, three weeks since Jessica's release from the hospital and one week to the day since he dropped all charges against her. Sherri had been livid. Nathan thought she might ban him from her island paradise. In the end, she agreed that it was his life and he had to do what felt right for him. There was no denying that Jessica's actions were criminal, but all things considered, Nathan couldn't have a clear conscience if he put a pregnant woman behind bars. The mental facility she'd been mandated to for six months was probably more of what she needed anyway. He'd been through a lot. Jessica had been through worse.

He missed her. That was the crazy part. When Nathan arrived at the hospital, he didn't stay long. Vincent was clearly upset that he'd come, and Nathan needed to see Jessica alone. The next time he called before coming over. Jessica was sitting up and her color had returned. She was remorseful, quiet, with a fearful vulnerability filling her eyes, reminding him of the woman he first fell in love with. Feelings he'd buried rushed to the surface. He'd buried the feelings, but they hadn't died. During his third and final visit, he'd almost shared this with her, until their conversation about the pregnancy and paternity tests, when she dropped the bomb that exploded his emotions all over the place. Her words rang in his ears to this day: "Vincent and I are getting married. The baby is his."

Sherri had been ecstatic at hearing the news. He should have been shouting, too. Who knew that finding out she was not carrying his child would leave him feeling so cut off, deprived, as if something that belonged to him had been taken away? Only after her announcement did he realize that somewhere in the back of his mind he'd actually been entertaining the idea of getting back with her, of their raising the baby together. He'd never forget what she tried to do, but after reading her letter and the stuff from Mrs. Hurley, he'd definitely forgiven her. Through her sister's manipulations, Jessica had felt killing him was the only choice. Though he and Sherri had decided to tell their mother about the breakup but not the reason, he could still hear what she'd say if she knew his thoughts: *You're planning to marry the woman who tried to kill you? I don't know who's crazier, her or you.*

The thought made him laugh out loud.

Everything happened for a reason, and in the end, he was glad that all of the stuff that had been done in darkness had come to light. His relationship with Jessica had taught him some valuable lessons. He'd taken the plunge and gotten engaged.

Making a commitment and navigating an exclusive relationship hadn't been as stifling as he'd envisioned; in fact, it had felt very good. So much so that now, that's the only kind of connection that Nathan was looking for . . . a forever kind of relationship, with a forever kind of girl.

This thought in mind, Nathan enjoyed a quick swim before heading back to the house. Mouthwatering smells of the islands—fried conch, johnnycakes, crab salad, and a vegetable stew with a name he couldn't pronounce—smacked him in the face as soon as he walked through the door, followed by a forever kind of girl.

"Good afternoon, Nathan! I hope you're hungry!"

"Hello, Develia." She stepped into his arms and Nathan wrapped them around her. He noticed her body fit perfectly with his. She felt soft, smelled good, too. He released her, and viewed the abundant display. "All this for me?"

"Absolutely. I hope you brought an appetite."

"I did. Everything looks and smells amazing."

Develia walked to the bar and brought back a colorful drink. "Especially for you, Mr. Carver."

"Ah yes, a Goombay Smash! This brings back some of my fondest memories on this island."

She raised her glass. "To making many more fond and wonderful memories in the Bahamas."

"Indeed."

They fixed their plates and on a veranda sat facing the ocean, enjoying the breeze and lively conversation. Nathan didn't know if he'd ever felt so stress-free. After dessert there was a companionable silence, as they sipped tea and watched the birds fly.

"Develia."

"Yes?"

"New Year's Eve, the night we met, I asked a question, remember?"

"You asked many questions that night."

"But there was only one you didn't answer." She raised a brow. "I asked how a lady as lovely as you could be alone at the club. Do you remember your answer?"

"No." She erupted with the melodic chuckle that he loved. "But I have a feeling you'll tell me."

"I don't remember it verbatim." He rubbed his chin in thought. "I think you said it was too good a night to talk of anything sad, something like that."

"That very well could have been what I said."

"Well, I'm back on the island with nothing but time, and I'd like to hear your story."

"I'll tell you, but later on just remember, you asked."

Nathan settled more comfortably into his chair. He could listen to Dev's beautiful accent all night.

The wedding ceremony was simple but elegant, attended only by Jessica, Vincent, Vincent's best friend, and the minister. The chapel was so beautiful that one could forget that the bustling neon-filled Vegas strip was right outside. Only May, yet the weather was balmy. By the end of June forecasters predicted Sin City might see three-digit degrees, a roasting usually reserved for August. Thankfully, the chapel's temperature was just right for Jessica, looking positively radiant in a yellow lace Coco Chanel classic, with an empire waist and flare at the knee. Vincent's handsome looks were shown off in a black Armani tux. They had only eyes for each other as their original vows were said. When Jessica said "I do" there were tears in her eyes, one cascading down her face. Before Vincent touched his new bride's lips, he kissed the tear away.

Later that night, in their penthouse honeymoon suite, Jessica stared out the window that overlooked the strip. The day seemed surreal, as had her life ever since she'd met Nathan. He'd changed everything. Finding out the truth about Jacqueline had transformed her even more. And Vincent? There's no way she could ever pay him back for his kindness: helping to nurse her back to health, promising to stay by her side during her mandatory six-month mental hospital stay, backing these words with a marriage proposal that he insisted happen before her admission next week, and being more excited to have a baby than any man she'd ever met. For these reasons, she became Mrs. Givens. She absolutely adored him. Love could come later.

"There you are." He eased up behind her, wrapping his arms around her waist. "My sweetheart and my baby," he added, his voice low and sexy as he kissed her neck and patted her barely noticeable baby bump. "Enjoying the view?"

She turned and put her arms around his neck, looked him deep in the eyes. "I love this one much better."

They kissed, temperatures rose. It was time to take this celebration into the bedroom. They undressed. Jessica excused herself to go to the restroom. She handled her business, then stepped to the sink and washed her hands. When toweling off, she caught her image in the bathroom's mirrored wall. She eyed her profile in the mirror, viewing her sheer silk-covered stomach as she turned this way and that. Stepping closer she looked again. The baby bump wasn't noticeable, but she knew that a human being grew inside her. This alone made her life worth living.

When she caught a final glimpse of herself in the mirror, a melancholy expression looked back. But she wouldn't second-guess her decision. It was for the best.

"We're pregnant," she whispered, placing her hand on the part of her abdomen where she imagined the baby to be. "I'm having your baby, Nathan. Too bad you'll never know."

THE PERFECT DECEPTION

Lutishia Lovely

ABOUT THIS GUIDE

The suggested questions that follow are included
to enhance your group's reading of this book.

DISCUSSION QUESTIONS

1. The central conflict of this novel plays out in the very first line. If presented with these two options, which would be your choice, and why?

2. Shortly after meeting Jessica, we learn about her background and some of the experiences that have shaped who she is today. After reading the prologue, what were your feelings about her? Was there an affinity? Empathy? Anger? Disgust? Nothing? Why or why not?

3. What were your first thoughts about Nathan and Jessica as a couple? Did they seem like a good fit? Is theirs a love you'd root for? Why or why not?

4. Nathan's family and friends were quite vocal in their opinions of who he dated. How much should we listen to other people's opinions about our relationships? If you were in love with someone your family hated, would you continue to date them?

5. During the holidays, an incident happened on the beach that was considered inappropriate. Do you agree with how this situation was handled? Do you think one has a right to express oneself however one chooses?

6. Once Jessica found out how she was to help a family member, the first line of this novel takes on new meaning. Knowing now what you didn't know when you read the first line, would your initial choice change? Why or why not?

7. Did the events in Jessica's past affect the way you felt about her handling of the present?

8. At times, Nathan and Jessica's relationship was tumul-
    tuous, yet neither could seem to let the other go. What
    are your thoughts on this unexplainable connection?

9. Did Nathan and Jessica truly love each other? Is it pos-
    sible to love someone yet still behave in the ways that
    they did?

10. Should Nathan have been more observant of what was
    happening around him? Would you have suspected
    something that he did not?

11. Jessica loved her sister, whose influence greatly im-
    pacted her decisions. What do you think about her sis-
    ter, and how Jessica felt about her?

12. How do you feel about Vincent? Throughout the novel,
    were his actions appropriate? Does the woman he loves
    deserve him?

13. Are you curious about Dev, and would you like to know
    more of her story?

14. Are you curious about Renee, and would you like to
    know more of her story?

15. Jessica made a decision that affects many lives. How do
    you feel about what she decided? What would you have
    done?

Don't miss the first book in The Shady Sisters Trilogy

The Perfect Affair

Available wherever books and ebooks are sold.

CHAPTER 1

"Let's toast to Jacqueline!"

A group of five fashionably dressed and vivacious women, seated in a trendy Toronto eatery, lifted their champagne flutes in the air. The atmosphere was festive. Even the April showers had paused, allowing bright, warm sunshine to surround them.

"To you, Jacqueline Tate," Rosie, the speaker, continued. "A woman who has finally gotten what all of us want."

"A good man?" The plus-size cutie with dimples and curves kept a straight face as she asked this. The others laughed.

"No, Kaitlyn, money. The next best thing."

"Or the best thing," Jacqueline countered, "depending on how you look at it."

"We wish you tons of success on this new venture. Go get 'em, girl!"

"Cheers!"

The ladies clinked their glasses and took healthy sips of pricey bubbly before questions rang out.

"What, exactly, will you be doing?"

"Is this full-time or freelance?"

"How did you get this job?"

Jacqueline laughed as she raised her hands in mock surrender. "All right, already! I'll tell you everything." She took another sip of her drink, eyes shining with excitement. "First of all, it's a freelance writing contract—but," she continued when the other writer in the group moaned, "it's for three months and . . . it's with *Science Today!*"

"What's that?" Kaitlyn asked, looking totally unimpressed.

"It's the magazine for scientists like *Vogue* is for models," Jacqueline replied.

Kaitlyn cocked a brow. "Really? That big, huh?"

"It's a huge deal," Molly, the other writer, commented. "Doing articles for such a prestigious journal will look great on the résumé."

"Wow, that's wonderful!" Rosie said. "Will you work from an office or from home?"

Jacqueline sat straighter, barely containing her excitement. "That's the best part, guys. I'll be spending most of this assignment in America, traveling to events and interviewing the movers and shakers in the science world."

Kaitlyn reached for the champagne bottle. "Somehow 'mover,' 'shaker,' and 'scientist' sound weird in the same sentence."

"That's because your world revolves around Hollywood," Jacqueline countered. "And you consider tabloids real reading and their content true fact."

"It isn't?"

This elicited more laughter from the group, and more questions. Finally, the successful-but-shy one in the group, Nicole, spoke up. "I'm really happy for you, Jacqueline. After what you've gone through, you deserve to have some good stuff come your way."

It was true. Last year had been a doozy. On top of losing a high-paying job due to downsizing, she'd found out that the love of her life was someone else's love too. Walked in on them in her house, in her bed. Guess he'd not counted on the fact that the interview she'd been called out to do might wrap up early. It did, and so did the relationship. They'd been dating for months. Jacqueline had even confided to her friends that he might be "the one." The one to break her heart, maybe, but not the one for lifetime love.

Rosie sensed Jacqueline's sadness, and placed a hand on her arm. "At least he's out of your life."

"I wish."

Kaitlyn cringed. "He's not?"

"Occasionally we'll cover the same event. You guys remember that he's a photographer, right?"

"I remember he's a jerk," Kaitlyn replied.

"And an asshole," Molly added.

Jacqueline laughed, and it was genuine. "Thank you, guys. You sure know how to make a girl feel good."

Kaitlyn peered at her friend of more than five years. She began shaking her head.

Jacqueline noticed. "What?"

"I don't get it. You're smart, funny, and the most beautiful woman I've ever seen in person."

"Oh, girl . . ."

"Seriously? If it weren't for you, I'd think those chicks posing on the magazine covers were make-believe."

"They are," Molly said. "It's called Photoshop."

"My point," Kaitlyn continued, "is I can't understand why you're not married. I'm with my third husband and I look like a whale!"

Jacqueline frowned. "You do not. Stop exaggerating and putting yourself down like that."

"That analogy may have gone a bit overboard. But I don't look like you."

No one would argue that Jacqueline was a natural beauty. Tall, slender, with creamy tan skin, long, thick hair and perfectly balanced features, she was often thought to be a model when out on assignment, and once had even been mistaken for the pop star Rihanna.

"Maybe Kaitlyn's right," Rosie offered. "Maybe in addition to finding great stories, you might find love."

"Oh no. I'm not even going to think like that, and set myself up to be disappointed. I'm going to stay focused and disciplined, never forgetting the reasons for why I'm there. I'll be going to some great places—LA, Vegas, New York—so, sure, I plan to have fun. But guys? Not interested."

"You say that now." Kaitlyn was obviously not convinced.

"True. Anything can happen. So if I do see a hottie and want a good time, I'll view it as just that, a good time, nothing more. For me, when it comes to men and relationships, using words like 'love' and 'forever' only leads to a broken heart."

Rosie gazed at Jacqueline with compassionate eyes. "You've been through a lot and you're still smiling. You deserve to be happy and to find true love. I, for one, will be rooting for that happiness to come your way."

Kaitlyn reached for the champagne bottle and, noting it empty, flagged down the waiter to bring another one. Already outspoken and boisterous, the bubbly loosened her tongue even further and made her talk more loudly. "I'm with you, Jacqueline," she said, trying to further drain her already empty glass. "I say get wined, dined, and screwed out your mind, then tell the muthafuckas to kiss your ass. Don't even give them your phone number if they can't pass the shoe."

Every face showed confusion. "The shoe?" Jacqueline asked.

"That's right. The shoe. Y'all haven't heard of that? It's a test." Noting her very interested audience, including some from surrounding tables, Kaitlyn lowered her voice as if she was about to drop secrets from Camp David. "Okay, here's what you do. Have him take you out, buy you dinner, and then, after a night of partying, when he's trying to get in the panties, take off your stiletto, pour a drink in the shoe, and tell him to drink it. If he can't do that, then he's not a coochie connoisseur."

Ms. Shy, Nicole, was suddenly not shy at all. "A what?" When the waiter brought out the second bottle, hers was the first glass raised.

"Coochie con-no-sir. One who'll lick it, kiss it, nip it, and flick it before he fucks it."

Rosie's cheeks turned as red as her hair. "Oh my," she whispered with a hand to her mouth.

Molly pulled out her phone to take notes.

"Thanks anyway," Jacqueline responded. "But the last man I'd give my phone number is one who'd drink out of my shoe. That's just foul."

"Whatever." Kaitlyn's countenance was one of pure confidence. "I'm just sayin' . . ."

Jacqueline sat back and crossed her arms. "And you know this because?"

"Because when I met the man who drank out of my shoe? I married him!"

This comment sent the table into another vocal frenzy.

"You're lying."

"No, he didn't!"

"Sounds like a wild and crazy date!"

"Geez! I'll never look at good old Harry the same way again."

Jacqueline sat back and took it all in. These were her girls; some she'd known for years and others a few months. Their sisterhood and support were genuine. Only one of her besties was missing. Kris. Her ride-or-die BFF who'd been there forever. She couldn't wait to share this great piece of news with the main one who'd been beside her during both good times and bad.

"Okay, maybe asking him to sip from your heels is a bit extreme."

You think? Jacqueline's raised brow seemed to imply.

"But there are still good men out there. I finally found one, though it took me three tries."

"Evidently my radar on good men is in need of repair."

"My mother always told me that when you meet him, you'll know." Kaitlyn sat back, thoughtful. "I have to admit, it wasn't until Harry came along that I knew what she meant."

Intrigued, Jacqueline eyed her. "How was he different?"

"It was natural, easy," Kaitlyn said with a shrug. "He felt like an old shoe."

"Ha! What is it with you and shoes?" Rosie asked.

Kaitlyn laughed. "I don't know. Probably time for a new pair." Her voice became serious as she looked at Jacqueline. "I didn't have to try with Harry. I was just myself. He felt right, and good, from the beginning. That's how I knew it. Maybe that's how you'll know it, too."

"Sounds easy, but again, with the bad luck I've been having, I'm just not sure."

"I understand your being cautious. Just don't shut totally down. Leave a little space in your heart open to love. A little light, so the right man can find it."

They toasted to that and once the entrées arrived, the conversation moved around to other things. Later, however, Kaitlyn's words still echoed. Jacqueline wanted to find love, really hoped that it would happen. But during this assignment and over the next three months, at least? She wouldn't go looking for it.